"By rights I should turn you over my knee and punish you for coming into my room like a thief in the night."

As the words left his mouth, Connor was overcome with a desire to do just that. He broke off the thought while his desires were still under control.

"But naturally I shall not. You could have been killed. I might have shot you."

"But you didn't." Emily's voice was a mere whisper.

He pushed her back so slightly so she had to tip her head in order to meet his gaze. He drew a ragged breath as he stared down at the lovely eyes gazing so trustingly into his. *Emily,* he thought wildly, *darling Emily, if only you knew . . .*

An Unusual Inheritance

REBECCA ROBBINS

AVON BOOKS ◆ NEW YORK

AN UNUSUAL INHERITANCE is an original publication of Avon Books. This work has never before appeared in book form. This work is a novel. Any similarity to actual persons or events is purely coincidental.

AVON BOOKS
A division of
The Hearst Corporation
1350 Avenue of the Americas
New York, New York 10019

Copyright © 1994 by Robin Hacking
Published by arrangement with the author
Library of Congress Catalog Card Number: 94-94092
ISBN: 0-380-77670-7

First Avon Books Printing: October 1994

AVON TRADEMARK REG. U.S. PAT. OFF. AND IN OTHER COUNTRIES, MARCA REGISTRADA, HECHO EN U.S.A.

Printed in the U.S.A.

RA 10 9 8 7 6 5 4 3 2 1

For Craig

1

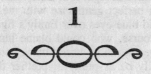

"**E**mily, there is no need for you to leave. We'll get along all right, even if Lord Marsden does spread his petty little rumor about." Mrs. Etta Lou Harriman's voice was sincere, but quavered slightly as if from fear that her young friend would actually agree to stay at Harriman's Academy for the Betterment of Young Ladies of Quality, rather than seek a new life for herself.

Shifting in her chair, Miss Emily Hastings smiled sadly at the woman seated behind a desk in one of the school's back offices. "Little? I would hardly call His Lordship's claims that I tried to seduce him a 'little' rumor." She sighed heavily. "And while I appreciate your friendship and willingness to hazard His Lordship's wrath, I cannot allow one man's spite to destroy everything you've worked for."

Etta Lou gave a small dissenting murmur, but Emily waved a hand to silence her old friend. "If I stay here Lord Marsden will not rest until the school is forced to close. He told me as much when I refused to . . . to . . . well . . . you know."

Emily watched with bittersweet fondness as the elderly woman ran an agitated hand through her short, fluffy white curls, displacing a narrow violet riband in a familiar gesture that always made Etta Lou look as if she'd been caught bonnetless in a high wind.

"But where will you go, my dear? It breaks my heart to think of you all alone and friendless, chased from our happy home by that beastly man." Without waiting for a response, Etta Lou gave an exasperated, unladylike oath that was at odds with her genteel appearance. "How can

1

anyone be so spiteful?" she cried. "Or so morally corrupt? I would never have thought it of Lord Marsden. He always behaved like a perfect gentleman with me."

She ran vivid blue eyes over Emily's figure, then spoke frankly. "Of course, who could blame him? If only you would cease wearing those horrid black bombazine gowns, you could easily be as pretty or prettier than any of our charges." She sighed. "Anyway, if you are determined to leave the academy, perhaps you should have some nice, colorful gowns made up for wherever your journey may take you." Etta Lou fluttered one wrinkled hand. "And perchance you might leave off wearing those horrid spectacles. You never know. You might meet the man of your dreams quite unexpectedly one of these days. 'Twould be a pity if you were to lose him because you look so unattractive. It pays to remember that you catch more flies with honey than you do with vinegar."

"If I ever decide to catch flies, I'll try to remember that advice," Emily answered wryly. "But seriously, Etta Lou, I don't need anything but the gowns already in my wardrobe—I have six exactly like this one, all in perfect condition. Maybe I'll buy something new when they have all worn out. Maybe. I cannot help but think it would be silly of me to squander my wages on girlish fripperies when I am long past my last hopes."

"One does not have one's foot in the grave at twenty-six!" Etta Lou responded adamantly.

"Perhaps not, but I am not so deluded as to think brightly colored clothing would make me look either young or desirable. Besides, if I had looked more desirable, I might not have escaped Lord Marsden's clutches for as long as I did. As for my spectacles, unless I wish to stumble about London blind as a bat, I'd best leave them where they sit."

Etta Lou threw up her hands. "I should think you'd rather be sightless than be an old maid, Emily. And don't try to tell me you are nearly blind. I've seen you without your glasses on many occasions."

"It is true that I see distant things perfectly well," Emily acknowledged, "but I cannot read or do needlework or see anything within three feet of my outstretched arms without them. Now let us have no more of this nonsense."

Etta Lou pretended not to hear. "You know, I'm sure you could find a husband if you'd only put your mind to it. I'll have you know Lord Marsden isn't the only man to find you attractive. I've seen other girls' fathers looking at you many times. Perhaps one of them is a widower. If you have a preference, I would be happy to put a bug in his ear . . ." Her voice trailed off suggestively.

"Don't you dare!" Emily said with a start. "I'd never forgive you!"

Etta Lou sniffed. "Naturally I would do nothing of the kind without your permission." Ignoring Emily's skeptical glance, she sailed on airily. "You know, what I don't understand is why Lord Marsden didn't just ask you to marry him. After all, his wife died giving birth to the last of his twelve children, so I know he must want another bride. If he was able to see your attractions behind those glasses and that awful gown, he should have been able to imagine you in fine silks and linens and thus have seen that you'd have made him an admirable spouse. You are Quality, after all."

"I hardly think being the daughter of a sea captain makes me Quality," Emily countered. "We have no idea who my mother was, remember. She might have been a scullery maid. But even if she'd been the daughter of a duke, it wouldn't have mattered—not only would I never have accepted Lord Marsden, but the *on dit* has it that he lost nearly everything he owned a little over a month ago, on an unfortunate turn of a card, and will be forced to marry an heiress."

Etta Lou clapped her hands to her cheeks. "No!" she said, with genuine shock.

"Yes," Emily insisted. "And as for my being attractive, only you would think so, Etta Lou. You and Lord Marsden, that is."

Swallowing the lump in her throat Emily tried not to think of how the "gentleman" in question had cornered her in her tiny office, backed her against a wall, and ripped her gown off one shoulder before a maid had fortuitously entered the room to make up the fire and put an end to his overtures. *That* particular bombazine gown Emily had ordered burned.

"But my dear," Etta Lou persisted, "your father was not just a sea captain. He was also the younger brother of a baron—I remember that from the application his sister, your Aunt Gussie, filled out before she died."

Emily nodded, fondly remembering the aged female relative she had lived with on and off while her father was away at sea. She had never even met her father, since, apart from the time with Aunt Gussie, she had spent her entire childhood at various private schools.

"And with your bones and classic features," Etta Lou continued, "your mother must also have come from good stock. You could not look so aristocratic and have had a mother whose family was composed of cits."

Emily shrugged. "It doesn't matter to me if I am a princess or a peasant. And I have no desire to lure a man into marrying me simply because I have good bloodlines or pretty clothes. I shall never marry unless I find a man who will not scoff at my scholarly pursuits. I will not give up the study of astronomy for any man," she finished resolutely.

"Emily!"

"Besides, I hardly think remaining unwed is cause for alarm. Perhaps someday I will meet a man who will accept me as I am, but if I do not, I do not. I shall survive perfectly well on my own."

"But how will you live?" Etta Lou asked. "You cannot want to be a schoolteacher for the rest of your life!"

"Why shouldn't I? That is what you have done, and you seem to be perfectly happy. Besides, thanks to Lord Marsden, I shan't be a schoolteacher much longer. To tell you the truth, I was thinking of looking for a position as a companion. Possibly to an elderly, bedridden woman who sleeps all day and has a magnificent library that I might study at my leisure."

"Our situations are nothing alike," Etta Lou declared. "*I* had a husband for thirty years. And men do exist who want more from their wives than a pretty face. My

Wilberforce was just one such. You mark my words, Emily, one day you will meet your dream man, and when you do, you will be sorry you did not heed my advice and make yourself a bit more presentable."

"Can we not discuss something else?" Emily snapped, her patience finally reaching its limits. "This conversation grows tiresome."

Etta Lou looked hurt. "There's no need to shout. If you want me to drop the subject, you've only to say so."

Emily sighed. "I am sorry. But you know, my getting married just to have a husband to take care of me isn't even to the point. I have money—perhaps not enough to live in luxury for an extended period, but at least enough to survive if I am unable to find another position—and I do have a place to go."

"Where?" Etta Lou asked curiously. "I remember your father left you a small quarterly sum upon his death ten years ago, but I did not think you had property as well."

"I don't. What I meant was that I recently received a letter from a Mr. Simms, my father's old solicitor. For some reason he wants me to come to London. He says he has something for me."

"How exciting! What could it be?"

"I haven't the slightest notion."

Etta Lou's eyes glistened. "If you're determined to leave, I won't try to stop you, Emily. But I want you to remember that any time you wish to come back, your position will be waiting. If you want to fight Lord Marsden, you've only to say the word and we'll fight him together. I'll not see you cast upon the world without a friend to your name. You've been like the daughter I never had."

Emily's heart constricted and she suppressed a strong urge to weep. "Oh, Etta Lou. You are so dear to me."

Clearing her throat, the old woman spoke briskly. "When do you plan to leave?"

Breathing deeply, Emily blinked away a film of tears. "The letter asked that I be in London at noon on the twenty-third—in two days. Since it takes half a day to travel the twenty miles to Town, I've booked passage on a mail coach for the day after tomorrow. Oh," she added as a thought occurred to her, "I'm taking my largest tele-scope with me but am leaving the other three for you to use in your astronomy classes. Perhaps whomever you hire as my replacement will have some knowledge of the sub-ject."

"That is kind of you, dear, but I cannot think many other women will have the knowledge necessary to teach the class. It is a pity we must wipe astronomy from our curriculum when you leave since, as far as I know, ours is the only school that teaches girls of Quality anything be-yond watercolors, embroidery, and how to plan a full-course meal."

"You're right. It's so unfair!" Emily said miserably. "Why do we allow society to force us to behave like mindless idiots concerned only with how much cream goes into crème brulé? Why are we at the mercy of unscrupu-lous men like Lord Marsden, who can ruin our reputations without anyone doubting their word, just because they are men?"

"I don't know, dear," Etta Lou said wistfully.

"Someday things will be different," Emily avowed. Then she smiled faintly. "Wouldn't it be wonderful if the solicitor were to tell me I had inherited a vast sum, so that we could promote the study of the sciences at girls' schools all over Britain?"

"Truly," Etta Lou asserted. "But for now I will simply pack your telescopes away until you return. I am sure all this trouble will blow over and, after you have taken a nice holiday, you will be able to return to us."

Remembering Lord Marsden's fury, Emily doubted it. "Perhaps," she replied noncommittally.

Etta Lou patted her hand. "I'll have the chef pack a nice luncheon for you to nibble on. Oh, and you'd best take Maggie along. Don't argue," she said quickly, as Emily opened her mouth to protest. "I know you're quite capable of traveling alone, but it simply isn't done. I'm sure the mail coach will be able to fit one more passenger, even if Maggie has to sit on the box. I'll pay her passage myself. You must have a companion, as no respectable hotel would give you a room, were you alone."

"Well, I had planned to stay at one of the inns just outside the city," Emily informed her. "Surely no one there will care that I have no maid."

Etta Lou gave a mortified gasp. "Stay at an inn? Impossible! You might be accosted—if they let you in the door! No, you must stay at Grillon's in Town. It is the only proper place for a young woman." Then she flashed Emily a rueful smile. "I'll worry about you, you know. You will write often, I hope. I'll be waiting to hear what your father's solicitor has to tell you."

"Of course I will. And thank you for letting me take Maggie."

The women exchanged wan smiles, then hugged when Etta Lou came from behind the desk and enveloped Emily in her lavender-scented embrace.

After a few moments Emily pulled away. "Well," she said briskly, "I must pack before we both turn into watering pots."

As soon as Emily arrived in London she took a room at Grillon's, as Mrs. Harriman had instructed. She found the hotel to be every bit as respectable an establishment as the older woman had claimed.

Once her single trunk of clothing and the two large packing crates containing her telescope, along with its mounting apparatus, were delivered and the carrot-haired, freckle-faced Maggie was settled in the chamber the two of them would share, Emily made her way directly to the solicitor's office.

Since the day was balmy and bright, and since she'd been informed that Mr. Simms's office was only a few blocks away from her hotel, she set out walking. In no time at all she neared the joint offices of Simms and Simms, Attorneys-at-Law, and climbed the gray stone steps leading the way into the elder Mr. Simms's domain. As she reached for the door handle, a deep, masculine voice spoke from behind.

"Please, allow me."

Turning, Emily settled a polite smile on the stranger standing a few paces away. She stepped back so he could open the door for her—and abruptly froze as she looked up into his face. Etta Lou Harriman's words roared through her mind: "You never know. You might meet the man of your dreams quite unexpectedly one of these days."

2

A flutter of excitement and warmth flickered in Emily's breast as she blinked up at the stranger's astonishingly handsome face. The man looked to be about thirty-two, and his eyes were the brilliant azure of a sunlit sea. A lazy smile framed teeth of gleaming white, and his chin, although shaven, was faintly shadowed, giving him a rakish appearance. His hair was as golden as sand on a tropical beach.

Although she hadn't given any thought to her appearance in years, Emily suddenly found herself wishing she had taken Etta Lou's advice and left off wearing her black bombazine gowns. Why, she must look a positive dowd! One hand fluttered to the battered chip straw bonnet perched on her head, but froze in mid-air as the man's smile broadened and his eyes danced with amusement.

"Miss?"

Realizing she was making a perfect cake of herself by staring at him over the bridge of her glasses as if she'd never seen a man before, Emily flushed and stepped through the open door. "Thank you," she muttered.

Once inside, she forbade her gaze to drift back toward the handsome stranger, heading instead toward a door on which the name "Silas Simms, Solicitor" was emblazoned in gold-leaf letters. But when the man behind her spoke again, she glanced back, unable to quell a surge of elation at the opportunity to hear his smooth voice once more.

"I'm sorry to trouble you," he remarked. Somehow his voice reminded Emily of being wrapped in a down comforter on an icy winter day. "I see you are here to see Mr. Simms. I, also, am here for that reason."

Still gazing raptly into his glorious blue eyes, Emily replied without quite realizing what she was saying. "Yes. Mr. Simms sent me a letter instructing me to visit on the twenty-third at noon. That is today's date, is it not?"

"It is indeed," he answered.

Emily started. "I do hope Mr. Simms has not mistakenly scheduled our appointments for the same time."

The man shook his head. "Never fear. I do not have an appointment. I am a seaman, and Mr. Simms left a note near my dock, informing me that he must see me immediately upon my return."

"Oh," Emily said with a frown, "it sounds important. Please take my appointment. I will just sit there until you are finished." She pointed to a low bench just outside the office. "If you would be so kind as to inform Mr. Simms that I am waiting, though, I would be most appreciative."

"Don't be a ninnyhammer," the man said firmly, tempering his order with a delightful smile. "Let us go in together. Whatever Simms has to tell me shouldn't take long. Please, allow me, once again." He moved forward and pulled open the office door, stepping back so she might enter.

Emily couldn't keep a warm glow from rising in her chest at his chivalrous gesture. Smiling, she prepared to step over the threshold, then froze as an unseen voice unfurled a bloodcurdling shriek.

"And the sun stood still, and the moon stayed, until God had avenged Himself against His enemies!"

Jumping back, Emily fell against the stranger, who put out two hands to catch her as she began to fall. Then, without warning, the stranger gave a harsh gasp and his hands went limp.

Emily landed on her backside with a thud in the middle of the marble-tiled hallway. Blinking in surprise, she noticed the man's handsome face had gone very pale. As though oblivious to her presence, he stepped over her prostrate form and hurried into the solicitor's office.

Emily squelched an angry retort with great difficulty.

"Polly!" the stranger said in a stunned voice. "Polly!

What the devil are you doing here? You've never been away from the captain since the day he bought you."

Curiosity *almost* overcoming ire, Emily smoothed her black bombazine skirts over her bared ankles, pushed her spectacles up more securely onto the bridge of her nose, grasped her reticule tightly, clambered awkwardly to her feet, and scrambled through the door in hot pursuit.

The stranger stood near one wall. On his right hand perched the oddest-looking creature Emily had ever seen. It was obviously a bird, but the feathers on its head were a vivid goldenrod color and stood straight up. The rest of the bird's body was white, with just a tinge of persimmon under its wings. Its eyes blazed.

"And the Lord punished the sinner, casting him into outer darkness so that the moon and stars were his only companions!"

This second outburst was undoubtedly aimed at Emily, for the bird, raising its head feathers even higher and snapping its huge beak, thrust its wings out from its body and hissed pointedly in her direction. Emily retreated several steps.

"For shame, Polly," the stranger chided, "that's no way to behave." Then he blinked at Emily with dawning mortification. "Oh, my dear lady, I must apologize for releasing you so precipitously. You see, Polly here belongs to a friend of mine. She must have escaped from him, somehow, and I suppose that is why Mr. Simms contacted me—so that I might claim her." He looked worried. "Although why he did not just send for Polly's owner, I cannot imagine. Please, forgive me?"

With his handsome face smiling so ingratiatingly at her, Emily was unable to remain piqued. "Of course. I understand," she replied stiffly, although she didn't really and, as the bird let out another rancorous hiss in her direction, didn't think she wanted to.

At that moment another man, short and thin, with wiry gray hair, appeared behind Emily in the doorway. "Ah, good. Miss Hastings, I presume," he said coolly, barely glancing at her as he fluttered a sheaf of important-looking papers. "You are right on time. I am Mr. Simms."

Emily opened her mouth to speak, but the solicitor suddenly noticed the golden-haired stranger, and, after hesitating a moment, smiled brilliantly. "And Lord Connor as well. How convenient that you have arrived at the same time as Miss Hastings. I *am* glad to see you. I see you've found Polly."

"Yes. How are you, Mr. Simms?" the younger man asked.

"Tolerable. Although I must say, it is a relief to have you come for Polly. Bird doesn't seem to like me above half."

Lord Connor scratched Polly's head with one finger. The bird responded to the young lord's ministrations by arching her body and making guttural noises which, Emily supposed, were indicative of pleasure, but which sounded as if Polly were anticipating a finger coming close enough that she might separate it from its owner's hand.

"She doesn't like anyone, really," Lord Connor replied. "She merely tolerates those of us who make her life comfortable. How does she happen to be here, anyway?"

The solicitor frowned. "I am afraid I have bad news, my boy. Captain Hawke is dead. As I wanted to be the one to break it to you, rather than have you discover it in an unpleasant, surprising way, I sent a letter to the harbormaster, to be given to you immediately upon your return to port." He opened a filing cabinet and thrust the papers he'd been holding into a drawer. "I see you got it.

"At any rate, when old Captain Hawke died Polly developed the nervous tendency of swooping down on the servants at Hawke's Nest when they least expected it and taking swipes at their ears with her beak. The old man, Cracker Jack, nearly lost one of his, poor chap, when it was ripped clean off his head. Doctor had to sew it back on, and I understand he put it on crookedly."

Emily cast a nervous glance at the bird's oversized beak and backed up yet another step.

"So," Mr. Simms continued, "after several of the servants were severely bitten, they managed to trap Polly in a basket and ship her to me, to deal with as I could. And I am returning her to you."

Lord Connor's face had gone deathly pale. "I see. How did the captain die?"

The solicitor turned to Emily. "If you'll just take a seat, Miss Hastings, I'll be with you shortly." He turned back to Lord Connor. "Captain Hawke and Cracker Jack went fishing in a dinghy. A sudden squall blew in and the boat capsized. The captain was lost, and Cracker Jack barely escaped with his life. The captain's body was not recovered. I'm truly sorry, my lord."

Despite feeling sorry for the young lord, Emily couldn't help but admire the fluidity of his muscles as Lord Connor settled comfortably into a leather chair. He moved as if he were made of liquid—smooth and supple and flowing. As she watched his thighs flex and relax, she felt an unfamiliar trembling in her breast and a weakness in her legs. Taking a deep breath, she dropped into another chair and forced her eyes to leave His Lordship's lower half and focus on her hands, folded demurely in her lap.

"Thank you for contacting me so soon," Lord Connor replied. He was silent for several moments. "Things won't be the same without the old man around yelling at everyone. We'll all miss him like the devil."

"I daresay. I'll miss him as well," Mr. Simms said reminiscently. "We'd known each other for years, you know."

The conversation continued in the same vein for several more minutes. Then, at last, the men seemed to remember Emily's presence and looked at her. Abruptly Mr. Simms's eyes widened and Lord Connor's face registered shock and dismayed recognition.

Just as Emily was considering the very real probability that Lord Connor's bird had been carrying some rare tropical illness, which both the solicitor and His Lordship had contracted and thus lost their reason, Mr. Simms spoke. "Miss . . . er . . . Hastings. Please forgive my ignoring you."

"Perfectly understandable under the circumstances, sir." Emily glanced toward Lord Connor, whose brows had lowered forbiddingly over eyes that had turned the color of a storm-washed sea. He looked as if he had just realized that, rather than a human female, Emily was instead a particularly virulent species of spider.

An icy ripple skittered over Emily's skin and, unable to hold Lord Connor's frigid gaze, she turned back toward the solicitor.

Mr. Simms's stare remained glued to her face. "By God. She is the spitting image of Lady Caroline. Is she not, Lord Connor? I'd not expected her to be so identical. Remove that awful hat, get rid of those dreadful spectacles, and let down those rich, dark curls, and you'd have Lady Carrie to the life.

"Look at her eyes, man!" Mr. Simms insisted breathlessly when Lord Connor did not reply. "Behind those awful glasses they're precisely the same shade of greenish-gray, and the eyelashes are just as thick and black. Of course, she doesn't look like much dressed as she is, but put the chit in an evening gown and give her the services of a good maid, and she could be every bit as attractive as Lady Carrie was—or at least a close second."

Emily wasn't sure which bothered her most: being compared to a dead woman, having her suspicions about her dowdy appearance proven correct, or being spoken of as if she weren't even present.

"I suppose she resembles Lady Caroline a trifle." Lord Connor's voice was rough and brittle. His face had regained some of its previous healthy color.

"A trifle?" Mr. Simms cried. "Are you blind, man?"

Emily's agitation grew by leaps and bounds. Confused, she alternated her gaze between the two men. What was going on?

Lord Connor glared at the solicitor and ground out, "Simms, I confess to a nasty suspicion that you didn't call me here merely to tell me about the captain's demise and to fetch Polly."

The solicitor jerked his gaze away from Emily's face. "Er . . . what did you say, my lord?"

"I asked why you called me here," Lord Connor said shortly. "I am convinced you're up to something. Since the captain is dead, and this woman looks like his deceased wife, I assume it is something concerning Captain Hawke's estate and this particular female."

After one last glance at Emily's face, Simms shook his head. "Amazing likeness. Absolutely amazing. Well, if you and Miss ... er ... Hastings will both come into my back office, I shall be happy to explain." With that he left the room and moved into a tiny chamber toward the back of the building.

Emily watched him go, then hurried to her feet and followed the solicitor. As she neared the door leading to the back room, Lord Connor spoke sharply from behind.

"I don't suppose you'd just go back to wherever it is you came if I asked nicely?"

Unable to think of a suitable response to this outrageous inquiry, Emily merely gaped at him.

"I didn't think so. Well," the young lord grumbled, "come on, then." With that he passed Emily and moved away. Climbing to his shoulder, the bird glared back at Emily and clicked her beak balefully.

3

Emily stared after the two men and the bird, thinking that, without a doubt, both men had gone as mad as poor King George. Too perplexed to do anything else, she trailed after them, taking care to stay well out of nipping range of Polly's bladelike beak.

Then, remembering Mr. Simms's rude comments about her appearance, she removed her spectacles and slipped them into one black bombazine pocket before entering the room, wishing all the while that she had the nerve to dispense with her battered chip-straw bonnet as well.

When they all stood in the back room, the solicitor smiled at Emily. "Please," he said, motioning toward a comfortable chair, "be seated, Miss . . . er . . . Hastings."

Lord Connor had already installed himself in one chair, and had placed Polly on the back of another, nearer the window. The bird kept her eyes on all of them, every now and then mumbling something unintelligible and snapping her beak as her large gray claws dug into the burgundy velvet backrest. As she watched the bird out of the corner of her eye, Emily kept her fingers wrapped tightly about her small black reticule, ready to use the bag as a weapon if Polly took to the air.

After seating himself behind a large oak desk and rummaging about in one of its drawers, the solicitor extracted a folder, set it on the desktop in front of him, flipped open the cover, and removed several papers. He unfolded a pair of glasses, perched them on his sharp nose, and began to peruse the documents.

Shortly thereafter Simms removed the spectacles, cleared his throat, and looked back and forth between

Emily and Lord Connor. "I shall start with you, my lord. As you know, while you were on your last voyage to Africa, your friend and benefactor, Captain Erastus Hawke, was lost at sea."

Lord Connor said nothing.

For a moment Mr. Simms looked decidedly uncomfortable, then asked abruptly, "You must be aware that, being a very cautious man, the captain employed two solicitors. I don't suppose the captain saw the other and signed over half the shipping company to you, as he was always promising, did he, my lord? I would have inquired myself, but do not know the second solicitor's direction. I know only of his existence, and the fact that he received copies of my documents and I of his."

"Not as far as I know. It wasn't necessary," Lord Connor said with a shrug. "We always understood between us how the shipping business stood—half being his and the other half mine."

Instead of looking pleased at this approbation, Mr. Simms frowned. "There is no gentle way to say this, my lord, so I may as well be blunt. Unless you can provide me with a notarized document stating that the captain signed half of the business over to you, I fear that legally you were merely an employee and have no right to any part of said establishment. As I would have received copies of any such document if it had been drawn up with Captain Hawke's other solicitor, I am quite certain such a document does not exist."

Lord Connor shrugged. "I don't suppose it matters. I know the old man meant to leave everything to me, anyway."

The solicitor shook his head. "I'm afraid you have been suffering under an unfortunate misunderstanding, my lord. I have the distasteful duty to inform you that your assumption that the captain intended to make you his sole heir was mistaken."

Lord Connor sighed heavily and glared at Emily. Eyebrows lowered, he muttered, *"She* has something to do with whatever it is you're leading up to, I'll wager."

"You are correct." The solicitor glanced uneasily at

Emily. "You must be wondering what all this is about, aren't you, Miss Emily—may I call you that for the moment, for simplicity's sake?"

"That is fine. And yes, I certainly am curious," Emily replied, wondering what was so very complicated about the name "Hastings."

"Do you recall some ten years ago, Miss Emily, when you received word that your father had died?"

"Naturally. I was most disturbed, but not heartbroken as I had never even met him. I don't think I received above three letters from him, either, during the entire time I was growing up."

She cast a glance at Lord Connor, whose countenance was growing more forbidding by the moment. "You see, my lord," she said politely in an attempt to explain, "my mother died at my birth, and, since my father was a naval officer and always at sea, he apparently felt it wisest to send me to an elderly relative for my early years and to a series of private schools when I grew older.

"When my Aunt Gussie—the relative with whom I lived while a young child—died, I had recently graduated from a minor school and been enrolled at a secondary academy for young ladies. After her funeral I went to live there. Four years later, shortly after my sixteenth birthday, I learned of my father's death and of a small competence he'd left me.

"My inheritance—which I have since invested and which has grown considerably, although I am still by no means wealthy—was not large enough to enable me to take up a residence by myself, not to mention that it would have been socially unacceptable. So, after I graduated from the academy, I decided to stay on as an instructor."

Emitting a disgusted snort, Lord Connor demanded, "What has this young woman's vastly interesting life to do with anything, Simms? Get to the point. Tell me the worst of it."

Thoroughly embarrassed, Emily fell silent but held her head high.

"Come now, my lord," chided Mr. Simms, "there's no need to be rude. You are a gentleman, sir."

Glancing down at her reticule, Emily said quietly, "That's all right. I am sure His Lordship is not interested in the autobiography of a young woman whom he had never even met until today. Please, Mr. Simms, just do as he asks."

Flinging Lord Connor a reproving stare, the solicitor recommenced. "As it happens, Miss Emily, your father did not die when you were sixteen. He passed away only a short while ago. And his surname was not Hastings. It was Hawke."

Emily's gaze flew to the solicitor's in questioning surprise. "I beg your pardon?"

"He was the captain of whom you have heard His Lordship and me speak. *Your* name is also Hawke—not Hastings as you have been led to believe these many years. Lady Caroline, the woman to whom we compared you a short time ago, was your mother. As you told us, she died when you were born. She was the last of her line."

"Are you trying to tell me that my father was alive for the past ten years?" Emily shook her head. "I am sorry for any inconvenience you may have suffered in sending for me, Mr. Simms, but you must be mistaken. That is not possible."

"I'm afraid it is," interjected Lord Connor testily. "Although Hawke never told me he had a daughter, I once caught him speaking with a portrait of Lady Caroline which hangs over the fireplace in the library at Hawke's Nest, begging her forgiveness for sending you away.

"From what I overheard, it seems he went all to pieces when your mother died and couldn't bear to look at the baby—at you. So he shipped you off to one of his relatives. An apparently penniless one, or you might have inherited her wealth and stayed away from here, where you're definitely not wanted," he finished coldly.

Avoiding Lord Connor's glacial stare, Emily turned her attention to the solicitor. "But if my father was alive all these years, Mr. Simms, why did he not contact me? Why did he want me to think he had died? What about my name? What possible reason could he have had to let me believe my name was Hastings if it is really Hawke? And

why would my Aunt Gussie have gone along with such a
lie? She must have known the truth."

The solicitor looked uncomfortable. "Both of them
probably felt it best that you weren't associated with the
name 'Hawke.' You see . . ." He fell silent, then sighed.
"Your father had a good reason not to tell you his true
identity. Not long after he'd sent you away, he took up a
rather unusual trade. He was . . . that is to say . . ."

Lord Connor emitted a rude grunt and waved a hand at
Simms in dismissal. The solicitor leaned back in his chair
with a relieved sigh. "What Simms is trying to say is that
Captain Hawke, your father, was a pirate. A buccaneer. A
sea dog. A sea wolf of the most dangerous sort. You know,
'avast matey' and 'walk the plank' and all that rot.

"That's when he picked up Polly here." Lord Connor
nodded toward the cockatoo. "Old Hawke had some crazy
idea that any pirate worth his salt must have a parrot."

Nonchalantly he brushed away a white feather that had
floated down to his sleeve. "As for your name, the old
man probably didn't want your reputation sullied if he
were ever caught and hanged to death. As for your aunt,
you can hardly think she would have wished your person
associated with the scum of the sea."

Emily's heart thudded in her chest like a great lump of
lead as she relived in an instant all the hours she'd spent
as a child making believe that her father was somewhere
at sea fighting the dreadful French. She'd been so certain
he would return to England, earn a medal from the king,
and send for her that they might make their home together.
When she'd heard of his supposed death, she'd found solace in the belief that he'd died a hero, serving his country.

She swallowed as her comforting dreams disintegrated
into harsh reality. "Is it true, Mr. Simms? Was my father
no better than a common criminal?"

The solicitor flushed. "Well, miss, I'd not have put it
quite like that, although he *was* involved in illegal activities. But he only preyed on those who had preyed on others, even though he never got legal permission from the
king to act as a privateer. In my opinion his only real
crime was not returning his ill-gotten gains to their rightful

owners. Of course, that would have been quite impossible since there was no way to know to whom everything belonged."

"So," Emily said grimly, finally accepting the awful truth, "how does it happen that he lived another ten years after leading me to believe him dead? And what part does Lord Connor play in this little melodrama? I take it all this has something to do with His Lordship's 'inheritance'?"

Mr. Simms nodded. "Ten years ago, when your father asked me to set up a small fund for your future well-being, he gave me every cent he possessed to put into that fund. Since then, however, he amassed quite a substantial fortune. I must tell you, before you feel that he deserted you, that the captain kept abreast of every move you made. He just didn't feel worthy of declaring himself your father."

"I would have accepted him with open arms," Emily said softly.

"How perfectly charming," Lord Connor remarked blandly, buffing his nails against his coat.

Ignoring the snide remark, Mr. Simms smiled at Emily. "I believe you would have. Anyway, although your lives were separate for the last ten years, he thought of you always, and that is why I have called you here. Captain Hawke had no intention of allowing you to scrape your way in a girls' school while he possessed such riches."

"Wait a bloody minute, Simms!" Lord Connor erupted. "Are you saying Hawke left everything to her? What about my shipping firm?"

Mr. Simms cleared his throat. "He did not leave everything to Miss Emily; however, I have some bad news about the shipping business. Before he died, Captain Hawke had me draw up a codicil stating that the shipping business was to be sold."

Polly let out a frightened squawk as Lord Connor leaped out of his seat. "Sold? I've spent years making that enterprise successful. It will only be sold over my dead body!"

"My lord," Mr. Simms said quietly, "please sit down. I don't like it any better than you do. I assure you it makes my job quite uncomfortable."

Pinning Emily with a baleful stare, Lord Connor did as he was told.

"As I was saying," Simms continued, "the shipping business is to be sold. However, you might yet have a chance to own it, my lord."

"And the moon is really a hunk of green cheese," Lord Connor said with a growl. "You know every cent I made from the shipping ventures was reinvested in the business. Now I find out that not only is the business I spent much of my life and all of my funds building not going to be mine, but that I have no money whatsoever with which to buy it back. You needn't think my brother Markus will ever advance such a sum. If I fell down in a street and were about to be trampled by a coach and four, he'd not lift a finger to help me. He'd be more likely to stand on the roadside and cheer. Furthermore—"

"You may yet have the wherewithal to buy it," insisted Mr. Simms, interrupting the younger man's tirade, "if you will just permit me to explain."

"If you don't mind, Lord Connor," Emily inserted bravely, "I would like to hear what else Mr. Simms has to say."

"I'm sure you would," Lord Connor retorted.

The bird chose this moment to interject a comment of her own, hissing in Emily's direction.

"And the earth trembled and was dark, and the moon became as blood, and molten fire consumed the bringer of injustice!"

"My thoughts precisely, Polly," Lord Connor remarked. He clamped his mouth shut and sat back, arms folded uncompromisingly across his broad chest. He kept his eyes trained on Emily's face.

Emily trembled with fear and anger. How could she ever have thought Lord Connor charming?

The solicitor cleared his throat. "Perhaps the best way to go about this would be simply to read the captain's will and let you two decide where to go from there. Also, as I stated earlier, the captain's other solicitor is in possession of these same papers, so he wouldn't be able to give you any new information. I tell you this to keep you from making a wasted trip to see him. If you like, Lord Connor, I would, however, be happy to visit him myself if you will give me his direction, in order to make absolutely certain the captain did not leave papers ascertaining your legal partnership in the shipping business in his care."

Lord Connor shrugged. "I hardly think it necessary."

"Very good," Simms replied. "Then let us read the will." He shot a glance at Lord Connor, who gave a gruff nod of approval. "Miss Hawke?"

"Please," Emily added.

Rearranging the papers on his desk, Mr. Simms picked up a document. Taking a deep breath, he commenced.

4

Mr. Simms read swiftly and quietly through the usual list of bequeathments to servants and the like, then his voice rose. " 'Having reached the age when I am not much longer for this world, I instruct my solicitor to send a message to my blood daughter, Emily, begging her attendance in London.

" 'At the same time, I would have Mr. Simms send another missive to Lord Connor Duncan, requesting his attendance on that same day to facilitate the reading and understanding of this last will and testament. You will find the section concerning their inheritances in the envelope, sealed with my personal crest, at the back of this document.' "

The solicitor looked up briefly. "I have already seen to the distribution of the other bequeathments, but even I have not yet read what the captain has in store for you two. Ah, here is the envelope." Mr. Simms retrieved an envelope, sealed with red wax and impressed with the seal from the captain's signet ring, from the pile of papers before him and ceremoniously removed the document. He glanced over the page and began.

" 'Allow me at this time to send both Connor and Emily my greetings and best wishes. Before we get started with who gets what, let me give you both a bit of advice: Keep your eyes looking toward Heaven, and you will find your just reward.' "

Emily's brow wrinkled.

Lord Connor, seeing her confusion, informed her coolly, "The old man couldn't leave off preaching even after his death, I see. He seemed to become obsessed with Scripture just before I left on my last trip to Africa. Kept quoting the Bible—inaccurately, as I am certain a schoolteacher like yourself has noticed—every time I was with him, and telling me how important it was that I pay attention to his spiritual counsel." He looked thoughtful, then turned to Mr. Simms. "Is there any chance the captain had lost his senses and that, therefore, this will is invalid?" he asked hopefully.

"I fear not, my lord," Simms replied. "He underwent stringent mental examinations three weeks before his death. Besides, if this document *were* to be proven invalid, everything would go to Miss Hawke, as she is the captain's closest blood relative. You would receive nothing. The mental analysis was performed by one . . ." He scanned another paper. "Doctor Dibble. He's the same medic who sewed old Cracker Jack's ear back on."

Lord Connor looked disappointed. "I know Dibble. He's a competent physician." He groaned exasperatedly. "For God's sake, Simms, there must be some way to get around the old man's desire to sell the shipping business."

Mr. Simms shook his head firmly. "The captain ordered me to make absolutely certain there was no way to break this will. Unless Miss Hawke chose to contest the document, there is no chance—"

"Well that's it, then!" broke in Lord Connor. Turning to Emily, he said, "You contest the will and we will divide everything equally when the legal dust settles."

Mr. Simms spoke up. "I don't know that you'd want to do that, Miss Hawke. Over time you might succeed in breaking the will, but the legal system moves like a snail stuck in honey. And there is the added problem that, since the estate would be frozen in the event of litigation, any money for legal fees would have to come from your own pockets."

"But I can't manage that!" Lord Connor protested. "I have nothing beyond a few pounds! Every other cent I possess is buried in the shipping business! How dare that old reprobate do this to me! He must have been planning this for years!"

Mortified by this evidence of Lord Connor's heartless

greed, Emily glared at him. "I can see why my father wasn't overly concerned with your welfare if you were his friend only because you stood to gain after his death, my lord. I am surprised he gave any thought to you at all."

Lord Connor gave her a frigid glance. "You mistake my sentiments, Miss Hawke; the captain was like a father to me. And I do not think, since we acted as partners in all things even though he failed to put our agreements to paper, that I am to be faulted for not wishing to be pauperized simply because he felt a belated and, in my opinion, *misplaced* sense of duty."

Although her fingers were trembling so violently that if she had not been clenching her hands together they would have rattled right off her lap, Emily held his cold gaze proudly. She did not trust her quivering lips to obey well enough to voice a retort, and so remained silently aloof.

"However," Lord Connor went on, "I would not have minded sharing everything with you, as you *are* the captain's daughter, if he had only left the shipping business out of it. Or given you his half. But I cannot graciously agree to give you everything I have worked for during the past ten years." He flushed. "I simply haven't the funds to be so magnanimous. If that is avarice in your eyes, then so be it."

"Let us read on," the solicitor said quickly, as if eager to avoid a confrontation.

" 'Emily, I imagine you wonder why I would go to the trouble to find you after my death. Since I consciously concealed my identity from you while I was alive, you must think I did not care about you. However, I have kept abreast of your interests for the last ten years, and have always loved you and kept your welfare in mind. Had you shown any sign of being unhappy or in want, I'd have taken care of matters immediately.

" 'Now to you both: Finding myself the possessor of an extremely large and valuable fortune, I am at odds concerning what to do with it upon my demise. On the one hand, I have Emily, who by law deserves everything I possess. On the other, there remains the fact that without Connor I would have next to nothing to even think of dividing. Therefore, I have decided to let fate determine your fortunes.

" 'Hidden somewhere in or near my Cornish estate, Hawke's Nest, is a cache of wondrous treasures. In Mr. Simms's possession are two more envelopes, sealed with my mark, each containing half of a treasure map. Each of you is to receive one of these packets, but neither is to open it until you reach Hawke's Nest—this is my final wish; I beg you not to disappoint an old man and open your envelopes in haste.

" 'Besides the map there are other clues which will become apparent as time passes. Whether you choose to work together or on your own is at your discretion. Winner takes all; the division of the treasure depends on the whims of the victor. And now good-bye, and good luck.' "

Lord Connor leaped to his feet, disturbing Polly again. "This is an outrage! I earned every shilling of that old fool's fortune while he sat in his castle gazing at the stars, and now he plans to send us off on a mock treasure hunt! I won't stand for this!"

"I do not think you have any choice, my lord, unless you want to forfeit the victory to Miss Hawke." As Lord Connor did not reply, Mr. Simms fished about among his papers, then drew forth two unmarked, sealed envelopes. "Who shall choose first?"

Lowering himself back in his chair, Lord Connor waved a hand wearily. "Ladies first, by all means."

Mr. Simms turned the packets in Emily's direction. "Miss Hawke?"

After Emily took one and sat clutching it in her lap, the solicitor passed the other to Lord Connor. Emily watched as His Lordship tucked it into his coat pocket without giving it a single glance. She looked back at Mr. Simms as the solicitor spoke again.

"Who knows? Besides the captain's loot you might be lucky enough to find the lost treasure as well—you remember the tale, Lord Connor, of the cache of jewels a Norman king hid somewhere near Hawke's Nest?"

"I remember the tale but am not fool enough to believe it is true."

Simms gasped. "Not true? Of course the story is true. Tales of the treasure's magnificence have been passed down in Cornish history for hundreds and hundreds of years."

Lord Connor raised a brow. "How is it that you know so much about it?"

For a moment Simms stared at the young lord. His face seemed quite pale. Then, clearing his throat, he seemed to recover his composure. "Oh, I have always been a student of history. And that particular story is quite fascinating." He turned to Emily. "Have you heard it, Miss Hawke?"

Emily shook her head. "No. Please, tell me."

Lord Connor gave a breathy sigh but leaned back in his chair.

Simms beamed and quickly launched into the tale. "Hundreds of years ago, a very rich Norman king built the castle now known as Hawke's Nest. He had not lived there long when he met a young maiden and fell in love with her. At first she refused to marry him, and he began showering her with jewels; one new jewel or exquisite gem for every day that passed.

"When the girl finally accepted his offer of marriage, he sent for the best jewelers and goldsmiths in the land and had them create two gloriously beautiful crowns for them to wear on their wedding day.

"Unfortunately, as the story goes, on their honeymoon night, Saxon invaders stormed the castle. There was no time to pack up the castle riches, so the king ordered them hidden in a place where the invaders, if they succeeded in taking the castle, would never find them."

Emily listened breathlessly. "What happened?"

Mr. Simms's eyes grew somber. "The Saxons took the castle and massacred everyone inside. Not a soul escaped. Ever since, people have searched for the treasure. Except for your father. To the best of my knowledge, he never bothered. He never seemed to see any reason, since he had plenty of blunt."

Emily sighed. "How romantic, and how very sad."

"Mm-hm," Simms agreed, echoing her sigh with his own.

Lord Connor sat up abruptly. "I hate to be a killjoy, but we do have some decisions to make, Miss Hawke. If you and Mr. Simms can drag yourselves out of dreamland, perhaps we might get down to business."

Emily felt her cheeks heat. She directed her comments to the solicitor. "Of course. I'm sure, Mr. Simms, that if Lord Connor and I put aside our differences and work together all will turn out admirably. After all, the captain meant for us to find his treasure, so surely he wouldn't have made the task impossible."

"Quite right." Mr. Simms cleared his throat and removed his glasses. "There is one other thing."

Lord Connor put his head in his hands, then raised a resigned countenance. "I might have known the old man wouldn't be satisfied with merely turning our lives upside down. What other method of torture has the old fool come up with?"

Mr. Simms rubbed the bridge of his nose where his spectacles had left a red mark. "You have exactly one month in which to find the treasure. Captain Hawke left instructions that the shipping business was to be sold on the twenty-third of next month. If I were you, I would start my search as quickly as possible."

As if to punctuate his sentiments, Polly let out a shrill squawk before launching into another quote.

"The stars in the heavens shall lead you out of the darkness, but if you do not follow them you'll stay in hell forever!"

Emily jumped, but not quite as high as she had the first time she'd heard the bird's clamorous declarations. Turning to Lord Connor, she gave him a brief look-over, and then nodded. "I daresay I can stand your boorishness for one month. What do you say, my lord? Shall we enter this venture as partners rather than opponents? It seems to me that two heads are definitely more likely to find a hidden treasure than one."

"If we must," Lord Connor grumbled. Then he brightened. "We will outwit the old man and, having found his pirate's booty, divide our spoils and part forever."

Ignoring a painful twinge at his blatant disinterest in her, Emily directed a question to the solicitor. "Where is Hawke's Nest, Mr. Simms?"

"In Cornwall. On the tip of Lizard Point. It's rugged, but very lovely, country."

"I quite agree with Mr. Simms; the high coast, as it is known, is indeed beautiful," Lord Connor volunteered, "if you like savage storms, forbidding, rocky beaches, and gloomy moors. And of course the place is widely known for being a veritable magnet for shipwrecks and smugglers.

"Often ships trying to round the point are simply blown off course by one of the numerous sou'westers and smash onto the rocks surrounding either Lizard Point or its neighbor, Land's End. And of course there are the wreckers, those families who make their livings tricking ships into smashing to pieces on the rocks offshore."

Emily shuddered.

"You know," Lord Connor continued with a speculative glance at her horrified face, "sometimes the gales off the Atlantic blow so fiercely that a man daren't venture outside without two friends to hold his hair on his head.

"And the lightning! On Lizard Point it consistently strikes what scrubby trees and small cottages are nearby, so most houses are built of native stone. That way only their roofs and interiors are destroyed. There are very few trees left anymore, either. Of course," he finished glibly, "Hawke's Nest is equipped with lightning rods, although I've never had much faith in their ability to deflect lightning's deadly force from its desired victim."

"Are the storms truly that bad?" Emily asked shakily.

"Oh, yes," Lord Connor answered. "But if you'd like, I'd be happy to take your half of the map and find the treasure myself, Miss Hawke. Then I would send your share to your banking establishment, and you need not brave Cornwall's deadly environment at all."

Emily hadn't missed the faint, satisfied smile that crossed Lord Connor's countenance when she'd felt the blood drain from her face at his description. In a sudden surge of rebellion as the handsome young lord lifted a hand and casually examined a fingernail, she returned firmly, "It sounds fascinating. I look forward to my visit."

Lord Connor straightened in his chair. "As you wish," he said curtly. "Mr. Simms, not that I mean Miss Hawke any harm, but would you mind telling me what happens in the event that either myself or the captain's daughter should meet with an untimely demise?"

Emily's gaze flew up to the young lord's angelically handsome face. Good God! Surely he wasn't suggesting . . .

Mr. Simms didn't bat an eyelash. "In that event, the survivor inherits everything."

"I see." Lord Connor studied Emily cryptically. "Are we agreed, then, Miss Hawke? We work together to find the treasure and then part ways?"

Emily returned his examination. If she went to Hawke's Nest, would she leave it in a carriage or in a pine box? And even if Lord Connor meant her harm, did she have any choice but to go to Cornwall and try to find her father's treasure?

Even though the competence the captain had settled on her years before had increased considerably, she still wouldn't be able to exist for long without finding a position. And, although she'd put on a brave front for Etta Lou, she very much doubted she would find another position of any kind once word of the fiasco with Lord Marsden got out—which it undoubtedly would.

No, she had no choice. She had to go to Cornwall.

As for Lord Connor, she mused, it was indisputable that she stood a far greater chance of finding the treasure *with* His Lordship's help than without it, whether he wished her ill or not.

Her fingers tightened on the envelope in her hands. She tucked it into her reticule. One thing was certain: She wasn't about to hand over her half of the treasure map to this man who seemed scarcely able to conceal his wish for her demise.

"Miss Hawke?" Lord Connor prodded. "Have you decided to stay in London, then, while I search for the treasure? A wise choice. I'm sure you will not be sorry."

Meeting Lord Connor's splendid blue eyes, Emily forced a smile. "On the contrary, my lord. I look forward to seeing my father's home."

Mr. Simms smiled and got to his feet. "Excellent. Then, if you both will agree to accompany me to a nearby restaurant for a light luncheon, I will send one of my employees to see about procuring a suitable traveling vehicle. I do not believe you keep a carriage in London to use when you return from a voyage, do you, Lord Connor?"

"No, simply my stallion. I enjoy traveling to Hawke's Nest by horseback," replied Lord Connor. "The wind in my hair reminds me of the breezes on the ocean. I am staying at the Templeton. Oh, and I also brought a groom along to care for my mount. You will find him in the stable."

"My maid and I are staying at Grillon's," Emily said. Then she started. "I fear I shall need the services of a cart, Mr. Simms. I will be taking two large crates with me."

"That will be no trouble at all," the solicitor said reassuringly. "I will have the carriage pick you up in the morning when you are both well-rested. Now then, shall we go? I swear I am quite famished."

5

They quit London the following day, amid a torrential downpour. Emily had decided to keep Maggie with her until they arrived at Hawke's Nest so that the maid might act as a chaperone. Once there they would hire a housekeeper, who would take up the responsibility of acting as duenna in Maggie's place.

Although Lord Connor vehemently decried the need for such action, after her experience with Lord Marsden, Emily had stolidly insisted that, unless a chaperone were present, she would not step foot inside the castle or, for that matter, into a closed carriage, with a man not related to her.

And, she had pointed out firmly, if she did not step foot inside, neither did her half of the treasure map.

They'd been traveling for several days and had just crossed the wide Tamar River and entered Cornwall when Emily put away a book she'd been perusing, leaned back, and rested her head against her seat. Although it was only past morning, she was tired and rather hungry, and longed for a cup of the hot chocolate with which Maggie had spoiled her each evening.

There was one comforting thing about their circumstances. To Emily's relief, Lord Connor's ill-tempered bird had been caged and placed beside the young groom on the back of the carriage. Both Lord Connor's mount and the groom's horse were tied to the back of the vehicle as well. Now and then Polly let out an angry squawk, which was accompanied by the groom's sharp cry of pain and rage.

Their progress had been slow, due to the second vehicle in their entourage, a low-slung wagon pulled by two decrepit, shaggy horses. The cart was driven by a sharp-tongued elf of a man who shouted curses and epithets over his horses' heads in an unsuccessful effort to make them move more quickly. At the driver's side sat his young apprentice, who was handsome in a rough-hewn way that made Maggie peek out of the carriage window every few minutes to gaze back at the fellow.

As another of the cart driver's raucous cries pierced the air, Emily wondered how the two large packing crates containing her telescope and its mounting apparatus were faring. Determined to have a look, she ignored the scowl marring Lord Connor's handsome face and wriggled past him on the seat, thrusting her head out into the drizzling rain that had plagued their journey from the start.

"Everythin' all right, miss?" the maid asked.

Emily craned her neck further for a moment, then moved back inside. "I think so. I don't see any problems. Mr. Crabbe was merely screeching at his horses again. Honestly, I don't think I've ever met a more ill-tempered human being." She paused, flicking a glance at Lord Connor. "At least, not more than once."

Maggie smothered a giggle.

Lord Connor glared and pulled his low-brimmed, high-crowned beaver hat down over his eyes. In a few moments he appeared to be deeply asleep. Shortly thereafter Maggie had also leaned back and was snoring pleasurably, her carrot-red hair disheveled and her mouth open, as her head lolled from side to side with each sway of the vehicle.

In actuality, Connor was wide awake. As he watched Miss Hawke sitting opposite him, he felt awash with conflicting emotions.

He was fully aware that another gentleman would have walked away from the whole situation upon realizing that his benefactor had had a legitimate heir. Or, he thought grudgingly, if he'd been financially unable to do that, a gentleman would at least have treated her with congeniality.

He had no doubt Miss Hawke was truly the captain's daughter, although the woman looked far more like Lady Caroline than old Hawke. Yet, the stubborn tilt to Miss Emily's chin when she'd refused to leave London unless

Connor agreed to hire a chaperone the moment they arrived at Hawke's Nest had been a shade of the captain himself.

For a split second when she'd made the balking gesture, Connor had been overwhelmed with sudden, piercing grief at the old pirate's death, suffering a pang so sharp it took his breath away and made his hands tremble so fiercely he was forced to clench them on his thighs.

God damn it, he missed the old man!

Shuffling on the seat, he pushed away a wave of melancholia. His movement caused the captain's daughter to turn toward him. Positive she could not see his eyes, he found this the perfect opportunity to study her features, as well as the myriad of emotions playing across them.

The only remarkable thing about the captain's daughter was her eyes, an extraordinary shade even behind her ridiculous wire-rimmed spectacles.

Mentally, Connor removed the glasses and set them aside.

Much better. Surrounded with thick black lashes, her eyes were huge, slate-gray touched with flecks of amber and green—like some tidepools he had once seen in Madagascar. Idly he wondered if, like the pools, her eyes hid unforeseen depths.

His gaze drifted upward.

Her hair, tucked up beneath a mobcap of white linen, was the precise shade of a dried pepper, a rich blue-black he had seen only on those of Asian descent. Of course, he reasoned, the captain had been a Cornish man, one of those short, dark-eyed, dark-haired people rumored to be of fairy stock.

Her light eyes, on the other hand, must be a gift from her mother, who, if memory served, had been one of those outrageously attractive people known as the Black Irish. Lady Caroline's hair had been equally dark, but her eyes were gray-green.

Just then a cool breeze wafted through the open window, brushing over Miss Hawke's body. Connor drew an appreciative breath as his body responded to her perfume. The scent reminded him of spice and sandalwood, and held murmurings of exotic ports of call—smells definitely at odds with Miss Hawke's unmistakably English appearance.

He breathed deeply again and was swept back through time and space amid memories of sunshine, palm fronds, desert oases. Of gleaming, white-hot sand, of natives riding proud white Arabians with flowing manes. Of pebble-sized rubies, emeralds, diamonds, and sapphires. Of flawless pearls suspended from a shapely harem girl's ears.

One silky lock of Miss Hawke's hair had slipped unnoticed from its pins and fell over her ivory brow like ebony satin. The remainder was tightly swept beneath a dowdy mobcap in a manner which, Connor decided, must certainly be painful. There was one benefit he could see to the unflattering hairstyle, though: it left her deliciously delicate earlobes exposed.

Tilted skyward, her rather long, aquiline nose appeared a trifle haughty, but her mouth, relaxed now that she believed herself unobserved, was more scrumptious than he'd have expected to find on a schoolmarm. While her top lip was quite narrow, the lower was very full and indescribably sensual.

In all, her mouth looked, he mused with surprise, as if it had been made to be kissed. He caught himself wondering if she had ever experienced such a pleasant caress. Of course, he thought just as quickly, given her matronly mode of dress and obviously schoolmarmish manner, it was unlikely that anything more enticing than daily sustenance had ever touched her mouth. Undoubtedly, no man had ever even considered kissing her.

It was impossible to tell what her figure looked like. Besides her neck, arching out of a high neckline with just a touch of lace at the collar, black gloved hands clasped demurely in her lap, and black kidskin slippers placed properly side by side beneath the hem of her hideous gown, Connor could see nothing of the remainder of her body. Hidden beneath the tent shaped, coal-colored gown, which looked as if it had been made to fit the proverbial circus fat lady, any bustline seemed non-existent.

And yet, he noted, the faint rise of her bosom beneath the voluminous bodice made him think that, perhaps, she was pleasingly endowed—she would *have* to be for her breasts to show at all beneath that hideous bombazine shroud.

And then, continuing along this pleasant vein, he recalled the moment which had only just passed, when she had leaned past him to look out the window. At first he had been irritated at being so crowded, but then, as she had arched her body, the flaccid bodice had pressed quite tightly against her chest and his irritation had vanished instantly.

Then, he thought with a hidden grin, *then* he had seen what treasures the woman kept hidden away from libidinous masculine eyes. One little movement and he'd have had his hands quite full!

At that moment and with that thought, one carriage wheel fell into a deep rut, bouncing its three occupants into the air. Miss Hawke's eyes widened and her cheeks blazed as she noticed his silent inspection.

"My lord!" she gasped. "I thought you were asleep!"

Pushing back his hat Connor grinned lazily and settled himself more comfortably against the carriage's velvet squabs. Really, she looked almost charming with that rosy blush washing her cheeks.

"Does my being awake mean you will feel unable to continue your study of my person?" he inquired smoothly. "If you like, I could close my eyes so that you might carry on."

Behind her glasses, Miss Hawke's eyes widened. "Yes. No! Thank you. That is—no!"

He raised an eyebrow inquiringly and, as her flush deepened and she shook her head violently, his grin widened. "Are you quite certain?"

"No—I mean yes. Thank you!" she stammered.

Connor felt a curious stab of regret at seeing her features go from pleasantly relaxed to stiff and proper. He sighed and frowned. "Don't be embarrassed, Miss Hawke. I suppose it is natural that we are curious about each other.

After all, until a few days ago we had no knowledge of each other's existence."

"That's true enough," she replied cautiously.

The corners of Connor's mouth lifted slightly. "Do you think we might put aside our dislike of each other for the time being? I swear I've found the last few days being unable to converse with another human being exceedingly tiresome."

Miss Hawke eyed him doubtfully, as though wondering if he was up to something or if he really wanted to let bygones be bygones. At last she nodded. "I suppose we could."

"Wonderful. While I'm on such a winning streak, I would also like to take this opportunity to apologize for my unforgivable behavior at the solicitor's office. It's just that your appearance quite took me by surprise. You must understand that I had expected to receive the captain's entire estate.

"Not because I was avaricious," he assured her quickly as her mouth began to tighten, "but because he practically raised me as his son and partner. Because our business was never legalized on paper does not mean it was not a partnership."

Miss Hawke's heavenly mouth relaxed and she almost smiled. "I quite understand, my lord. And I agree—it would be more pleasant, since we're going to be working closely together, if we could keep from lunging at each other's throat every moment."

Connor nodded.

"Not only that," Miss Hawke said, "but it also seems foolish to be perpetually at daggers drawn when it would obviously be more in our best interests to be on good terms. I am sure we'd be far more likely to find the treasure, and thus save your shipping business, if we could work together without bloodshed." Finally she did smile, shyly. "What say you? Shall we cry pax and be friends?"

Connor returned her smile. "I should feel honored."

One hour later Connor awoke to find Miss Hawke hurtling into his arms. His gasp of chagrin at being awakened in such a precipitous manner was mixed with delight at discovering that the captain's daughter was every bit as amply endowed as he'd suspected. "My dear miss—"

He didn't have time to utter another word.

6

Everything tilted precariously to one side and the world began spinning. A tremendous cracking sound echoed like a gunshot, and then the carriage was bouncing over and over, throwing its passengers back and forth against the cushions, the ceiling, the walls, and one another.

Connor groaned with pain as his head crashed against the carriage floor. Then he cried out as he and Miss Hawke were thrown through the gaping hole that was left when the carriage's door was ripped off and they landed with a heavy thud on the ground.

As they rolled down the muddy embankment, he instinctively held Miss Hawke's head to his chest, turning her quickly and protecting her with his body with each rotation so that she barely came into contact with the rocky earth.

When the world finally stopped spinning, he opened his eyes to find her stretched out on top of him, staring down into his face with blind horror. Her fingers clutched his cravat so tightly he could scarcely breathe. The rain had ceased, and in the sky beyond Miss Hawke's head, he noticed the sun peeping from behind a moisture-laden cloud.

When the captain's daughter made no attempt to stand, Connor managed a shaky grin and tugged her fingers free of his neck-cloth. "Dear lady, while I would ordinarily welcome such overtures, just now I think we might wish to see if our companions are hurt."

"Yes, of course."

Her voice was a frightened tremor; still she didn't move—didn't even seem to know him. Connor frowned,

40

regretting his flippancy. Squinting, he studied her eyes for signs of injury. "Miss Hawke? Are you hurt?"

Sliding off him and rolling away, she pushed to her feet and raised a trembling hand to her head. Brushing her fallen locks back from her face, she replied shakily, "I do not think so. Just frightened and confused and a bit dizzy. What happened?"

"I am not certain," Connor replied. He sat up and shook his head sharply. A stabbing pain accompanied the movement. Gritting his teeth, he tried to stifle the sudden gasp that slipped between his lips.

"Lord Connor!" Miss Hawke cried as he swayed precariously. "There is a deep gash along the left side of your brow. Please, sir, lie back down!"

Connor shook his head more gently. "That isn't necessary. Aside from a splitting headache, I'm sure I'll survive."

Miss Hawke didn't look convinced. "You're going to have quite a scar."

He laughed weakly. "I've always wanted to have a devastating scar that would make all the ladies swoon—although I never wanted to undergo the necessary trauma. But really, I feel much better. We must search for our companions."

He stood and gazed back uphill in the direction from which they had tumbled. First examining the gouges in the moist dark earth, he then turned and looked downhill for some sign of passengers—dead or alive. Then he swallowed. "My God. Climb uphill without looking back, Miss Hawke. I'll follow momentarily."

Ignoring his command, the captain's daughter whirled about and peered into the ravine. A sharp cry erupted from her throat and she threw herself into Connor's arms, pressing her face against his chest. Connor put a hand on the back of her head, cradling her gently as he continued examining the wreckage.

At the bottom of the crevasse, the carriage lay upside down with its wheels still spinning. Apparently the carriage horses had escaped injury, for they were not connected to the traces; indeed, the entire front end of the carriage was missing, as if it had been ripped clean away. Both Connor's and the groom's mounts, however, lay motionless, in a tangled heap.

The shattered pieces of timber that had once been the old cart, and the horses that had drawn it, lay near the chassis of Lord Connor's carriage. Nothing moved. The cart driver and his apprentice were nowhere in sight. Miss Hawke's belongings, which had been packed so carefully atop the dray, lay strewn from one side of the chasm to the other.

Numerous black bombazine gowns were scattered across the grass like huge dead crows. The two wooden packing crates, the loading of which Miss Hawke had so carefully overseen, now lay in fragments. Whatever had been in them was now smashed and broken, mere bits of wood and metal.

At last Miss Hawke pulled away from Connor's chest and turned back to study the scene. She said nothing, but gazed despairingly at the horses' bodies, the wrecked vehicles, and her scattered possessions. Connor watched her silently.

After a time he cleared his throat and spoke softly. "If you are certain you are unharmed, I'd best go look for my groom, the coachman, the cart driver, and his apprentice."

She nodded. "Do you think they're buried beneath the rubble?" Her voice was a raw whisper.

He shrugged his shoulders helplessly. "I pray not." Glancing back at Miss Hawke, he saw tears well up in her eyes. "Will you be all right while I'm gone?"

"Yes." Then her face blanched. "Maggie! She must still be in the carriage! I must go with you to see if she's all right."

Connor's jaw tightened. "You stay here. If she *is* there, I'd best be the one to find her."

Emily watched Lord Connor slip and slide down the muddy precipice. When he reached the bottom he paused and squared his broad shoulders before stepping toward the smashed vehicle. In a moment he turned and raised his hands, holding them out from his sides.

"She's not here," he shouted.

Relief flooded Emily's veins, making her legs quiver

like those of a toddler who'd just learned to walk. A second later she heard a low moan. Hurrying toward a scraggly bush, she nudged the branches away and peered into the thicket. "Maggie!"

From her position sprawled amid broken branches, the maid moaned again and raised a scratched hand to her brow. "Oh, miss, me 'ead feels like it's goin' to fall off! What 'appened?"

Emily quickly related the details of the accident.

"Is Andy dead, then?" Maggie whimpered, referring to the cart driver's apprentice.

"I don't know. Lord Connor went downhill to see what he could find," Emily said gently. "But we mustn't bury them yet; they may have landed in a bramble bush like you did."

After helping Maggie out of the bushes and brushing as many sticks and bits of debris away from the maid's skirts as she could, Emily turned to watch Lord Connor climb back up the slippery incline. As he neared the top, she offered her hand.

Grasping Emily's fingers, Lord Connor shook his head. "I couldn't find anyone. Perhaps they jumped off when the vehicles began to fall, and are up there." He nodded back up the hill in the direction from which they had fallen.

Just then, on the road far above, two men peered down at them and waved wildly. Maggie cried out hopefully and grasped Emily's hand.

"Thank God," Lord Connor said. "It's my groom and the coachman."

Maggie's face fell.

Removing a handkerchief from his pocket, Lord Connor dabbed away a bit of blood that had flowed down his cheek from the gash on his forehead. "I hope the cart driver and his boy were as quick." He looked back at Emily. "I'm afraid all your belongings are beyond salvaging. Whatever you had in those big crates has been smashed into a thousand tiny pieces, and your gowns are shredded beyond repair."

"My things don't matter," Emily breathed, simply relieved that the missing men weren't crushed beneath the battered cart. Then, remembering the maid, she motioned toward Maggie, who was now slumped on a flat rock, swaying to and fro and keening loudly.

Running an experienced eye over the maid's body, Lord Connor remarked tentatively, "She doesn't appear hurt, just hysterical. Though she may have sustained some injury not visible to the eye."

"She is fine," Emily said in an undertone. "Just scratched a bit and worried about the driver's apprentice."

Lord Connor frowned. "I can't imagine where he and the driver are," he said softly. "I didn't see them amid the wreckage, but they may still have been killed. Come, let us climb back up to the road. Best let me go first, to help you over the rough spots and keep an eye out for . . . anything amiss."

Emily nodded, then each of them moved to take one of Maggie's arms to support her as they climbed. Once, Emily stumbled over a protruding tree root and Lord Connor quickly moved to help her over it, reminding her of how personable he'd been before he'd become aware of her identity.

Really, she thought with a rueful twinge, he could be a very charming gentleman. And he was *so* handsome. If only he had not taken such a disliking to her at the solicitor's office. At least they seemed to be on more solid ground now. But it did hurt to know he thought her so unappealing.

Then she scolded herself silently for even considering his charms at such a time. Instead, she concentrated on soothing Maggie's shattered nerves, supporting and encouraging the maid as they continued up the hill. They reached the crest of the gorge without seeing either of the missing men.

Lord Connor's horses, having been released from the carriage traces, stood tied to a bush at the roadside. Polly's cage rested near the horses—apparently the groom had managed to grab the cage as he jumped from the falling carriage. As if realizing how nearly she had come to death, the bird sat, silent and subdued, on her perch.

Emily, Maggie, the coachman, and the groom stayed beside the animals while Lord Connor moved toward the carriage traces still lying in the center of the road. Lord Connor leaned toward the structure and ran a hand over the wood. Momentarily he straightened, a dark frown creasing his brow. When he returned, Emily looked up questioningly.

Drawing her aside, Lord Connor drew a deep breath and spoke so the others could not hear. "The trace has been cut almost clean through. This 'accident' was no accident."

"Are you saying someone tried to murder us?" she gasped.

Lord Connor shook his head and glanced over at the others. "I do not know."

Emily glanced back down the hill. "What about the dray? Did you notice if it had been sabotaged as well?"

"It didn't appear so. It looked, rather, like the cart horses were startled by our carriage splitting in two and careening down the hill. Poor beasts must have slipped on the weakened bank and taken the cart with them. Look there. Do you see what I mean?"

Looking where he pointed, Emily noticed several deep gouges where the sidehill had given way beneath the combined weight of the rain-saturated earth and the heavily laden vehicle. She shuddered. "Have you any ideas what might have happened to the cart driver and his boy?"

Lord Connor gave her a speaking glance. "One does have to wonder why they have so conveniently disappeared."

Nodding, Emily looked back downhill and grimaced. "What about the horses? Shouldn't we bury them or . . . or something?"

Lord Connor shook his head. "I'll pay someone in Launceston—the next city on our route—to take care of it. You've been through too much today to have to stand here in the cold while my men and I do the job." Suddenly he frowned. "By the way, where are your spectacles?"

Emily's fingers flew to the bridge of her nose. "I must have lost them in the accident!"

"You don't seem to be having any trouble seeing," Lord Connor remarked.

"No. I am farsighted. I only need glasses to see things up close. Like needlework, or books. I can barely see anything that isn't nearly an arm's length away unless I wear them." Then she sighed. "But I suppose I'll have to make do until I return to London and can have another pair made. The hillside is much too vast to search for them."

"I would be happy to try, nonetheless," Lord Connor offered.

Flushing, Emily realized her comment must have sounded like an entreaty. "Oh, I didn't mean—"

"I am at your service, ma'am." Lord Connor interrupted. Without waiting for her response, he climbed back down the muddy hill. He returned shortly. "I found them, but I fear they won't be much use to you."

He put a mangled object in her hands. Holding it out at arm's length, Emily squinted at the crumpled mass. In a moment a half-hysterical giggle erupted from between her lips. "Oh, dear. I see what you mean."

The wire rims were bent almost out of recognition. One lens was missing, and the other had cracked, resembling a spider's web. As Emily turned her glasses over in her hands, the remaining lens disintegrated with a musical tinkle.

She shrugged and tossed them back down the hill. "Oh well. I suppose it's no great loss. My friend at school, Mrs. Harriman, was forever telling me to throw them away in order to better my looks."

To her discomfort, Lord Connor gazed at her intently, then murmured, "Although I cannot agree that it is better to be blind than bespectacled, I must say that you *do* have exceptionally beautiful eyes, Miss Hawke."

Emily's breath caught in her throat as something feminine and almost forgotten welled up inside her. Her cheeks grew warm. Unschooled in playful flirtation, she turned away and contemplated her scattered, torn dresses. " 'Twould seem Mrs. Harriman has had two wishes fulfilled. She also hated my black gowns."

As though sensitive to her discomfort, Lord Connor didn't reply. Instead, waving to his groom, he called out, "Bring the horses over here." Turning back to Emily, he cocked an inquisitive brow. "Unless we want to remain here we'll have to ride bareback to Launceston. If you prefer, though, I shall send the coachman and my groom to town to procure another conveyance while you, Maggie, and I wait here. You should be aware, though, that it gets rather cold in Cornwall when night falls, and though the sun is shining right now, it may begin raining again, soon."

Emily shook her head. "At this point I'm just happy to have transportation. And to be alive so that I need it. Let's go."

Suddenly Lord Connor's eyes widened and his hand flashed to his coat pocket. He sighed with relief, but then turned his worried face toward Emily. "Your half of the map! Do you still have it or did you lose it in the fall?"

Luckily, Emily's reticule, which she was in the habit of lacing over one wrist, was still in place. Although covered with mud, the handbag was closed, with the map still safely inside. "I have it right here," she replied, tapping her reticule.

"Thank God."

Emily frowned as Lord Connor moved away to finish helping ready the horses. Was that the only reason he'd been concerned with her safety? So that he wouldn't lose her half of the map in case she died without telling him where she had put it?

Although ashamed at such thoughts after his kindness, she could not forget his cold question to the solicitor: "What happens in the event that either myself or the captain's daughter should meet with an untimely demise?" If she had died, he'd have become sole proprietor of the captain's treasure.

She watched Lord Connor's tall, muscular form bend to pick up a dropped rein. With his gleaming golden hair falling over his forehead like that of a rambunctious schoolboy, he didn't look malevolent, but looks could be deceiving. Was he, even now, wishing he'd procured her envelope at the start of the trip and not been so careful of her safety during the fall?

At that moment Lord Connor turned toward her and

held out his arms. Avoiding his gaze, she moved forward and tried not to notice the heat of his fingers at her waist as he deftly plucked her from the ground and settled her lightly on the gelding's broad back. Then he removed his ripped coat and draped it over her shoulders to ward off the damp chill.

In a few more minutes Maggie was mounted behind Emily, her arms clasped around Emily's waist. Both women straddled the horse's back so that their stockinged legs hung, uncovered, down the animal's sides.

Embarrassed at having to expose her limbs, Emily felt her cheeks burn. Despite her misgivings about Lord Connor's motives to her person, she was grateful (and perhaps secretly a trifle miffed) that he kept his warm blue gaze to himself.

While she was ruminating on the confusing dichotomy of why a man who might wish her dead would be so solicitous, she found herself unable to keep from staring at Lord Connor's handsome white-shirted back and well-muscled legs as he swung onto one of the remaining horses and gripped its bare sides with his thighs. Once the groom and coachman were likewise mounted Lord Connor clicked his tongue, and the small party started on their way.

They reached Launceston in the early afternoon. Solicitous of the ladies' feelings about having the townspeople gawk at their less-than-proper transportation, Lord Connor suggested they stop at the Owl and Mouse, an inn on the outskirts of town, while he made his way to the magistrate's office to report the unfortunate accident and their two missing traveling companions.

By the time he returned to the Owl and Mouse, the rest of the party had already eaten a hearty luncheon. While he donned his coat, which Emily had discarded in favor of a thick blanket procured from the inn's mistress, and ate his own repast, the coachman obtained another carriage. After a quick discussion, they decided to drive on in order to come to Hawke's Nest by nightfall.

Thus, ensconced once again in a carriage, Emily felt the

day begin to catch up with her. Visions of the poor dead cart- and riding-horses flashed in and out of her mind, making her queasy, chilled, and light-headed. She pulled her blanket more closely about her shoulders.

Pressing her fingertips to her head, she tried to massage away the dull ache that had begun to torment her. When the pain had eased somewhat, she glanced up to find Lord Connor's sympathetic gaze upon her.

In a comforting voice, he murmured, "It is quite natural for people involved in accidents to react with abnormal calm during and immediately after the incident, only to find themselves quite overwrought several hours later. I've seen it before on ship."

As great warm tears began sliding down her cheeks, Emily pressed her palms to her eyes. "I'm sorry to be such a booby," she whimpered. "It's just that I can't stop thinking about those poor horses. How awful to die like that."

"Yes. But everything happened so quickly I doubt they suffered overmuch," he said reassuringly. He was silent for a moment, then went on softly, "Why don't you come sit by me? I promise to be a pattern card of propriety. I think you need a strong shoulder right now."

Emily glanced over at Maggie, whose raucous snoring indicated she would not be easily disturbed, then gave Lord Connor a watery smile. "It would be nice, if you are sure it would be all right. You don't think I'm just a spineless ninny?"

"On the contrary. I think you the bravest woman I've ever had the honor to meet. Any other gentlewoman of my acquaintance would have taken refuge in a fit of vapors long ago." He returned her smile and patted the seat beside him. "Come, Emily."

Emily felt a surge of warmth in her cheeks at his use of her Christian name, but did not reprove him since it felt surprisingly wonderful to hear the word slip from between his lips. She moved to sit on his side of the carriage, then boldly slid closer so that she just touched his shoulder.

Lord Connor's smile deepened. "There. Isn't that better?"

"Yes."

Truly, it did feel most comforting to feel his solid strength beside her. Although he made no attempt to put his arm around her shoulders or touch her in any fashion, his shoulder was as hard as steel beside hers, and the steadfastness of it was remarkably soothing. In a few seconds her tears lessened, then stopped altogether as she drew warmth and solace from his body.

Despite the disturbing sensations that touching him evoked in her, she yawned. "Oh, dear. Please forgive me. I am suddenly very sleepy."

"Also a perfectly natural response to a very trying day."

They rode along in silence for the next several miles. After a time, Connor opened his mouth to speak. As he did so, however, Miss Emily Hawke's dark head tipped precariously to one side, coming to rest on his shoulder. Her blanket slipped to her waist.

Gazing down at her tearstained features, Connor smiled and felt a pleasant warmth pervade his body. It felt so nice to have her beside him. Almost as if she belonged there.

Despite his certainty that it was improper, he raised one arm and placed it around her shoulders, telling himself it was only so that Miss Hawke would not take a chill. The carriage continued swaying smoothly to and fro, like a baby's cradle, and in no time at all Connor slept as well.

7

Some time later, Connor turned to look at the woman once more seated opposite him. Overcome by a charming, pink-cheeked shyness upon waking in his arms an hour earlier, Miss Hawke—Emily, as he had come to think of her—had practically leaped back across the narrow aisle to sit beside Maggie. She had resolutely avoided his gaze for the last several miles.

Her evasion did not trouble Connor, though, for he found it quite delightful to watch the combined emotions of wonder and delight dance across her face as she gazed out at the Cornish countryside.

Just then, as the carriage passed close by the sea, Emily leaned her head out the window. She gasped and pressed a hand to her throat. "Merciful heavens!"

Connor turned to see what had caused her alarm.

As the carriage swept around the southernmost tip of Lizard Point, it passed by a rough swatch of ground where the sea had undercut the cliff. More than a hundred feet below the sharp drop-off, the ocean, like an energetic washerwoman, scoured the granite outcrops and sandy beach with unflagging determination. "Ah. Maiden's Leap," he said. "We're almost there now."

"Maiden's Leap," Emily breathed. "How utterly romantic. Was there actually a maiden who leaped from the cliff in Cornish history?"

He grinned. "Not that I am aware of."

"I'm glad." Emily closed her eyes and breathed deeply. When a faint spray misted her cheeks she opened her eyes and laughed delightedly. "Why, I can taste salt!"

"Have you never seen the sea before?" he asked.

"No, never. And yet it is strange," she added confidingly. "Somehow I feel almost as if I were coming home." Turning, she looked dreamily toward the west, where the clouds had parted to offer a superb Cornish sunset.

Connor watched her gaze follow the sun as it sizzled down into the sea like a ball of molten wax spreading a crimson and gold sheen across the water. His own eyes shifted back and forth between Emily's face and the vivid horizon. At last he abandoned his study of the sky and fixed his attention on his companion.

There was no comparison. With her ebony curls glowing faintly red from the reflected sunlight, and her face shining with an aura that seemed to flow up from her very soul, no sunset could ever compare with the captain's daughter at that moment. Connor felt an odd sense of satisfaction and comfort rise up through his chest.

"Look at all the colors!" Emily cried ecstatically. "Red, purple, violet, blue, orange, even green. I've never seen anything so lovely."

"Nor have I."

Catching his eyes on her face, Emily blushed prettily. Connor reluctantly looked out toward the sea. "Sunsets on the sea are stunning, aren't they? Of course, they are even more so when one is on board a ship out in the middle of the ocean."

"I can imagine. They must be truly remarkable." Craning her neck further out the window, Emily peered up the coast. "When will we be at Hawke's Nest?"

"In a few minutes."

"I can hardly wait. To think that my father was alive all these years. It seems impossible, and yet . . ." Her voice trailed off and Emily was silent for a few minutes, then she looked up. "How did you come to meet my father, my lord?"

Connor paused, wondering where to begin and how much to tell her. Too much would mean opening himself wide to her possible scorn, something he had not done since—

He ruthlessly suppressed the memory that rose like a fire-breathing dragon in his mind. "I suppose you might say that if it weren't for the captain, I might be dead now. He saved me from a press gang."

"A press gang? I have heard the term but am not certain what it means."

"It is a group of men who kidnap young lads and send them off to foreign ports to fight with the Royal Navy. They operate in coastal towns. After kidnapping their victims, the press men rob them of their worldly goods, knock them unconscious, and fling them into the hold of a ship until the vessel is far enough out to sea that the lads cannot escape. Frequently they are paid by the navy to gather new recruits. Your father came along at the very moment I was accosted by one of these gangs and . . . took issue with their methods."

Emily's eyes widened. "Please, my lord, tell me all about it!"

To his surprise Connor found himself almost longing to share his past with her. A lump rose in his throat and he pretended to cough until it was gone. "Well, if you're sure it will not bore you," he said hesitantly, still stunned at the revelation that he *wanted* this woman to know all about him.

"Oh, no!"

Unable to withstand the plea in her exquisite eyes, Connor glanced momentarily at Maggie, who was still snoring. Then he nodded, fiercely suppressing the cloud of mistrust that had kept him, for so many years, from letting any female come close enough to see the pain he'd kept hidden away in his heart since his youth.

"Very well. The series of events that put me in contact with your father all began when I was eighteen." His cheeks grew hot but he pressed on. "Many youths on the threshold of manhood fancy themselves in love with the girl next door. I was no different. My neighbor's name was Bettina Findlay—Lady Bettina Findlay—and I was utterly head-over-heels about her. I thought she felt the same. I found out, however, on the evening of my elder brother's twenty-fourth birthday, that she did not.

"My brother and Lady Bettina announced their betrothal at my brother's birthday supper, in front of one hundred and sixty-four guests. Bettina didn't even pretend to feel regret at discarding me like so much garbage."

His gaze flew to Emily's eyes to see if she would laugh at his misfortune and stupidity for believing in a faithless woman. When he saw his own pain reflected in her face, he was nearly undone. He dragged his gaze away and looked down at his hands.

"How awful!" Emily murmured, voice heavy with sympathy. "And how heartless of Lady Bettina. Didn't your brother know you loved her?"

"Oh, yes, he knew. In fact, I think Markus offered for her for that very reason."

"Surely a brother would never knowingly cause his own sibling pain!"

"This one would. He always hated me because I was better at sports, hunting—you know, the usual male pursuits—than he was. He was never able to best me at anything, and that made him nearly mad with envy. So he chose to best me in the way he knew would hurt me the most."

"How could Lady Bettina have married him, if she loved you?"

Bitter gall rose in Connor's throat. He laughed humorlessly. "If she had truly loved me I suppose she could not have done so. However, she later told me that I had completely mistaken her warm sentiments of sisterly affection for something she had never intended," he ground out between clenched teeth, remembering Bettina's impassioned kisses.

"Then she laughed and said that she far preferred being Lady Duncan to being a mere Lady Connor. My brother was Lord Duncan, you see, our father having died several years earlier."

Eager to be away from the subject of Bettina, Connor's voice strengthened as he redirected the conversation toward Emily's father. "A few days after the betrothal dinner I got some notion into my head that I would join the army. I asked Markus to purchase my regimentals. He refused."

"Why?"

"Jealousy again, I suppose. Markus never gave me anything without a fight—especially if it was something I really wanted. But I was determined to leave home even without his aid. There was nothing left for me there once I lost Bettina.

"I made my way across country to Dover. Although I had no concrete plans, I suppose I hoped I could find passage on a ship to some foreign isle, make my fortune, and return to steal Bettina out from under Markus's superior nose."

"Did your brother come after you?"

"No. I'm sure he was glad to see me gone. At any rate, I was in Dover but a fortnight when I was set upon by the press agents. Just as the men were taking me to the holding ship, the captain happened by. All by himself he beat the gang to a pulp and nursed me back to health. I had several broken ribs, a broken collarbone, and a serious concussion.

"After I had recovered I became a sort of apprentice to him, turning a blind eye to his more nefarious activities. I told myself his pirating was all right, since England *was* at war with France."

Emily frowned. "Precisely what sort of 'nefarious activities' was the captain involved in? And did you ever take part in them?"

"Well, as you already know, he considered himself a privateer. A privateer owns his own ship and attacks foreign vessels in order to take possession of whatever valuables are on board. But I was never allowed to take part in the attacks, since the captain was always very protective of my interests. You must remember I was but a lad when we first met, and I suppose he did not want me corrupted."

"Is privateering illegal, then?"

"Not if you have a royal writ of permission. The captain did not. He did not want me implicated in case he were ever caught. I don't know why he worried. Since it was in King George's best interest, the king was wont to ignore even those privateers who did not carry a royal writ. You see, anything that weakened France would have been acceptable, under the circumstances."

Emily nodded thoughtfully.

"We had a splendid time sailing the seas," Connor said, "although I always had the feeling the captain had more kettles over the fire than he was letting on."

"What do you mean?"

Connor narrowed his eyes. "I'm not certain. It's just a feeling I had. But I never actually heard of the captain having interests other than the privateering and, later, the legitimate shipping business. Anyway, when I got older he decided I should attend a university. He sent me to Cambridge, and when I graduated I took over the running of the present-day business. And that," he finished, "is how I met the captain, and how I came to view him as more of a father than an employer."

"And you were with him until his death?"

"More or less. Although I spent more time on voyages than at Hawke's Nest. When the captain got too old to sail—his gout and rheumatism had become very painful during my school years—I sailed without him while he stayed here in Cornwall. Every time I came home he made me go over every detail of the journey."

Emily sighed wistfully. "How I wish I had known him."

"You must not think he had no interest in you, Emily. Or that he was an evil man. He was undoubtedly the finest man I've ever had the honor to know." Connor frowned. "I shouldn't have implied he was a bad man by saying all those negative things back at Simms's office. The captain was a good, decent person. God knows he saved my skin, and he always had a coin or a comforting word for those in need."

"I still can't help feeling a little betrayed."

"I understand, but I assure you that if the captain hadn't felt your reputation would have been hurt by being associated with an ex-pirate, he would have loved having you at Hawke's Nest," Connor said earnestly.

Emily gazed at him searchingly. "Honestly?"

"Honestly." Emily opened her mouth to speak, but at that moment he pointed out the window. "Look! Hawke's Nest!"

His exclamation woke Maggie. She mumbled and rubbed her eyes, her carroty hair standing up in all directions.

Emily stared at the huge, sea-battered fortress, open-mouthed. "I've never seen anything like it in my life! It's enormous!"

"Yes," Connor said. "As the solicitor, Mr. Simms, already told you, it was originally a Norman stronghold. Your father won it in a card game just after I met him. He moved in when his doctor forbade any more voyages. He loved it here."

"I can see why," Emily replied sincerely. "It is magnificent."

"I have always thought so. The castle is constructed of granite. The stone was cut in rectangles which were fitted together so tightly one would be hard-pressed to slide a knife blade between them." He lifted his hand. "Up there are the battlements that line the entire upper story. There is a narrow walkway just past them."

"It's very high, isn't it? Aren't the windows awfully small?"

"It is extremely high. Nearly five stories. And though the captain added on some new windows on the balconies outside the bed chambers, the original windows are tiny because they were more for shooting arrows out than for letting sunlight in. Do you see the window up there, on the highest tower in the center of the castle?"

He pointed, and Emily's gaze followed the gesture to one odd segment that stood several meters above the rest. Connor watched her study the structure, noting her gray-green gaze take in the high tower directly in the middle of the old castle, and the four other, shorter towers that surrounded it.

"Yes."

"During thunderstorms, the captain used to climb that tower and sit at that window with the rain slashing his face and body. He wouldn't come down until he was completely drenched. He had a special room up there. He loved to watch lightning strike the rods placed strategically on the other four corners of the castle. He'd sit there for hours until the storm had passed, just gazing out at the water and watching the waves lash the cliffs. During those storms the water rose maybe ten feet, and the waves would almost reach the castle itself."

Speaking for the first time since she'd awakened, Maggie shuddered. "I can't imagine anyone wantin' to live 'ere. Sooner I gets back to London the 'appier I'll be. 'Tis as cold as death." Pulling her heavy gray woolen cloak more securely about her shoulders, she sniffed and wrinkled her nose. "And it smells like dead fish."

"That's the sea," remarked Connor with a smile. "It's odd that people either love the briny smell of the ocean or they hate it. There is never any in-between."

"How can you say it smells bad, Maggie?" Emily protested. "It just smells like salt and fresh air. But don't worry. As soon as I can find someone to take your place you can go back to London on the first coach."

"What about you, miss?" Maggie demanded. "You won't be wantin' to stay on 'ere, will you? You'd best come back with me. This ain't no place for you, mark my words. This 'ere place is evil."

Emily laughed. "Evil? Don't be ridiculous. It isn't evil, just old. Besides, I must stay here." She snapped her mouth shut as Connor shot her a speaking glance reminding her that Maggie knew nothing about the real reason they had come to Hawke's Nest. "I mean, I must stay at least until I learn something more about my father."

Maggie harrumphed and turned away.

Leaving the edge of the cliff, the carriage swept through a thick stand of wind-bent trees, rattled up a short drive, and swooshed between two granite pillars made of the same silver granite as the castle. In seconds the vehicle slowed before an impressive walkway leading to two vast oak doors, complete with brass fixtures and huge iron ring-style knockers.

Leaping out before the vehicle came to a full stop, Connor held a hand out to the women as soon as the carriage paused, and helped them step down to the rough cobblestone drive. Maggie grimaced at the vision of the dark castle, but Emily's face shone as she stared up in fascination and open delight. Connor, too, looked up, again trying to see the castle through her eyes.

Hideous stone gargoyles danced all across the door-way's frontispiece. Some had wings, some hideous faces with several-inch-long fangs, some enormous ears, and some long, sweeping forked tails, like small demons protecting their domain. From two of these gargoyles, placed strategically at each end of the twenty-foot portico, water gushed out of pursed stone lips in a steady stream, indicating it had rained here recently, as well.

Seeing Emily's astonished gaze settle on these two spewing monsters, Connor chuckled. "Ugly, aren't they? Nearly a foot of water collects up there after a good storm and they serve as admirable rain gutters, although their mouth openings are so small it takes several hours for all the water to drain away. Originally, all the gargoyles across the roof had open mouths, and they were used to pour hot oil on intruders. Now, obviously, the only mouths remaining open are the two on the end, and they are almost closed off due to mineral buildup."

"They are wonderful," Emily replied sincerely.

Connor felt a warm glow at her approval.

Maggie shuddered again. "Can we go inside, miss? I feel like they're starin' at me." Hurrying forward, the maid ran up the steps and waited beside the door.

Connor motioned for the groom to join the driver on the front of the carriage so he could direct the way to the stables, and once the boy had settled there, the vehicle moved back around one corner of the castle.

Studying the intricate stone carvings adorning the old fortress, Emily heard a low groan suddenly rumble from high amid the gargoyles, as though one of them had whispered to his companions. Raising her head, she glanced up toward the roof, mouth half-open in surprise.

She didn't have time to utter a word, though, for at that moment Connor flew into her, slamming into her ribs and knocking the air from her body as he pushed her violently to one side and pressed her to the ground. As they hit the earth her eyes opened wide with indignation and she managed to squeak, "What are you—"

There was a terrific crash as a granite gargoyle, loosened somehow from its perch just above the landing, smashed onto the drive, shattering into hundreds of pieces and cracking the stone where Emily had stood only moments earlier.

Although he had braced his body for the impact, several large chunks of rock glanced off Connor's body, making him grunt with pain. When all was quiet, he demanded harshly, "Are you all right?"

Pushing out from under him, Emily stumbled to her feet and brushed bits of debris from her black skirt. "I think so. What happened?"

"One of the gargoyles fell. It must have been loosened by the rain."

Emily blinked. "If you hadn't pushed me when you did I would have been crushed."

They stared at each other for a moment, then abruptly moved apart. Neither wanted to say what had occurred to each of them.

If the stone had struck her, Emily realized, she would now be dead and Lord Connor would be the sole heir to Captain Hawke's treasure. While she didn't *think* His Lordship had deliberately set up this little ploy to kill her, there was a minute chance he had gotten this idea after the carriage accident. Had he perhaps written ahead with instructions for someone to push the gargoyle off the edge when they arrived, and then changed his mind at the last minute?

Could he really be so greedy?

She remembered his insisting that his anger at her unexpected arrival in his life had not been due to avarice, but how well did she really know him? And if he *had* planned her murder, why then had he rescued her? Second thoughts, perhaps?

She didn't miss the flash of some unrecognizable emotion that passed over Lord Connor's face and was quickly masked.

As for Connor, his expression was more one of shock at the discovery that he would have been severely disturbed had even a hair on Miss Emily Hawke's pretty head been displaced.

And further, the suddenly cold expression on Emily's

face made him wonder if perhaps she were not wishing that one of the pieces of granite that had struck his back had been a little closer to his head, thus removing the necessity of sharing the treasure altogether. He stared at her, contemplatively.

Surely she couldn't be so bloodthirsty and uncaring. Could she?

She certainly could if she were of similar temperament to Bettina. *That* experience had shown him that, beneath their protestations of friendship or, worse yet, love, women had no hearts. How well did he really know the captain's daughter? She had seemed sympathetic and sweet, but was she, really?

Suddenly the day seemed very dark and gloomy, and the gash on his head, as well as the bruises he'd sustained in the carriage accident, and now the aches from the impact of falling rock were all beginning to throb painfully. A low moan further up on the doorstep drew his attention. The maid, Maggie, had swooned. "Come on," he growled brusquely. "Let's see if Maggie is all right, and then let's get inside before something else happens."

8

Maggie was fine although, even once she stood beside Emily, she emitted intermittent moans. Emily and Connor were distracted from their maudlin thoughts as well as the maid's whimpering when the heavy doors swung open with an ominous creak and a wizened man with peppery hair, a dirty bandage wrapped around one ear, and eyes like chips of obsidian emerged. His gaze was directed toward the noisy door hinges, which he proceeded to wiggle back and forth, scowling angrily. When he shouted, Emily was so surprised she almost leaped into Lord Connor's arms.

"Nipper! Didn't I tell 'ee to oil them 'inges? Get your butt out 'ere and do it or 'is Lordship will be back afore ye're done! 'Ee can't expect me to do everythin'."

Moving away from Emily, Lord Connor touched the odd fellow on the arm. "Hello, Cracker Jack."

The old man let out a second, even more bloodcurdling, shriek and whirled about.

"Lor' love us, it's Master Connor!" he cried then, his leathery skin splitting into a thousand fractures as his mouth opened in a crooked grimace of delight that exposed a huge, wet lump of dirty brown chewing tobacco. He didn't notice the shattered gargoyle littering the drive. "Ye scairt me and good!"

"My apologies, old friend."

Cracker Jack waved a hand dismissively, shifted the moist wad from one side of his mouth to the other, and then spat off the edge of the steps. "No matter. Sorry I didn't 'ear yer carriage pull up the drive, but my 'earin' ain't what it used to be a-cause of this bandage I'm wearin'."

Lord Connor cocked a brow. "So I see. Is that where Polly got you?"

"Aye. Nasty beast. I 'ope 'ee left 'er in Lunnon where I sent 'er. Are 'ee here to stay?"

"For a while, at least. And I'm sorry to tell you I did bring Polly back with me. I felt the captain would have wanted me to."

Both men were quiet for a time, obviously sharing a moment of silence for Captain Hawke. Then Lord Connor cleared his throat. "There is someone I think you'll be interested to meet." Reaching back, he gripped Emily's arm and pulled her forward. "Miss Emily Hawke, allow me to introduce my good friend, Cracker Jack."

The old man's night-dark eyes went wide with horror, and he almost choked on his dank-smelling wad. Making the sign of the cross, he backed up several paces. "Lor' love us," he whimpered. "It's Lady Caroline back from the grave! Ain't there enough trouble 'round 'ere without 'ee bringin' dead 'uns back to 'aunt us, Lord Connor?"

His Lordship chuckled. "Relax, my friend. Miss Hawke is no apparition. She is Captain Hawke's long-lost daughter."

"The divil 'ee say!" the old man exclaimed.

"Yes. And that nervous young woman with her"—Lord Connor pointed to Maggie, who had leaped behind Emily when the old man had screeched—"is her maid. I was introduced to Miss Hawke at the solicitor's office in London where Mr. Simms notified me of Captain Hawke's recent death. And now," he remarked with a conspiratorial glance at Emily, "she has decided to visit Hawke's Nest to learn more about her father."

The old man edged closer to Emily, his gimlet gaze inspecting her from head to toe. Then he backed off again and spat out another dark brown stream of tobacco juice. Emily fought off a wave of nausea.

"Are 'ee absolutely sure she ain't a ghostie, sir? Look at that dress, now. Looks like it could have been given to 'er by the divil 'imself. All black and ugly. Don't look like no dress any woman of my acquaintance would be caught dead in—unless she *was* dead."

Lord Connor patted the old man's shoulder. "Now Cracker Jack, you know Lady Caroline was a pure saint. She could never have been banished to the fiery pits of hell. I'm sure she is even now garbed in white and singing with the angels."

"May'ap," Jack muttered grimly. "But I weren't told the cap'n 'ad no datter, and 'e surely would have told me, seein' 'ow close we was in the old days and then wi' me livin' 'ere like this. I was prob'ly the best friend the old duffer 'ad. Many were the nights we sat up drinkin' brandy and playin' at piquet. 'Tweren't no secrets a'tween us. No sirree, no secrets a'tall.

"I don' believe 'e 'ad no datter. That gal is an 'aunt, pure and simple, even if she 'as managed to fool Yer Lordship. But don' 'ee worry, Lord Connor. I knows 'ow to get the best o' 'er. Got to invite 'aunts in afore they can do any 'arm—they be like vampires, they do." With that he crossed his arms in front of his chest and backed up, effectively blocking the entrance.

"All men have their secrets, Cracker Jack, even the captain. Perhaps he merely forgot to tell you about Miss Hawke," Lord Connor replied comfortingly. "But come, all you need do is look at the chit to know she's of the captain and Lady Caro's blood."

Although he spat a third time, the old man didn't budge.

Lord Connor sighed. "Listen, my friend. We are tired and hungry and would like to freshen up, so I must insist you remove yourself from the doorjamb and let us pass."

Seeing that Cracker Jack gave no indication of even having heard Lord Connor's polite entreaty, Emily forced her stiff lips into a pleasant smile. Sweeping forward, she grabbed the old man by his gnarled hands, holding tightly when he tried to pull away.

"Dear Mr. Jack," she cried gaily, "I am so delighted to meet you. Please, call me Miss Emily. May I call you Cracker?"

Lord Connor gave a muffled chuckle. "Call him Cracker Jack, Miss Hawke," he said. "Cracker isn't his

Christian name. Nobody knows his surname, including Jack himself."

Emily blinked, her attention deflected for a moment from her intention of charming the servant. "Then why on earth is he called Cracker?" she asked, puzzled.

"In mariner terms, a cracker is one who is recognized at being an expert at some special skill. Since Jack is a master sailor, he has been called Cracker Jack for as long as I've known him. It's a common enough moniker for a seaman. I'm surprised that, being a schoolmarm, you weren't aware of the term."

"No, Lord Connor, I was not aware of that fascinating bit of information," Emily snapped, losing patience as her feet started to ache. "I hardly see where I would have acquired such information since I've spent nearly my entire life at seminaries for young ladies. Perhaps you think such discussion suitable for gentlewomen? Now please be quiet while I convince this good man I am not an 'aunt—a haunt—so that we might go inside!"

Lord Connor's eyes sparkled. "Lord, woman, don't cut up at me. I didn't mean to put your petticoats in a tangle."

"There, you see, my lord?" Cracker Jack challenged before Emily could deliver a blistering set-down to Lord Connor. " 'Ow can she be the cap'n's datter if she don't know nothin' 'bout the sea?"

Emily's temperature was rising rapidly, and she was ready to cuff Lord Connor up the side of his handsome head when her eye was caught by the dingy bandage tied over Cracker Jack's ear. It was partially concealed by his peppery hair and was liberally sprinkled with dark brown spots that surely must be dried blood.

Good heavens! Hadn't he changed the bandage since the accident? Lord only knew what vermin the cloth harbored!

Her attention was instantly diverted. "My good man!" she cried. "You'd best let me or Maggie change that bandage before you get a terrible infection."

The alteration in the old man's demeanor was immediate. Tipping his head back, he gave Emily a rueful smile and shook his head, obviously delighted with the attention to his affliction. " 'Tis all right, missus, truly. It don't 'urt much anymore," he intoned in a slightly tremulous voice, as if recovering from Polly's attack had robbed him of his remaining strength.

" 'Tain't the worst injury I've ever 'ad, and I've never 'ad an infection afore even with the worst of 'em. 'Ee know, Lady Caroline always took an interest in my ailments, too. Angel of mercy, she was, an' a real looker." Cracker Jack tipped his grizzled head to one side and threw Lord Connor a glance. " 'Ee know, Yer Lordship, I *am* beginnin' to see a few differences between the two of 'em, now that I look 'arder."

Uncertain whether that was good or bad, Emily smiled and rushed on before Lord Connor could tear down the bridges she had so carefully built. "Oh, I am so glad." Her pleasure was dampened only slightly by the snicker from Lord Connor's direction.

"Why, I remember back in sixty-nine when I took a saber in the thigh durin' a voyage," Cracker Jack said reminiscently, "and the cap'n brought me back to 'is 'ome nearly dead. Lady Caro nursed me back to 'ealth and sat by my bedside day and night.

"I'll tell 'ee now," he said to Lord Connor in a loud whisper, "if she 'adn't been the captain's woman, I'd have married her in a trice. A face like a Madonna, and the *biggest* pair of buoys 'ee ever did see! Like watermelons, they was, and I'll wager they tasted just as sweet."

Emily's cheeks flamed.

Between snorts of laughter, Lord Connor interjected, "Now that you realize the young lady is not a ghost, Jack, perhaps you will save your tales for another day and grant us admission. As Miss Hawke mentioned, we are all very tired, and I, for one, am somewhat hungry."

The old seaman stepped aside instantly and they moved into the castle.

As they walked through the main foyer Cracker Jack scratched his bandage and said, "Don't know what I can feed 'ee tonight, my lord. I think there's a bit of bread and an 'unk of cheddar in the pantry, but the cook left just after the cap'n died. Said she weren't stayin' on with a bunch of no-good 'oodlum smugglers overrunnin' the place. I'll go into Lizard for supplies at first light."

"Smugglers?" Lord Connor said quickly. "What made the cook think there were smugglers about?"

"Oh, there were some strange goin's-on for a while after the cap'n's death. But I think t' old biddy was just scairt of the castle. 'Tis a bit creepy sometimes, the way the wind moans around its tiny windows and strange noises echo through its dark 'alls in the night.

"The sounds seemed to 'ave started up since the cap'n's death—when you were away, my lord—I s'pect that was what made the cook leave. Thinkin' there might be intruders, I started lockin' the doors in a secret way so I'd know if anyone was comin' or goin' undetected. Nowadays, although I still 'ear strange noises betimes, I know 'tis just the wind. Can't be anyone sneakin' in, not with my system."

"Why did you think, at the beginning, that the noises were caused by intruders?" Lord Connor questioned.

"I used to find sand scattered all over the place, and sometimes I found the doors standing wide open and an army of footprints on the floor, as if they'd been a party in the 'all. O' course, I still see footprints, but they must be left from before. You know, the floor 'asn't been cleaned in quite some time."

"Ah. Quite astute of you to rig up a special lock system, old fellow. What did you do?"

"I stuffed a bit of paper between the door and the jamb. If anyone opened the door, the paper would fall out onto the floor. I never worried about anyone comin' in through the windows, since, except for those on the bedchamber balconies, all the other windows are much too narrow for an intruder to 'ave climbed through. Not to mention that scalin' the castle walls and riskin' death would 'ave made that avenue an unappealin' prospect."

"Brilliant," Lord Connor said approvingly. "You have my thanks for keeping the place safe in my absence. Did you ever discover who the intruders were?"

"No, but, if 'ee ask me, 'twas Nipper lettin' that group into the 'all. I think 'e 'ad gotten into the 'abit of invitin' 'is friends in for a bit o' yer rum, my lord. I'd check the cellars first thing tomorrow, if I was 'ee."

"Nipper?" Lord Connor said, surprised. "You think my valet was responsible?"

"Aye. There was only the two of us 'ere, you know, and the prints in the 'all continued showin' up long after the cook 'ad gone. So I told Nipper that if I saw any more indications of intrusion, I'd tell 'ee and see that Nipper was turned off. Since the trouble seems to 'ave stopped since I threatened 'im, I'd say that's a pretty good admission of guilt."

"I see," Lord Connor remarked, obviously not convinced.

"Now then, 'ow bout that bread and cheese, my lord?"

"Bread and cheese will do nicely this evening. I think we are all too fatigued to want much anyway," Lord Connor reassured him. "We'll see about hiring another cook tomorrow."

"Good. You know, my lord," Cracker Jack said then, "Milo 'as been missin' for quite a while. I've been a bit worried, since 'e usually comes back afore now. But the ugly blighter is probably just off carousin'—though where 'e'd find a woman of 'is kind I can't imagine. 'E wanders off and comes back when it suits 'im. This time 'e's been gone for over a month."

Suddenly Jack looked thoughtful. "Didn't 'ee bring any luggage 'ome?"

"We had a slight accident and our bags were lost," Lord Connor explained.

" 'Ee don't say!" Cracker Jack came to a stop below an enormous stone staircase. "Well, if 'ee can show the ladies where to drop their anchors so they can refresh themselves, I'll go find that food. I'll put it in the library and lay a fire."

As the two men talked, Emily's gaze drifted over the great hall in open dismay. Huge clusters of spiderwebs clung to the corners of the room and hung like dusty lace between the grand staircase's banisters. Even the ancient, cuplike bronze chandelier in the center of the room was barely visible beneath a gray shroud. As for the castle floor, a layer of dust at least half an inch thick covered every square foot, making little puffs with each step they took.

Once they reached the cobwebby staircase, Cracker Jack departed for other regions of the castle. Lord Connor turned to face Emily, who instantly schooled her shocked features to hide her revulsion. She allowed him to take her by the arm and lead her aside while Maggie gazed about the vast, tapestry-hung hall in openmouthed horror.

"I thought it best not to elaborate about our carriage accident. Although I certainly do not suspect Cracker Jack, I think that if we want to find out who is responsible, just on the off-chance it's someone here at Hawke's Nest, we'd be best served to keep our own counsel."

Emily nodded, but frowned. "I understand, my lord, but I feel compelled to inform you that I am not the fool you obviously think me. I assure you I am not going to spill any details of our venture to the first curious pair of ears.

"First you gave me that look when I told Maggie I needed to stay here at the castle rather than return to London, and now you treat me as if I had noodles for brains. Do you have such a low opinion of all women, or am I the only lucky one?"

Holding up his hands, Connor conceded, "You are absolutely right. I apologize. As the captain's daughter you must have a good head on your shoulders. The old man was as cagey as they came, and if you inherited half his wits you must be a veritable genius."

He hesitated and looked down at her oddly. "Just look how he's brought us together. We started on this journey blood enemies, and now we are laughing like the best of friends. Of course, it always did feel like he knew what was best for everyone in his orbit. Odd thing was how often he was proven correct."

As twilight had fallen shortly after their arrival, and everyone was utterly exhausted, the travelers made a skimpy repast of the bread, cheese, and apples Jack had laid out for them in the library, and then made their way to their beds. Fortunately for Emily, who had lost all her clothing

in the accident, Cracker Jack had managed to locate one of
the old cook's discarded night rails, which the woman had
banished to the rag-bag. He handed it to Emily while
flushing beat red. Emily was too tired and grateful to be
embarrassed. The nightgown, while huge and somewhat
threadbare, would do nicely.

Afraid of the dark old castle, Maggie had wanted to
sleep near Emily, but, since the only other clean bed was
in the old cook's chamber near the kitchens, the maid had
agreed to sleep there for the first night until a bed could
be made ready in Emily's own room.

Cracker Jack led Emily to her chamber, which he chat-
tily informed her had belonged to the captain himself and
had been unentered since the old man's demise—except
for Nipper, who had removed most of the dust and laid a
crackling fire in the grate.

After Cracker Jack left, Emily turned the door key in its
lock and began examining the chamber. The first thing she
noticed was a mug of hot chocolate awaiting her pleasure
on a table beside an enormous canopied bed. Emily
smiled. How like Maggie not to forget her nightly cup of
cocoa, even with so much happening. She must have explored the kitchens since they were near the old cook's
bedchamber, and heated the milk on the kitchen stove.

Besides the bed and side table, the room also held an
Italian-style bureau, an empty armoire, and one high-
backed chair of dark mahogany carved into intricate drag-
ons, lions, and griffins. Full-length curtains of rich
crimson and gold velvet cloaked nearly all of the huge
blocked granite walls, and a thick Oriental rug covered
most of the flagstone floor. But the most enthralling item
in the room was undoubtedly the portrait of an exquisitely
beautiful woman in an elaborate ivory brocade gown, that
covered a large section of wall.

Emily gasped and backed away. She sat on the mahogany chair, from which she could study the painting. It
could only be Lady Caroline.

Scrutinizing the portrait, Emily failed to see how Mr.
Simms and Lord Connor had ever likened *her* to this gloriously lovely, almost otherworldly creature. Lady Caro-

line was the most transcendently beautiful female Emily had ever seen.

To be sure, Emily thought, she might resemble Lady Caroline in a *small* way, but the resemblance ended almost before it had begun. Her eyes drank in this depiction of her mother's beauty.

Tiny pearls and diamonds glinted amid daintily embroidered silk flowers decorating Lady Caroline's gown. A few ebony curls hung over delicately sloping shoulders, while the rest of the woman's thick mane was wrapped into an elaborate pile atop her head.

A superb necklet of the same gems decorating her gown lay about Lady Caroline's slender neck. From the center of the pearl and diamond choker, an enormous pearl the size of a small egg hung suspended between her full, creamy breasts.

One of her hands was raised, her long fingers lovingly caressing the gem. Her smile was beguilingly crooked. Her eyes, the same silvery-green as Emily's, seemed somehow teasing.

At last Emily sighed and turned away to remove her black bombazine dress and put on the cook's night rail in preparation for bed. Clad in the voluminous bedgown, she filled a shallow basin on the bureau with water from a white enameled pitcher and began washing the travel dust from her face and neck. Then she unpinned her serviceable chignon and, finding a man's silver-backed brush and hand mirror, which she assumed to have belonged to her father, atop the bureau, began smoothing the tangles from her hair.

Seeing her image clearly in the hand mirror proved nearly impossible without her spectacles, so she propped the glass sideways on the bureau and backed away until she could see her reflection fairly well. She glanced briefly at the portrait, which was also reflected in the mirror. Then, feeling quite dowdy beside her mother's glory, she shifted her body so she could no longer see the painting.

When she finished brushing her hair, she replaced the brush beside the mirror and turned thoughtfully. Picking up her reticule, she pulled out the envelope containing the map.

It was almost overwhelmingly tempting to break the imprinted red wax seal, tear into the paper, and study the map, thus gaining a head start over Lord Connor in the treasure hunt. But at last she sighed, shook her head and placed the map on the bureau beside her reticule. Her act was not wholly prompted by honorable intentions; without her spectacles she knew she'd have been unable to see the map well anyway.

Picking up her cup of chocolate, she moved to the long windows and spread aside the sumptuous red velvet curtains. The windows, really double doors, opened outward. She stepped onto a narrow stone balcony.

The evening breeze was chilly and fresh, smelling of the salt as it brushed her cheeks and hair. A few clouds hung forbiddingly against the corner of the sky, and the black sea shone like wet mink, sparkling as it tossed the moon's reflection about like a young boy with a silver ball. She let her gaze drift in, closer to shore, then narrowed her eyes as a flickering light caught her attention.

At first she didn't realize what she was seeing. Then she gasped. It was a ship! A single ship, moored just off shore.

Someone was signaling to the castle.

The light shone. Vanished. Then reappeared. Turning left and right, Emily scanned the other castle windows but saw no answering signal. Craning her head, she leaned over the balustrade and looked up in the direction of the captain's favorite tower.

Yes, sure enough, an answering light shone once, twice, three times.

Emily looked back at the ship and sipped her hot, sweet chocolate. Though barely visible in the moonlight, the vessel seemed quite elegant. Perhaps it belonged to Lord Connor, and he had gone for a nighttime sail. Or could he be the one who had answered the signal?

Then she caught her breath. Could Lord Connor be a smuggler?

It was not unthinkable. He had, after all, been her father's partner. Could Lord Connor's smuggling have been why the thought of selling the shipping business had sent him into such a furor?

Had the captain perhaps discovered that, despite his efforts to keep Lord Connor out of his privateering ventures, Lord Connor had developed a penchant for even more felonious activities? Was that why the captain had left instructions that the business be sold?

Then Emily laughed at her fanciful suspicions. They were ridiculous. If it was, indeed, Lord Connor out on the ship, he was surely just taking a night-time sail. She did not dwell on the mysterious signal from the fifth tower.

As the small vessel sailed out of sight, she turned away from the window and swallowed the remaining hot chocolate. A few glowing embers from the fireplace threw a rosy illumination over the chamber. Hurrying across the cold floors, icy despite the thick rug, she flung herself into bed.

As she relaxed into the mattress, her thoughts turned back to Lord Connor, whose rooms were at the opposite end of the castle. Although she felt quite comfortable, she suddenly wished she had not been put quite so far away from everyone else, or at least that Maggie had been able to sleep with her rather than in the servants' quarters.

Not wanting to give her imagination fodder for nightmares, she thrust all thoughts of dangerous intruders or ghostly apparitions from her mind, snuggled down beneath the faintly musty-smelling comforter, and soon felt her body begin relaxing into sleep.

Seconds later an odd sound brought her eyes open with a snap.

It sounded for all the world like an intruder had unlocked her chamber door and was entering her room! The muffled echo of footsteps reached her ears. Something *was* in the room with her.

And it was coming toward the bed.

Clamping her eyes tight, Emily pretended to be unconscious. Perhaps if the creature, or person, or ghost, thought her asleep, it would leave.

But it did not.

When the footsteps paused at the side of her bed, Emily

thought her heart would explode. She kept her eyes closed as long as she could. When she could take the suspense and terror no longer, she looked up—

—and blinked in stark disbelief. Before she realized it, her mouth tore open and a scream ripped out of her chest.

Standing several feet from the bed was the ugliest creature Emily had ever seen. A bristling white beard covering its cheeks, a mouthful of teeth like yellow blades gleamed in the firelight, and eyes like flaming coals peered at her malevolently. A great tricorn hat topped the entity's head, and colossal ears fanned out from its face like gigantic sails.

When the monster opened its mouth and joined her in screaming, Emily's mind slid effortlessly into oblivion.

Long after everyone else had retired for the evening, Connor sat in the library. It was an opulent chamber, with gaudy tapestries dating from the twelfth century, and a fireplace large enough to hold an entire tree trunk. It was the place he always came when he needed to sort out his thoughts or feelings. Tonight his attention was centered on the person of Miss Emily Hawke, and why he should feel so out of kilter at the possibility she had wished him dead.

Irritated with himself, he shook his head.

There was really no earthly reason he should feel depressed. It was not as if Emily Hawke was an important person in his life. She was merely a slight inconvenience. She would be gone in no time and his life would return to order.

He made a strong attempt to remove Miss Hawke from his thoughts.

The lady refused to go.

Connor had been dismayed at the expression of repugnance on her face when she'd gotten her first glimpse of the interior of the castle, although he had also noticed her efforts to hide her revulsion. He could not help recalling the disgust in her eyes upon seeing how utterly filthy everything in the place was, from the cobwebs decorating the chandelier in the main hall to the thick carpet of dust on the floor.

Apart from his and the other residents' rooms, the kitchens, and this library, Connor had to admit that the castle was not what any female would have wished for in an abode. After all, Cook, who had steadfastly refused to be placed in the position of both housemaid and food provider, was the sole woman ever to have stepped foot inside the place.

None of the men living there had cared enough to pick up a dustrag. The captain, for example, had never minded the filth, and had, therefore, never found it necessary to hire anyone to maintain cleanliness.

With the situation as it stood now, it occurred to Connor that perhaps the captain's reticence had been the result of his wishing to keep his treasure hidden. Too many people scurrying about, poking into corners and closets, would surely have been dangerous.

The squalid living conditions of the rest of the castle had never before concerned Connor, since his valet, Nipper, had always kept Connor's own things sparklingly immaculate. Nipper was superb in his calling, quite possibly the most skilled gentleman's gentleman in England. The valet's only drawback was his staunch refusal to set foot outside Cornwall, where he had lived ever since the captain had hired him shortly after Connor's graduation from Cambridge. This had not been a serious problem, however, as Connor spent most of his time away from Hawke's Nest at sea. The only time he visited his London clubs was after returning to the London port after a voyage. Thus, since he did not take his valet to sea, he dressed himself while in Town.

Since no one in the castle could be called upon to act as housemaid, Connor decided abruptly, he would hire a boy to help tame the overgrown jungle of a garden and a girl or two to clean up inside and help the new cook, once one had been found.

Once that item had been cleared up, he walked to the sideboard, poured a large brandy, and plopped down in a comfortable armchair with his boots propped before the blazing fire. After draining his cut-crystal goblet, he rose to his feet, left the library, and made his way to the staircase in the center of the great hall.

The passage at the staircase's head ran from east to west. Connor's rooms were in the east wing, while Miss Hawke had been placed, for both propriety's sake and because the captain's old room was the only empty chamber that was habitable, in the west.

He had almost reached his chambers when he heard the bloodcurdling screams.

9

S pinning on his heel, Connor raced toward the west
wing. It seemed to take forever to run the distance
to Emily's room, but once he arrived he pounded violently
on the heavy oak door. "Miss Hawke! Are you all right?"

There was no response.

"Let me in or I'll break down the door! Miss Hawke!"
When only silence met his demand, Connor took a deep
breath, backed up a few steps, and threw his weight
against the door. The wood splintered. Backing away, he
repeated the action. This time the door gave way completely, separating from its hinges and smashing against
the bedchamber floor.

Stepping over the rubble, Connor squinted in the darkness. "Miss Hawke? Where are you?"

A low murmur came from the enormous bed. Moving
swiftly, Connor approached and leaned forward.

The captain's daughter lay beneath her comforter, her
long hair draped over her bare shoulders like a swath of
ebony silk. Reaching out, Connor touched one bare arm
that peeked out of the blankets. He shook it gently. "Miss
Hawke?"

Emily's eyes opened slowly. For a moment she looked
disoriented, then gasped, "Is it gone?"

"Is what gone?"

Emily sat up and the comforter slipped to her waist.
With difficulty Connor tried to shift his gaze away from
her full breasts, covered with only the old cook's threadbare nightrail. His eyes got as far as creamy shoulders that
looked as if they would be heaven to touch, then flickered
back to her breasts and lingered there.

Emily's dark nipples were easily visible behind the thin fabric. Connor was overwhelmed with the urge to caress them. He backed away from the bed, turning slightly to hide the evidence of his rampant thoughts. Then Emily spoke and he redirected his attention away from her body to her words.

"There was something here. Some kind of monster."

He blinked. "A *what?*"

"A monster. I locked my chamber door, but it had a key. It came toward the bed and screamed at me. Its teeth were like enormous yellow knives. It had long fingers, a bushy white beard, big ears, and it was the ugliest thing I've ever seen."

Connor looked around skeptically. "Well, it isn't here now."

She frowned. "Do you suppose it could have been a ghost?"

He stifled a relieved grin. "I doubt it. I think you must have been dreaming. Or you could have seen Maggie coming in to check on you and, due to your inability to see close things without your spectacles, thought *she* was a monster."

Emily's face flamed and her fingers clenched on a pillow. Connor could see she was suppressing a desire to hurl it at his head.

"I was not dreaming. I had just gotten into bed when it came into the room. And it was more than an arm's length from me, so I saw it quite sufficiently to know it was not Maggie. It was real, I tell you!"

The grin he'd been hiding curled Connor's mouth. "My dear girl, I hardly think it likely that ghosts and monsters are running free around the castle. Come now, do you not think it more likely that you fell asleep and didn't *realize* you were dreaming? That sort of thing happens all the time, you know. I have experienced it often myself, especially when I was overtired, as you are now."

Emily's mouth formed a stubborn line. "I *was* awake."

Connor bowed slightly. "I must accept your word."

Pushing the coverlet aside, Emily climbed out of bed. Then, realizing his gaze was pinned to her nearly bare bosom, she pulled the comforter from the bed and wrapped it around her shoulders.

"Well?" she demanded. "Aren't you going to help me look for it? If it isn't here, maybe it left a trail."

Connor sighed, more disappointed by the girl's covering her luscious body than by her failure to accept his hypothesis. "Oh, very well. I'll check the window. You check the door." He paused. "Never mind the door. I knocked it down when I heard you screaming."

Emily flashed him an incredulous glance. "Why? It was not locked. The monster opened it with its key. Never mind. I'll build up the fire so we can see better."

After a few seconds Connor turned away from the long windows. "Nothing here. It couldn't have gone out this way. See? The windows are closed and locked from the inside."

Clutching the blanket to her throat, Emily hurried to join him. "Then it must have gone back out the way it came in. Did you see anything when you came down the hallway?"

Connor shook his head. "No, and I was standing on the staircase when I heard you scream. If it'd been there, I'd have seen it."

"Then it must have been a ghost," Emily said triumphantly.

"Again, I must cede to your opinion. Though it seems odd that a ghost would use a key."

Since his voice did not sound mocking, Emily's gaze flew up to see if he was being facetious. She caught her breath. Connor's eyes gleamed down at her with an expression she had seen only once before, on Lord Marsden's face. This time, however, rather than being terrified, she discovered that she was utterly delighted.

The thought that Connor might find her attractive was like nectar of the gods.

His eyes glowed like two of the coals in the grate, and a slow, sensuous smile touched his lips. Wearing only top boots, fawn leather breeches, and a cotton peasant shirt open at the throat, he resembled nothing so much as the pirate her father had once been (and Lord Connor might still be). He looked as if he were intent on stealing her away to his quarters.

Emily's treacherous body longed to be stolen.

A tiny flame flickered up from the pit of her belly, flared into a roaring inferno, and surged through her chest and over her cheeks, making her face hot and her skin seem too tight.

What had they been looking for a moment ago? Why had he come to her room in the first place? She could not remember, could remember nothing but how his body, hard and warm and male, had felt, and the scents, of leather and tobacco and man, had clung to him as he pressed against her during the carriage accident and again when the gargoyle had fallen from the roof. At that moment she wanted nothing more than to feel his closeness again.

Suddenly she felt much too warm, and allowed the comforter to slide from her shoulders. It pulled the over-large neckline of her nightrail with it, so that both blanket and nightgown pooled around her elbows and draped over the rise of her bosom, barely concealing her nipples.

Like a woman bewitched she watched Connor's eyes glitter, almost as if he had the power to lower the blanket even further just by willing it to move. His mouth tightened as his gaze slipped caressingly over her throat, the neckline of her nightrail, and settled in the shadowy hollow between her breasts.

Oh, God, she thought, agonized. *Let him touch me, now.*

All she could think of was how it would feel to be pressed close to him, of what it would be like to have her body and his separated only by a few layers of thin lawn fabric—or separated by nothing at all.

Her breasts tingled, their nipples hardening to eager points of fire. She parted her mouth slightly as her tongue slid over her oddly parched lips. In mere moments the schoolteacher she had been had disappeared, and was replaced by a woman of flesh and blood, bone and muscle, flame and desire.

She knew her eyes were begging what her lips could not say. As if it had a life of its own, one of her hands rose to touch his face, sliding up over his whisker-shadowed jaw and hovering gently over the head wound he'd sustained in the carriage accident.

Connor felt his body respond to her obvious hunger. *Good God,* he thought feverishly, *does she know what she is suggesting?*

Although his fingers itched to stroke her smooth flesh, he stood motionless, his hands stiff at his sides. If he kissed her, would she scream and run away as any woman of propriety knew she must? Or would she melt into his arms?

More importantly, was he fool enough to allow such an opportunity to slip past without finding out for certain exactly what she *would* permit?

Emily watched the battle raging in his eyes. Then there was a sudden movement at the open door, and the moment was gone. Pulling up both blanket and nightrail, and pressing her fingertips to her burning cheeks, she whirled away, scarcely noticing that Lord Connor was addressing the newcomer.

Breathing unsteadily, she tried to calm herself. Good heavens, what had happened to her? She had behaved like the most wanton trollop! Then someone spoke and, remembering what had brought Lord Connor to her room, Emily pushed all embarrassment from her mind.

Her eyes met Maggie's as the maid rushed into the chamber.

"Good gracious, miss!" Maggie stepped over the splintered remains of the door. Seeing Connor standing at Emily's side, the diminutive maid bristled like a bantyhen. "What's 'Is Lordship doing 'ere? What on earth is goin' on? What 'appened to your door?"

"Lord Connor broke the door down because he heard me screaming. I thought there was something in the room with me. His Lordship was kind enough to help me ... search the room." Emily's cheeks flamed again, and she was thankful for the darkness of the chamber.

Maggie gasped. "What did you find, my lord?"

"Nothing. But I intend to have another look around in the morning when there is better light. I'd like to ask you a favor, Maggie. I know it may not be too comfortable, but

I would like you to bring your things up from the cook's room and sleep here tonight. We can rig a temporary pallet on the floor beside Miss Hawke's bed."

"I'll get my things and be right back," Maggie said. "I never should have agreed to sleep downstairs in the first place. If anythin' had happened to Miss Emily I'd never have forgiven myself."

Passing by Nipper and Cracker Jack, who had burst into the room, the maid said quickly, "It's nothin'. My lady just had a bad dream about a monster comin' into her room. Must have been the exhaustion of travel." She disappeared down the hall.

Nipper's eyes widened in an expression akin to shock. For a few moments he walked about the chamber as if searching for clues. Then, turning abruptly, he left the room. Muttering, Cracker Jack also departed, leaving Emily and Connor alone once more.

Emily cleared her throat. "Well," she said haltingly, "I guess I'll go back to bed now, my lord."

"A good idea," Connor replied. "I shall do the same." He glanced at the splintered door. "I'm sorry about your door. I'll have it replaced tomorrow. It's just that I'm not used to women having nightmares and screaming."

Emily looked at him squarely. "It was not a dream. There really was something here."

Connor shrugged. "This castle is a gloomy old place, isn't it? Maybe you really did see a ghost. Who knows? The estate is certainly old enough to have a few. I mean, what self-respecting castle would be without its resident haunt?"

Gazing down at Emily, he was suddenly struck by the thought that, unless he left immediately, he would take advantage of their next few moments together in a most indiscreet way. He turned and was halfway to the door when her gasp made him whirl about. "What is it? Did you see it again?"

Emily stood beside the bureau, staring down at it with obvious dismay.

"My map!" she cried. "It is gone! It was lying right here, beside my reticule! It's been stolen!"

"Could you have misplaced it?"

"Certainly not," she retorted, pointing at a spot on the bureau. "I left it right there and now it is gone. I tell you it was stolen. And I know by whom!" She glared at him, her recent desire turning to blazing hostility.

"Now wait just a minute," Connor said. "Surely you don't think that I took it."

"What else am I to think, my lord?"

"Perhaps your intruder—" Connor began.

"I hardly think a ghost or a monster would be likely to carry off a sealed map. No, my lord, whoever took it did so because he wanted what was contained within that envelope. And the only person who knew that was you!

"You took my half of the treasure map and then tried to trick me into not noticing by giving me those heated glances and awakening my carnal desires. Don't even try to deny it, you blackguard. Give it back!"

Connor's temper flared at her accusation. "I don't have your damned map. As for your 'carnal desires,' it would be impossible to awaken them since you have no more passion in your body than a barley cake!" he snapped. "You, madam, are a veritable icicle!"

With that he swept through the doorway, reached a hand behind him to slam the door, realized it was not available, threw her a last, challenging glare as if daring her to laugh at his mistake, and disappeared down the hall.

Emily watched him go. Of course he had taken her map, the dirty bounder. And she certainly was *not* an icicle. Returning to the bed she picked up a pillow and pounded it mercilessly, pretending that its feathery softness was Lord Connor's muscular chest.

And, as she lay back down, she wondered why she was more troubled by Lord Connor's pronouncements of her lack of sexuality than about losing the treasure map.

10

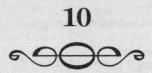

Blinking blearily at her distant reflection in the tiny hand mirror the following morning, Emily pinned her hair into a heavy, braided coil low against the back of her neck, allowing a few curling strands to frame her face. She had not worn the attractive hairstyle since the incident with Lord Marsden. She tried to forget his comments about how alluring he had found it—comments made just before he had informed her that she would become either his mistress or a social outcast.

As she briskly fluffed the feathery curls on her forehead she thought firmly that it was high time she forgot about that ugly incident. It was unlikely she would ever see Lord Marsden again. Even if she did, she refused to let thoughts of his near-rape force her into making herself look old just to avoid the interest of other men.

Surprising herself, she realized that if she ever *did* meet the man of her dreams, she wanted to be prepared.

She staunchly ignored the niggling suspicion that, even though she believed him to be a no-good thief, Lord Connor's reaction to her new style had everything to do with her sudden desire to banish the past.

With a final pat to her coiffure, she donned her freshened black bombazine gown. Her mouth twisted as she glared down at the ugly dress. Apparently Maggie had mended the several small rips the garment had incurred during the two accidents, for it looked as good as new.

Although she had never before given a thought to her mode of dress, Emily found herself wishing the gown had been beyond repair. She sighed. How nice it would have been to have had reason to purchase a more attractive ensemble.

Then she scolded herself. It really did not matter what she wore. She was not a ridiculous schoolgirl, eager to catch the eye of any available male. She was not trying to impress anyone.

She was not!

Besides, she mused dismally, as plain as *she* was, something so frivolous as a pretty dress wouldn't help her appearance much. Glancing out of the corner of her eye at her mother's portrait, beautiful clothes were meant for women like Lady Caroline.

With a final, squinting glance in the small mirror, she shrugged and turned away, stepping over the remains of her battered chamber door. Her heart did a flip-flop as she thought briefly of Lord Connor. How should she behave when they met that morning? How would he behave to her? Should she pretend that nothing untoward had happened? How could she possibly do so?

The tantalizing smells drifting up the great staircase proved that Cracker Jack had succeeded in his supply-trip to Lizard, and that Maggie was acting as temporary cook. Emily's stomach rumbled and she started eagerly toward the scent.

In the light of day the interior of the castle looked even filthier than it had the previous evening. With each step she took, clouds of dust swirled up to dance in the slender sunbeams that struggled to shine through the narrow, grime-smeared windows.

As she reached the middle of the staircase, she glanced back and noticed that her feet had left prints scattered amid many, older prints, on the carpet. The dull hint of lavender that showed through lent suspicion that the rugs would be a lovely royal purple if cleaned properly. Emily shook her head. It was amazing the way men would willingly live in such squalor if they didn't have a woman to look after them!

Dust tickled her nose as she resumed her downward journey, and she sneezed.

"Allergic, Miss Hawke?"

The deep voice made Emily spin about. Lord Connor

smiled enigmatically from the top of the great staircase, looking immaculate in gleaming Wellington boots, tan breeches, and a dolman-sleeved lawn shirt. He wore no jacket.

His eyes sparkled like the finest Ceylon sapphires, a flash of concern, as if he were afraid she would not deign to speak to him after last night's fiasco, glinting in their depths.

Feeling her chest constrict with the same unfamiliar longing she'd experienced the night before, Emily cleared her throat and forced herself to remember her stolen map. "Not a bit. I think anyone would sneeze in all this dust. It's quite overwhelming."

"It is, isn't it?" Lord Connor looked abashed. "My heartfelt apologies. I plan to see about hiring a cleaning crew this afternoon."

Emily raised her brows. "Are you sure that is wise, my lord? Granted the place is a mess, but are you quite certain we want servants in our way while we search for the treasure? What if they should come upon it accidentally?"

He looked uncertain. "Well, I do not want you to be uncomfortable."

"I think I will be able to bear the filth for a time," Emily replied. Unable to help herself, she grinned. "Perhaps the captain left telltale footprints, as we have, which we may follow right to the loot."

Lord Connor laughed. "Who knows? All right, if it is acceptable to you, then we will wait. However, if we find nothing within a few days, we must send Maggie to the nearest village, Lizard, to hire more servants. She cannot possibly manage this household on her own for long, although if the delectable scent wafting up the stairs is any measure, she seems to be doing an admirable job as cook. Speaking of that, shall we go down to break our fasts?"

Emily's stomach growled and she blushed, hoping he had not heard. "Certainly." Although still furious about her stolen map, she felt ill-at-ease walking along in silence and so tried to think of something else to say. Finally she asked, "Where exactly is Lizard, my lord?"

"Approximately seven miles to our west."

He said nothing more, so Emily resigned herself to the

uncomfortable silence. As they reached the bottom of the stairs, she once again saw the huge hall they had passed through the previous evening. She took the opportunity to examine the room more closely.

Numerous tapestries, faded with dust and grime, hung along the walls. Several suits of rusty armor that must have been added in the centuries after the Normans had disappeared held silent vigils in each corner. Wall sconces contained the remains of ancient torches that had dripped oily scum onto the flagstone floor.

High overhead, the ancient, cobweb-ridden bronze chandelier she had noticed the night before loomed like a colossal spider. The wax candles that ran around its perimeter were mere gray stubs, also thick with dust. A large chain was connected to the top of the chandelier and draped across the ceiling. It continued down one wall so that the servants could release the light in order to polish the bronze—although this obviously had not been done in a very, very long time.

Then a rustling noise attracted her attention and Emily noticed that Polly's cage had been hung upon a hook in one corner of the great hall. The bird glared and hissed as they passed and, just as they moved by her cage, screeched another of her declarations.

"And the sun and moon shall appear as nothing next to my glory. You shall be paupers unless you heed my words!"

Emily flashed Lord Connor an uneasy glance. "I'm glad she is locked up. And that she doesn't know anything more damning than misremembered Scriptures. I hate to think what she'd say if she were possessed of a more colorful vocabulary."

They rounded a corner and came to a small dining room set off from the rest of the building. The chamber's walls were made of numerous pale green panes. The ceiling was also glass, but it had somehow been slid back along a metal track to allow a fresh, faintly briny breeze into the room.

The sky was a breathtaking blue with only a few puffy clouds marring its perfect expanse. "Oh, my!" Emily murmured. "This is absolutely the most lovely room I've ever seen. It doesn't look like it's part of the castle at all!"

Lord Connor shook his head. "It isn't. Since the captain was quite fond of taking his breakfast while watching the sea, he had it especially designed. He brought in a crew of German architects to build it." He led her over to one of the glass walls. "Look out there."

Emily's eyes followed the direction in which Lord Connor pointed. About a hundred yards away the earth fell into the sea, forming a rugged cliff beyond which she could just see tentative fingers of ocean spray sparkling in the morning air. "Oh, how glorious!"

"Isn't it?" He turned as Maggie entered the room. "My dear girl, if your cooking tastes half as good as it smells, I shall never let you go back to London!"

Maggie threw him a dismayed glance. "Then perhaps I should take your breakfast back to the kitchen and feed it to Cracker Jack's cat," she threatened.

"Please, no!" Lord Connor exclaimed. "I'm so hungry I'd eat the cat himself if food weren't soon forthcoming."

Grinning saucily, Maggie placed a covered silver platter on the side table.

Remembering the maid's kind gesture the previous night, Emily said, "I wanted to thank you for the chocolate, Maggie. It was very sweet of you and I enjoyed it very much. I didn't expect it so soon after our arrival here."

"You're welcome, miss. 'Tis always nice to 'ave somethin' warm afore bed." Then Maggie disappeared again, only to return a few seconds later with a large tray of scones and two crystal bowls filled with butter and golden honey. "There you go, my lord," she said.

After Maggie left, Connor pulled out a chair for Emily. "Please sit down, Miss Hawke, and I will be happy to serve you."

"Thank you."

"You are most welcome. I also wanted to mention that I found an old trunk filled with ladies' clothing in one of the captain's storage rooms this morning—I thought I'd remembered seeing it years ago, and so I looked, thinking you might not want to be limited to one gown during your entire stay. I believe the dresses belonged to your mother. There's also a large mirror."

"A cheval glass would be marvelous! I must confess I was hard-pressed to make myself presentable this morning with only the use of a hand mirror. And I would be delighted to see my mother's clothes."

Lord Connor removed the lid from the breakfast platter and sighed blissfully. He picked up two porcelain dishes, first loading hers, and then his own, with a heavenly smelling concoction of fried fish with freshly diced scallions and pools of melted cheese drizzled over the top. Beside this he placed several scones smothered in butter and honey.

"There you are, Miss Hawke," he said cheerfully. "Enjoy your first, but hopefully not last, taste of a pilchard."

Emily picked up a fork and took a big bite. Then she took another, chewing slowly to savor every moment. "Oh," she announced at last, "it is the best fish I have ever tasted!"

Sampling his own, he agreed, "Mm, you're right. These are delicious. Of course, pilchards are a staple in Cornish cooking. I've had them cooked many ways, but never as good as this. Your Maggie is indeed a superlative cook."

Silence fell as they finished what was on their plates and Lord Connor refilled them a second time. At last Emily leaned back, blissfully sated, staring at the mound of food still on her dish. "I feel guilty leaving so much uneaten, but I can't possibly swallow another bite. I don't know if I'll even be able to move for an hour or so as it is."

"I thought perhaps we would take a ride around the estate this afternoon, to let you see some of the country and to introduce you to neighbors who knew your father. That should give you a chance to work up a new appetite. There are some lovely thoroughbreds, as well as a few Arabians, here."

"I would love it," Emily replied, "although I am not a very experienced rider."

"I promise to find you a nice gentle mare. When we return from our ride, perhaps we will have a look at my half of the map and go from there."

Emily grew sober. Pinning him with a direct gaze, she said quietly, "Last night you denied taking my half of the map. Can you look me in the eyes and swear that you were not responsible for its disappearance, my lord?"

He met her gaze squarely. "I swear I did not steal anything. In fact, if it will make you believe me, I will be happy to give you my half of the map. Although," he added with a faint grin, "without your spectacles it won't do you any good unless we work together. I suggest we begin considering my map 'ours,' and if we should find yours, we'll think of it as the same."

Emily stared at him for a moment longer, then nodded. "I agree. I'm sorry about last night." Her cheeks warmed as she realized she was not at all sorry about the more intimate emotions that had passed between them. "I mean," she stammered, "accusing you of thievery. It was most unfair."

"Don't say another word about it. Given the situation, you could hardly be blamed for jumping to the most obvious conclusion. I only hope you will forgive my hasty words. I spoke in anger and should have held my tongue."

"Of course." At that moment a bloodcurdling shriek rent the air like a saber. Emily blanched as the sound was joined by Maggie's terrified cry.

As Emily leaped to her feet, one of the jet buttons on her bombazine sleeve caught the lace tablecloth, tipping everything on the table toward her. In moments her half-full plate, a crystal bowl of honey, and a goblet of fresh orange juice slid in a sticky mess down the front of her gown.

Hardly noticing the chaos, she gaped at Lord Connor, then declared confidently, "The monster! I told you it was real! It's got Maggie!"

To her astonishment and chagrin, Lord Connor threw back his handsome golden head and roared with laughter. "Good Lord!" he managed to gasp finally. "I should have guessed!"

11

Hastily disentangling the tablecloth from her sleeve and using her napkin to brush as much food and drink from her bodice as possible, Emily glared at Connor. "How dare you, sir! I fail to see why my maid's being attacked is cause for humor!" Turning on her heel, she raced toward the kitchen.

Still chuckling mirthfully, Connor jumped up and followed. He entered the kitchen to find Emily staring with horrified fascination at the scene before them.

Standing atop a counter piled high with sliced vegetables, Maggie held a bunch of carrots in one hand and a clump of broccoli in the other. Waving them in a wide arc, she wielded the carrots like orange swords at the creature standing on the floor beside the table.

"Get away from me!" the maid screamed. "Get back!"

The "monster" roared with fury and pounded both fists on the buffet, sending bits of mushroom, endive, cabbage, and rutabaga flying.

"Get back, you 'orrid beast," Maggie screamed. Seeing Emily in the doorway, she cried out beseechingly, " 'Elp me, miss! 'elp me! It's tryin' to kill me!"

Emily didn't budge. Instead she continued watching the scene, and Connor watched Emily. The frightening beast didn't take its eyes from the redheaded maid.

The creature accosting Maggie was dressed in gentleman's evening garb, complete from polished, tasselled Hessians to an intricately tied white lace cravat. It looked quite fierce.

As it turned toward Emily, its black lips curled away from oversized yellow teeth and it snarled viciously. Emily backed up a step and collided with Connor, who, not un-willingly, slid his hands around her waist to steady her trembling form. She leaned back into his embrace.

Raising his fingers to brush the undersides of her full breasts, Connor sighed with pleasure. Glad the captain's daughter could not see his enjoyment, he made a silent vow to give Maggie's attacker an extra banana for lunch. Momentarily Emily appeared to realize the improper na-ture of the embrace, and, cheeks pink, pulled away forth-with.

Sighing, Connor picked up a chopped carrot, took a bite, and addressed Maggie's assailant. "Hello, Milo, what's to do? Taken to ravishing helpless young maids, have you?"

Immediately the creature's ire vanished. Turning away from Maggie, he strode forward and reached past Emily, putting out an extremely hairy hand. He shook Lord Connor's fingers politely. *"Eee, ee,"* he murmured as if in explanation.

"Now then, my good man," Connor demanded once the amenities had been observed, "Why are you terrorizing my cook?"

Milo turned back toward Maggie. There was an unmis-takable grin on his lips and a sparkle in his dark brown eyes. Winking, he waggled his bushy white brows extrav-agantly. Then, bowing from the waist, he seemed to beg her forgiveness for his crudity.

Obviously unappeased, Maggie stayed perched atop the table. "I'm not comin' down until 'e's gone," she insisted. "Dirty, womanizing brute. Look at 'is face! 'E's actually enjoyin' this! What is 'e, anyway? Some kind of—"

"Stop!" Connor shouted. "Don't say it!"

Maggie broke off in mid-sentence, her mouth forming a wide O. Then she frowned. "Don't say what?"

Connor smiled soothingly at Milo and lowered his voice. "The one thing you must never, *never* do, is call Milo an M-O-N-K-E-Y. If you do I guarantee he will do more than simply pound on the table."

"Lord Connor is right, Maggie," Emily added. "Milo isn't a mon—" She caught herself just as the animal's eyes began to widen and his lips drew back from his teeth. "He isn't an M-O-N-K-E-Y. He is a chimpanzee, if I remember my natural science correctly. From Africa, I believe." She looked to Connor for verification.

"Very good, schoolmarm." Connor smiled approvingly. "I am impressed. Milo was a favored friend of the captain's, and accompanied him everywhere. Long ago, while visiting London, Captain Hawke had a splendid wardrobe made up for him. As you can see, Milo loves to look like a 'top-'o-the-trees' gentleman."

Nodding, Emily turned to address Maggie. "Climb down slowly," she commanded. "Don't make any sudden movements."

The maid paled. "I'd rather stay 'ere, miss, if you don't mind."

"Don't be silly," Emily countered. "You can't possibly remain there all day. Get down. You are probably upsetting the poor chimp by being up so high. Most male animals prefer being higher than their female counterparts. They find anything else threatening to their dominance."

Connor's lips twitched with amusement.

Maggie wrapped her arms around herself stubbornly. "I don't see 'ow that would 'elp. Even if I got down I'd still be taller than 'im."

"Maggie!"

"And what if 'e grabs me, what then?" the maid argued. "No thank you, I'm stayin' right 'ere where it's safe."

Emily gave an exasperated sigh. "Oh, for heaven's sake. Here. I'll distract him; you can get down while he's looking the other way."

Crossing his arms over his chest, Connor leaned against the wall, settling back to watch what promised to be an entertaining show. Although he knew Milo wouldn't hurt either of them, he had no intention of enlightening the fair ladies to this fact and missing the spectacle.

Reaching cautiously past the chimp, Emily plucked a large rutabaga from the table. Holding it out, she waved it gently from side to side and called in a singsong voice, "Milo, here Milo sweetie. Come and get the lovely rutabaga."

Connor released a snort of laughter. "To the best of my knowledge, he's never been overly fond of vegetables."

Emily threw him a superior glance. "Do you have a better idea?"

Connor tried to look thoughtful. "You might try a banana. He'll do almost anything for one of them."

Emily looked around. "I don't see any."

"Neither do I."

"Well," Emily demanded querulously, "since you know his likes and dislikes so much better than I, what do you suggest I do, Mr. High-and-Mighty?"

Connor suppressed his mirth. Scratching his chin, he strove to look sincere. "You might offer him a kiss. He's very fond of ladies."

Emily's mouth dropped open. "I beg your pardon?"

"I said you might offer him your cheek," Connor continued solemnly. "If he finds you attractive he will come to you. Of course, I cannot claim to be privy to his tastes in women, but I do know he considers himself quite a ladies' man among the maidens of Lizard. They all spoil him quite dreadfully."

Turning away from Maggie, Milo gazed adoringly at Emily and made loud smacking noises with his lips as if he'd understood every word.

"Offer him my cheek?" Emily repeated. She eyed the chimp mutinously. "You've got to be joking."

"I assure you I'm quite serious."

"If you're so sure it will work," she retorted, *"you* kiss him, my lord."

"Oh, no," Connor said regretfully, "Milo isn't that kind of fellow." He bit back another chuckle. "I'm afraid that, since you have no banana, the only thing he will settle for is a kiss. Otherwise," he whispered ominously, "he might just attack your maid again."

"Oh, please, miss!" Maggie squealed. "Don't let 'im 'urt me!"

Emily stood her ground. "Why don't you kiss him then, Maggie? After all, it is *you* he has treed on the table."

The maid blanched and pressed herself against the wall. "Oh, I'm afraid that would never do, Miss Hawke,"

Connor insisted. "Look at the way Milo is staring at you. He seems to have transferred his affections. I doubt seriously that he would accept a kiss from Maggie now, any more than he would want one from me." Truly, Connor saw, the chimp was practically leering in Emily's direction. The smacking noises grew louder.

Emily chewed her lower lip. "Are you sure he'll settle for just one kiss? He won't grab me or anything?"

Connor shook his head. "Rest assured that although he enjoys stealing a kiss once in a while, Milo is nothing if not a gentleman. Isn't that so, my friend?"

The chimp raised a hairy hand to adjust his cravat and brush an imaginary fleck of lint from his coat sleeve as if to say he agreed wholeheartedly. Then he raised his head, pulled back his lips, and grinned with unabashed delight in Emily's direction.

Pursing his lips, he pushed his head away from his chest, closed his eyes, and waited expectantly. When no soft female cheek met his lips, he opened one eye and growled.

Emily swallowed visibly. "Well, I suppose one kiss won't kill me."

Step by slow step, she neared the splendidly dressed chimpanzee. Milo's eye closed again. Screwing up her face, Emily pressed her cheek against Milo's moist lips. Then, as though giving the chimp no time to decide he wanted another, she scurried away and scrubbed at her cheek with her sleeve.

Connor thought he would explode if he could not laugh soon.

Milo's eyes opened and he smiled triumphantly. Emitting a squeak of gratitude, he bowed low and held one closed fist in Emily's direction.

"I think he has something for you," remarked Connor with interest. "You'd better take it."

Obviously feeling much braver now that the kiss was out of the way, Emily smiled uncertainly and held out her hand, palm up. "I only hope it isn't something utterly disgusting," she muttered out of the side of her mouth.

"I'm sure it's not. I'd imagine he has picked up a pretty

bit of driftwood, a shell, or possibly a nice bit of sea-polished glass," Connor said reassuringly. "At least, I hope."

Emily winced as Milo opened his hand and pressed an object onto her palm. For a moment he held her fingers tightly, then closed them over the object and smiled sweetly. Then he turned and ambled out through a door that led onto the lawn.

Through the door, which Milo left wide open, the trio of humans watched the chimpanzee disappear around the corner of the house. Then Emily opened her fingers and glanced down at her hand. She gasped.

"What is it?" Connor demanded abruptly. "If that little terror has given you something revolting, I'll—"

Maggie's eyes grew wide. " 'Ow beautiful!"

Connor took Emily's hand. Nestled in the center of her palm was an enormous diamond, sparking red, blue, and green fire.

"It couldn't possibly be real," Emily said shakily. "Could it?" She looked up hopefully.

"It certainly looks real. And it's quite possible that it is," Connor remarked, gazing speculatively down at the precious gem but making no move to take it, "since the captain had numerous interests in Africa, which is where most diamonds come from. Unless I miss my guess, our hairy friend has beaten us to the treasure. Then again," he said thoughtfully, "it is possible *he* is one of the 'clues' to which the captain alluded."

"Treasure?" Maggie raised thrilled eyes. "What treasure?"

One of Emily's eyebrows rose and the corner of her mouth twisted mockingly as if she were remembering his admonitions about the need to keep their venture secret.

"Well," Connor faltered, wishing his cheeks did not feel quite so warm, "I suppose it won't hurt to tell Maggie. She's your maid, after all, and surely trustworthy."

Emily's expression didn't change. "Oh, surely," she replied dryly.

"Do you want to tell her, or should I?"

"You're doing a splendid job."

Decidedly overlooking the smug amusement in Emily's eyes, Connor quickly related the story. As he finished he smiled at Maggie's obvious excitement.

" 'ow thrillin'," the little maid gushed, wiggling like an excited puppy as her eyes sparkled into Connor's. "Where do we look first?"

Momentarily Connor's gaze dropped to the maid's plump bosom and rounded, wriggling body. His eyes gleamed with masculine appreciation. Then he smiled and opened his mouth to reply.

"*We* do not," Emily snapped, cutting him off. "*You* wanted to go back to London, remember? I'm quite certain your duties will keep you occupied until that time comes."

"Oh," Maggie said dejectedly, "yes, miss. Well, I can't stand 'ere gawkin' all day. There's still supper to prepare."

Connor blinked at this obvious display of feminine jealousy. Then he smiled, feeling quite pleased.

"Would you like to walk outside with me to see if Milo is still in view, Miss Hawke?" he asked as the subdued maid began chopping up more vegetables. Without awaiting a response he took her elbow and led her through the open door and out onto the lawn.

Emily chastised herself silently. Why had she snapped at poor Maggie, simply because the maid had looked extremely pretty just then, and Lord Connor had noticed? He'd have had to be blind to miss Maggie's feminine charms, the way they'd been bouncing around.

Besides, Lord Connor was nothing to her. Why, he would very likely have a good laugh at her expense if he knew she had been more antagonized by his attention to her maid than by his mention of the treasure.

She had been unfair. The only thing to do was to apologize to Maggie as soon as possible. Perhaps she could claim exhaustion or—or stress. God knew there had been enough of that the last few days. She certainly couldn't tell Maggie the truth, that she had begun feeling proprietary toward this man whom she had known for only a few days.

Although the sticky mess on her gown had dried and

was no longer uncomfortable, she remarked unsteadily, "I would like to wash before we go any great distance, my lord. Orange juice isn't precisely pleasant against the skin."

"Of course," he replied. "I just want to see if Milo is still nearby."

They had reached the edge of the cliff and stood above a wide, pale golden beach. Gulls wheeled and cried, and the surf roared. A mile or two out at sea, Emily noticed a small island. A tower or lighthouse sat upon its rocky crest. She was just about to ask what it was when Connor spoke.

"I don't see him. He must have wandered off."

"Does he have any favorite places?"

"Oh," Connor said, his gaze sweeping the beach, "he loves to collect shells and pretty stones—as you have noticed," he added with a grin. "But it doesn't really matter where he's gone, since he sleeps in the same place every night unless he's off on one of his adventures."

"Adventures?"

"Yes. You remember that Cracker Jack informed us of Milo's latest disappearance? Sometimes he just takes off and no one has the slightest idea where he has gone. But he always comes back. As for where he sleeps when he's home, I suppose you have noticed the old, bowl-shaped chandelier in the great hall?"

"The very dirty one?" Then, realizing her statement had sounded grossly rude, Emily flushed.

Connor grinned wryly. "The same. It's his bed. He scavenged some old blankets and moved up there the very day the captain took over this place. Uses the chain suspended along the wall as his ladder. Most chimpanzees in the wild also choose the highest places they can find for their beds—but then I suppose you already know that, being a schoolteacher."

"Yes. Which part of Africa is he from?"

"The Cameroon. His mother had been shot by mighty white hunters, and the captain found Milo huddled against his mother's corpse. Poor baby chimp was nearly dead of hunger and exhaustion."

Emily hesitated, then asked, "So my father really did have a heart, regardless of the fact that he was a criminal?"

Connor met her gaze squarely. "You must get these images of your father being a criminal out of your mind. Despite his slightly illegal business pursuits, he was the most estimable man I've ever had the honor to know."

Emily's heart seemed to swell in her chest and she felt embarrassed at having belittled the captain. "I'm glad," she said lamely, not knowing how to express her relief that her father had not been all bad. Wanting to change the subject, she remarked, "I hope the chandelier is a safe place for Milo to sleep. He could be killed if it fell. Or someone could be caught beneath it and crushed."

"I doubt it's truly dangerous. Milo doesn't weigh much, only about seventy-five pounds, I'd guess." His gaze turned speculative. "I wonder where Milo got a key to your chamber. Do you suppose he may have been the one who stole your half of the map?"

Though she still suspected Connor, himself, for the robbery, Emily gave a perfunctory nod. "Perhaps." Then she realized she still clutched the diamond in her hand. Opening it, she gazed down at the lovely gem. "Do you really think he might have found the captain's treasure?"

"I've no idea. Pity he can't tell us. It would make the whole thing much easier. We'll have to keep an eye on him and hope for the best."

"Mm," Emily agreed. "We'll also have to remove my bedchamber key from his possession as soon as possible. I'll die of fright if he makes another midnight visit." Then she pointed toward the island. "What is that?"

Connor followed her finger. "Oh, that's Star Island. An astronomical observatory."

Emily's heart did a flip-flop and continued thumping erratically as she realized that, since her arrival at Hawke's Nest, she had been so wrapped up in speculations of Lord Connor and the treasure that she'd given no thought at all to the one thing that had meant more to her than anything else in the world for almost her entire life: astronomy.

12

S teeling herself to be disappointed when she discovered that the observatory was in ruins, Emily remarked tensely, "Are you telling me my father *built* his own observatory? Or was it on the island when he won the estate?"

"He built it, though I don't believe he ever used it," Connor said. "Although he was indeed fascinated by the stars, and we had many interesting conversations on the subject, to my knowledge he never even went out to the island. It was too hard for him to climb the stairs to the tower.

"Actually," he continued, "he had the observatory erected for me. Astronomy was my main subject of study at Cambridge. I wanted to remain at school so I might continue my studies rather than come home to the captain, whom I knew had missed me and wanted me to take part in his shipping interests. How could I disappoint him? Especially since it had been his money that had sent me to school in the first place? Nonetheless, he knew I would never stay in Cornwall for long without some way to continue my studies of the stars."

Stunned, Emily gaped at him.

"When I am not on a voyage," Connor went on, "I spend much of my time out there on the island. But I haven't had a chance to do any astronomical research in almost a year. I had hoped to spend some time here after my last voyage, but now, with the captain's death, I'll have other responsibilities.

"I am forever wary that I will return after a long absence to find the telescope damaged in some way—you know, by a fierce storm or perhaps by lightning." Suddenly he looked at her, his face revealing inner embarrassment. "I hope you aren't too put off by my scholarly pursuits. Most women of my acquaintance would be. Intellectual interests are hardly what one expects from a gentleman. Most men of quality spend all their time gambling, shooting, hunting, or the like."

"I am not at all put off. Actually, I find it quite admirable," Emily replied lamely. "Then you are an amateur astronomer?"

Connor nodded. "Before I went to the university I made several voyages with the captain. On one such trip our ship got blown off course during a storm, and our compass and sextant were lost overboard. Fortunately, the first mate knew all about astronomical navigation and was able to get us back to land.

"I decided right then that, in the event I lost my navigational equipment again, I would not be lost at sea, so I took up the study of the stars." He grinned self-consciously. "Rather a cowardly reason to study one of the sciences, wasn't it?"

"Oh, no!" Emily contradicted with careful insouciance, not wanting to incur his disgust in case he was one of those males who disapproved of intelligent females. After all, she thought cautiously, teaching needlework and watercolors at a girls' school was one thing; teaching subjects taught mainly at boys' schools was another.

Nevertheless, behind a mask of ladylike interest, she glowed at the thought that she had finally found a man who shared her fascination. Her inner jubilation broke through in a smile. "Anything that caused you to devote your life to something more than those 'gentlemanly' pursuits could never be cowardly. It is wonderful."

"Thank you." Connor looked sincerely relieved. They said nothing more for a few moments, then he remarked, "I do not know how much you know about astronomy, but the telescope on Star Island was made by Sir William Herschel—one of King George's royal astronomers. It was quite a coup for the captain to obtain one of his instruments. They are in great demand among the scientific community." His eyes glinted. "My telescope is forty feet long and five feet in diameter. One of the largest ever made."

Emily gasped. "Why, that's huge! How do you manage to move it without a crew of ten or twenty men?"

"I designed the mechanism myself, using ball bearings and a system of levers," Connor said proudly. "If you think you'd enjoy it, we could go out sometime and I'll show you the stars. We could keep the trip as short as you like," he added, hoping that would help to persuade her to accompany him. "I know it can get rather boring gazing up at the night sky if one isn't interested in astronomy. We would stay only as long as you wished."

Unable to maintain her demure countenance any longer, Emily's eyes flashed and she nodded eagerly. "I would love it. And of *course* I have heard of Sir William Herschel. Hasn't everyone?"

Connor chuckled and shook his head. "Really, Miss Hawke. Why should anyone have heard of the man? Apart from his fame in the scientific world, he is hardly one to run about in society. Are you just trying to please me by telling a little white lie about knowing who he is?"

"Certainly not! I was fortunate enough to meet him, some years ago, while visiting Slough. His telescopes are said to be the finest in the world! Oh, Lord Connor," she said rapturously, "you must be envied by every other astronomer in the country for having a Herschel telescope of your very own right here at Hawke's Nest!"

Connor goggled. *"You* met Sir William Herschel?"

"Yes, indeed!"

"I'll be damned," he said oddly. Recovering, he asked, "What was it like looking through his telescope?"

Emily shrugged and made a face. "I do not know. His sister Caroline, although a most charming lady, seemed to think that I should retire with her when night fell, just as the men were going outside. She was quite adamant, and I was sent to bed like a young miss. I was most distressed, and have meant to return these many years but have been unable to get away from my teaching duties long enough."

"Miss Hawke," Connor said agitatedly, "never say you

have designs to become a scientist as well as a school-marm?"

Thinking he was mocking her, Emily glowered. "And what is wrong with that? Or are you one of those men who think the only thing a woman is good for is a man's comfort?"

Connor laughed. "Good God, no! Dear lady, I assure you I do not think women are only good for a man's 'comfort.' Hardly that. In fact, I've never met a woman who wasn't more trouble than comfort any day of the year."

Emily pressed her palms to her burning cheeks. "Oh, dear. I am so sorry for cutting up at you again. It's only that I get so angry when I feel like a man is talking down to me just because I am a woman."

Connor's chuckles faded and he gazed at her thoughtfully. "I assure you I neither took offense nor meant any. I was simply impressed with the depth of your education. While it is true that most men of my acquaintance are uncomfortable around intelligent females, I find it quite intriguing to carry on a meaningful discussion with a woman with more wit than hair.

"In truth," he continued, "the main reason I have never wanted to take part in a London Season—although I do admittedly belong to several clubs and enjoy visiting them when I am in Town—is because I've yet to meet a woman there who did not simper and behave as if she had nothing but air between her ears. That goes for matrons as well as debutantes. And, of course, why else does a man suffer through the Season if he is not interested in finding a wife?"

"I would not know," Emily admitted. "Having been at school all my life, I have never had a Season. And even if I had wanted one, I did not have the funds. Or anyone to sponsor me."

Leading her toward a small group of rocks near the edge of the cliff, Connor helped her sit on a smooth stone and then sat down beside her. "So tell me, how did *you* become interested in astronomy? You will agree, I think, that it is even less normal a lady's pursuit than a gentleman's."

"One of the few times he remembered my birthday, my father sent me a small telescope when I turned thirteen," Emily said. "Since I had never met him, I wanted to be able to impress him when I first had the chance, so I learned everything I could about the stars." She sighed. "Unfortunately he 'died' before I could dazzle him with my newfound knowledge. Or fortunately. I mean, what man would want a bluestocking for a daughter?"

Catching her arm, Connor looked into her eyes. "I assure you, Miss Hawke, your father would be most impressed if he were to meet you now. You are a captivating woman. Not only are you intelligent, but you are beautiful and enchanting."

Flushing, Emily pulled away and looked back at the island, uncertain how to respond.

Connor seemed to accept her retreat graciously. "I must tell you, Miss Hawke, I never hoped to find a female companion who shared my passion for the stars. It makes our friendship that much more precious."

Happiness fizzed through Emily's veins like champagne bubbles. Raising her eyes, she noticed that his gaze was fixed on her face. The sun glinted off his golden hair and his eyes shone. When his glance dropped suddenly to her mouth, her lips parted of their own accord.

Abruptly Connor turned to gaze at Star Island. He cleared his throat. "Have you, by chance, ever been to one of the king's star parties? I hear they are quite enjoyable."

Although uncertain what she had wanted him to do, Emily sighed with regret at his obvious change of subject. "No, although I have always longed to inveigle an invitation to Windsor when the king calls Sir William Herschel to London to entertain the royal court. His Majesty does that about once a year, I believe, although he entertains at the court less frequently now that he has been . . . ill."

Connor nodded his understanding of her reference to King George's recent bouts of madness. "We can hope the regent will follow in his father's scientific footsteps and continue the star party tradition."

"Even if he does I don't delude myself into thinking I will ever be invited," Emily replied regretfully. "But that is of no matter. Just meeting Sir William in Slough was the most exciting event of my life. And now to find one of his telescopes here at Hawke's Nest! I can hardly credit it."

"Speaking of the king's parties, I received just such an invitation about a year ago. Had I known you then, I would have insisted we attend together—as friends, of course," Connor said hurriedly.

"You received an invitation?" Emily said enviously. "Did you go?"

"No. I was to leave on a voyage to Africa the next day, and did not want to be up until all hours."

Emily nodded. "I know exactly what you mean. Sometimes, at the academy, I was so tired after spending the night gazing through my telescopes that I could scarcely remember the history lessons I was supposed to be teaching the girls the following morning. Therefore, with Mrs. Harriman's permission, I began teaching them astronomy instead. That way I could pursue my hobby and the girls could extend their education."

"An admirable notion."

"Thank you. May we visit Star Island as soon as possible?"

"I will make arrangements to sail this very afternoon, if you would prefer that to riding."

"Yes, please!"

Connor watched his companion, thinking her the most charming creature he had ever known. She would make some lucky man a superb wife. Especially if the man was interested in astronomy. Someone like himself, for example.

Startled, he shook his head. That was a ridiculous notion. He hadn't the time *or* the desire for a wife, regardless how appealing Miss Hawke seemed at that moment. Furthermore, she would not make a good wife for *him*. He intended to marry a woman he need never love, one who would raise his children and keep his house without making demands on his heart.

There was no way on earth he would allow himself to

fall into the same trap as he had with Bettina Findlay. Getting mawkish about a woman led to betrayal and pain. He would *not* feel that way about Emily. It would ruin a beautiful friendship.

Nevertheless, experiencing a preposterous desire to keep the gladness on his companion's face even if it took drawing the moon down from the sky to do so, he said, "We must pack a lunch and spend the day searching the island for treasure. After all, we have to start treasure hunting somewhere. It might just as well be there. When night falls we can have a look at the stars."

Emily clapped her hands together delightedly, like a child being offered a prized toy. "Will we take the ship I saw in the harbor?"

Connor frowned. "What ship is that?"

"Last night I saw a beautiful little sloop moored in the harbor. It shone a lantern at the castle, and someone in the fifth tower flashed a light back. Three times. At first I thought it might have been smugglers." Her smile faltered as she seemed to observe his change of mood. "Then I realized it must be one of your ships."

Connor's lips tightened. Smugglers?

His mind raced back to Cracker Jack's informing him of Cook's desertion. Had the old woman actually seen smugglers prowling about the castle? And if she had, might they still be around? He would have to look into the matter. If they were still present, they could pose a danger to everyone in the area. "It may indeed have been smugglers."

Emily was silent for a moment. When she spoke, the sparkle had gone out of her eyes and her voice was very soft. "Would it be best if I told no one else about this?"

Connor nodded. "Undoubtedly. If what you saw *was* a ship of smugglers," he explained gruffly, "speaking of them carelessly could endanger your life."

"I know how to keep a secret," she said quickly. Her face had gone quite pale.

Connor caught his breath as he considered Emily dying at the hands of smugglers. He was nearly brought to his knees as emotional pain, as strong as a physical blow, hit him in the stomach.

He swallowed. If there were smugglers working in the area, he knew they would not hesitate to kill anyone they thought a threat to their well-being. Emily must not die so needlessly. She was the most beautiful creature he had ever seen. The most alive.

"Please," he said harshly, "see that you do."

His heart throbbed as he gazed at her. Her hair shone blue-black and her eyes glimmered silver-green. As she looked out to sea, with her cheeks now flushed a delicate rose, he dropped his eyes to her mouth. Weakened by the thought of her in the clutches of smugglers, he was overwhelmed with a desire to pull her close, to protect her always, and to steal the kiss he had missed the night before.

The tip of his tongue swept across his lips.

To combat the urge to pull her into his arms, he forced his gaze away from her face, took several deep breaths, and clenched his hands into fists until his nails dug into the palms of his hands.

He would not kiss her. He would not allow himself to feel warmly toward a woman, only to be betrayed in the end. Love did something strange to women, something unpleasant.

Emily was his friend. To allow himself to feel anything else would be fatal.

A part of him whispered that this comparison was unfair, that Emily Hawke was nothing like Bettina Findlay, and that if he did not seize the opportunity to discover their differences, he would lose something precious forever. On the heels of this thought came the realization that it might be highly dangerous to be alone on Star Island, beneath a glittering sky, with this delectable female and her delightfully plump breasts, moist mouth, velvety curls, and huge, exquisite eyes.

As his body temperature rose, he drew another unsteady breath and tried to think of bland things: a pot of stew, shearing sheep, wildflowers, swine in a mud bath.

Then, as Emily took a deep breath and the color in her cheeks deepened, she raised her lovely eyes to the rapidly healing wound on his forehead. "How ... how is your head feeling, my lord?"

Connor felt a sharp, stabbing sensation in the area surrounding his heart. His fingers itched to release her ebony curls from their braided coronet and allow them to swirl in the fresh breeze sweeping in from the sea. His lips longed to slide over the silken softness of her cheek and inhale her sweet, spicy perfume.

And his hands ... his hands longed to slide over her lush female curves, delicious even beneath the ugly black bombazine gown, until she whimpered with the same longing that thundered through his veins.

Swallowing the heady passion that made his breath come in unsteady gulps, Connor cleared his throat and held out his arm. "It is fine, thank you. Hardly hurts at all. Come," he said huskily, "let us go inside. You'd best have Maggie help you change into one of those gowns I spoke of. Then, while Jack readies a dinghy so that we might row to the island, you and I will adjourn to the library where we will see what we can make of the half of the map we still have."

13

E mily and Maggie returned to the bedchamber to find that Jack had already deposited the cheval glass and the chest filled with gowns just inside the door. Too excited to wait a moment, they rushed to the chest and began pulling out gown after gown for viewing. Each successive ensemble was more lovely than the last.

The first was covered with chips of turquoise, others with bits of emerald, jade, chalcedony, and malachite. A few had fringes of topazes and yellow diamonds, while others hadn't a spare inch that was not drenched with pearls, sapphires, or rubies. Very soon brocades, satins, velvets, woolens, and silks so fine they seemed lighter than air were piled in vibrant heaps across the bed.

Behind an embroidered screen near the fireplace, Maggie prepared a steaming bath so that her mistress might wash away the stickiness covering her front. Emily stroked the fine fabrics while she waited for the water to warm. She shook her head.

"I cannot possibly wear such beautiful things while grubbing around this dirty castle looking for treasure," she said. "And I hardly think an observatory is likely to be much cleaner. Lord Connor told me no one has been there in over a year. There is bound to be dust. What if the gems fell off the gowns? They must be genuine; they are too exquisite to be paste. I'm sure they are worth a small fortune."

Then she caught her breath. Gazing speculatively at the glittering pile of dresses, she fingered one particularly splendid creation in sapphire-blue silk, sprinkled with diamond chips in the shape of miniature stars. Did Lord

109

Connor know how valuable the dresses were? she wondered.

Perhaps the gems might be sold in order to save his shipping business. Suddenly she blushed, realizing that she must feel more for him than she'd admitted even to herself, if she considered parting with something that could make the difference between a life of luxury or deprivation for herself in the event they never found the treasure.

But surely it could not hurt to sell the gems and give the money to him while they were searching for the captain's booty. They would find it, she was sure. Until then, although it would be a pity to destroy the exquisite gowns, it would be practical to make use of the jewels beyond enjoying their loveliness.

When Maggie spoke Emily jerked her head up with a guilty start, half-afraid the maid knew what she'd been thinking.

"But miss! Surely you will want to look beautiful for your afternoon with 'Is Lordship! Maybe if we removed some of the jewels from one of the gowns," Maggie said tentatively. "The yellow silk with the amber fringe, for example. It shouldn't be too 'ard to remove the stones. I think I could 'ave it ready by the time you finish your bath."

"I suppose you could try," Emily answered doubtfully. "Are you sure you could remove them without leaving gaping holes in the fabric?"

"I think so." Maggie wandered back over to the trunk and looked down thoughtfully. Suddenly she bent over, an excited expression on her face. "Look!" she exclaimed. "A hidden compartment. There are slippers and gloves to match everything. And here is a white silk parasol which I think could be used with almost all the gowns."

Emily sighed wistfully. "It *is* tempting."

"I'll see what I can do while you soak," Maggie said. "Come on now, the water is getting cold."

Emily undressed and moved toward the copper tub. By the time she finished bathing, the maid was holding the de-gemmed yellow gown up for her inspection. Emily smiled. "It is lovely. Thank you, Maggie."

"You're welcome, miss. I've put the other gowns in your armoire, but 'ave left out three dresses for your approval as dinner gowns. There don't seem to be any day dresses. I suppose that is why these gowns were saved after Lady Caroline's death—because they were so valuable. I thought this ivory satin with seed pearls acceptable as it is, and perhaps this sea-green sarsenet will be suitable if I remove its bodice of emeralds. They are a bit much, I'm thinkin'. And this scarlet silk with its overskirt of gold net and rubies might also prove useful."

"I had hoped some of the gowns would be suitable for everyday wear. I suppose I shall simply have to wear my black dress when I search for the treasure." Emily shook her head resignedly. "It seems a crime to deface such works of art, doesn't it?"

Maggie grinned. "Yes, miss, but I'm 'avin' a wonderful time."

Since Emily was still feeling a trifle guilty about snapping at the maid earlier that morning, she said quickly, "Then you must choose a gown for yourself."

Maggie gasped. "I couldn't!"

"Of course you can. I insist. Haven't you ever heard the old saying, 'The workman is worthy of his hire'?"

"Well . . ."

"Didn't I see another green silk in the trunk?"

Maggie's green eyes grew wide. "The one with the peridot chips on the sleeves and 'em?"

"Yes, I think so." Emily found the garment and pulled it out of the armoire. "Here you go."

"Oh, miss," the maid breathed. "I never dreamed to own such a thing."

"It will look lovely on you. With that red hair and your green eyes, I'm certain you will look quite beautiful."

Then, feeling much more charitable toward herself, Emily allowed Maggie to help her into the yellow silk gown. A glance in the cheval glass told her that she did, in fact, look quite striking. The color contrasted with her ebony curls and brought a sparkle to her eyes.

"Are you quite certain this is not too elaborate an ensemble for a picnic?" Emily asked the maid hesitantly as she stepped into the buttercup-yellow kid slippers and pulled wrist-length gloves over her hands. "It is so rich, even without most of the amber drops."

"Oh, it is fancy, miss, but you 'aven't anythin' else to wear and I'm sure 'Is Lordship will think you quite gorgeous. After all, it was 'is idea that you wear these gowns, wasn't it?"

Secretly delighted with the chance to shed her ugly black bombazine, even if only for a short time, Emily was forced to agree. Any doubts she might have had vanished as she descended the great staircase and saw Lord Connor gazing up at her in open admiration.

"You look lovely," he said sincerely.

Emily's stomach tickled nervously at his warm gaze. "Thank you. It is a pleasure to wear something other than black, I must confess."

"If I had my way," he remarked heartily, "the regent would decree that you must never wear black again. That color is perfect on you."

"You flatter me unmercifully, my lord," Emily said with a laugh, feeling carefree and gay in her new finery.

"I speak only the truth. Since Maggie was busy with you, I took the liberty of packing a light luncheon of bread, cheese, and wine. But first we shall adjourn to the library and discuss our search plans, if that suits you."

"Of course." Then she paused. "I was wondering about something, my lord."

"Yes?"

"All of my mother's gowns, except this one, which Maggie unadorned, are literally smothered with gems of all kinds." Her cheeks warmed. "I . . . I was thinking perhaps we might sell the jewels in order to save your shipping business. In case we do not find the treasure at all."

Lord Connor stopped dead in his tracks. "You would do that?" he asked incredulously. "You would deface your mother's dresses, and hand over a small fortune, without any qualms, just to save my company?"

"Of course," Emily replied sincerely, hoping her cheeks were not too pink. "You could reimburse me after the treasure was found."

A radiant smile spread across Lord Connor's face, like the sun after a storm. "Dear lady, I do not know what to say. I'm overwhelmed."

"Then you will agree?"

"I certainly would, if I thought it would do any good. But I am afraid the shipping business is worth over fifty thousand pounds. I am quite certain that, although quite beautiful, the gems on your gowns would be worth maybe a few thousand at best."

"Oh," Emily said, feeling quite deflated.

She shuffled after him as he moved into the library.

The first thing Emily noticed about the library, which she had been too exhausted to appreciate on the night of their arrival, was the size of the chamber. Its ceiling was twice as high as that in an average room, and its walls were lined with expensively bound books. The room smelled pleasantly of leather.

A second painting of Lady Caroline hung over the cavernous fireplace. Dressed in deep blue, she wore a strand of enormous star sapphires around her slender neck. More adorned her ears and hair, and covered the wrists of her long white gloves. If possible, she looked even more beautiful than she did in the portrait hanging in the captain's chamber.

"Oh, my," Emily breathed. "She is gorgeous. And those jewels! I've never seen anything like them."

"I have been meaning to write to Mr. Simms and inquire as to their whereabouts. I believe the captain placed them in a bank in London years ago. By rights they should belong to you." Connor grinned. "At least you'll have them if we do not find the treasure. You certainly won't starve."

Emily brightened. "Oh! If we do not find the treasure I insist we sell at least some of my mother's jewels. Maybe, combined with the gems on the gowns, they will bring in enough money to save your company."

"Absolutely not. I could not allow it," Lord Connor said firmly. "Your mother's jewels will not be sold. Most of them are undoubtedly family heirlooms. But I thank you from the bottom of my heart for even considering such a kindhearted gesture."

They moved toward a long oak table. Glancing back, Lord Connor studied the painting once again. "Your mother was a true Incomparable. You can see now why Mr. Simms and I were so struck by how much you resemble her."

Emily flashed him a disbelieving glance.

Either not seeing it, or perhaps just ignoring it, he helped her into a chair and sat beside her. "Now then. Let us see what clues the good captain has given us. Since your half was stolen," he remarked, "I've carried my half on my person at all times. I've even slept with it."

Emily watched as he removed the envelope, still sealed with the captain's mark, from his pocket. "I thought you'd have opened it by now."

"I thought about it," he said with a rakish grin. Standing, he moved toward a large oak desk, opened a drawer, pulled out a silver letter opener, and sliced through the wax seal on the parchment's fold.

Emily frowned as he unfolded the map, read its contents, and uttered a perplexed oath.

"What is it? What does it say?"

"See for yourself." His expression did not change.

With a dawning sense of dread, Emily took the proffered sheet of paper. She stared at Lord Connor for a moment, then holding the paper at arm's length, looked down and read aloud. "Make a wish upon a star, and you will find your heart's desire." She blinked. "Why, this is no map! What can it mean?"

"It seems utter nonsense to me," Connor replied dryly. "Which makes me wonder if there is really any hidden treasure at all. Perhaps this whole thing was just a ruse to bring the two of us together." He gazed at her speculatively. "Perhaps the real reason the captain has thrown us together was to play matchmaker. He always did have a romantic streak."

"Oh," Emily cried, "surely he would not have been so cruel. I cannot believe it! Why, if there is no treasure, that means you're going to lose the shipping business no matter what! Because if there is no treasure to be found, there is nothing we can do to keep it from being sold to someone else with sufficient funds! And to risk your future just to throw us together in the hopes we would fall in love would be absurd. No. I don't believe it."

Obviously Connor didn't trust himself to reply. Instead, he moved to a side table that held an assortment of cutcrystal decanters. Grasping one about the neck and picking up a glass from a second tray, he poured himself a generous brandy. He swallowed the alcohol in a single gulp, then turned to Emily. "Want a drink? I think you could probably use it."

Although it was not her usual habit to imbibe strong spirits, Emily heard herself answer, "Please." And even more astonishing, when he handed it to her, she also polished off the brandy in a single burning swallow. For several moments she coughed and sputtered while he patted her on the back.

"Another?"

"No, thank you."

One part of Emily was deeply chagrined to find they had been duped.

The other part of her wondered, suspiciously, if Lord Connor could have opened the envelope and replaced the map with the ridiculous rhyme.

Surely not. But would a man who was also a smuggler be above such deception?

How much of what he said could she believe? What of the way he had seemed to threaten her earlier that morning, when he'd insinuated that harm might come to her if she told anyone about the smugglers' ship she'd seen in the bay? Was Lord Connor the estimable gentleman he seemed or a blackhearted villain?

But if he was a villain, why had he not leaped at the opportunity to sell her mother's gems?

If he *had* lied, and had actually taken her half of the map, he now had in his possession the whole thing, and he might even already know where the treasure was hidden. That would explain why he didn't feel it necessary to take her mother's jewelry. Yes. That had to be the answer.

She forced herself to return his gaze calmly when he spoke.

"Well, it is a turn of bad luck, but I don't think this should preclude our going to the island for a picnic and some stargazing, do you?"

He managed, she noticed with bitter admiration, to sound almost crushed.

"After all," he said more spiritedly, "even though our maps have turned out to be a dead end, there is still a treasure of some kind, somewhere. Remember Milo's diamond."

The same thought had already occurred to Emily. Again the niggling fear that Lord Connor was behind the disappearance of both halves of the map, as well as the orchestration of the carriage and gargoyle incidents, surged through her. The only thing puzzling her was why he would have placed himself in danger, both times.

For a moment she was tempted to give him the diamond and leave, but just as quickly, she discarded the notion. He would never believe she would just walk away. And she needed the money too badly to run. If there were even the vaguest chance he was truly a knave, her only hope was to pretend she had absolutely no suspicions.

Who knew what he might do otherwise. Arrange another accident, perhaps, and this time fail to come to her rescue? She smiled weakly. "Quite so. You know, I am not feeling very well. I think I will forgo our trip to the observatory and lie down for a while."

Connor shook his head. "I think you are simply overset by disappointment. I insist we continue with our plans. If you feel ill once we get to the island I will bring you back immediately. But I think you will feel better once you get some fresh air."

Unable to look him in the eye, Emily gazed at her feet as he took her arm. He led her from the room, down the myriad winding hallways, and into the kitchens, where they gathered their picnic supplies.

"Will Maggie be accompanying us?" she inquired as Connor slung the basket rungs over one arm, suddenly eager to have protection of even the most fragile sort. If

Lord Connor guessed that she was suspicious of his smuggling, would she be safe going to the island alone with him? And how could he not wonder what she thought? It all seemed so obvious. Did he perhaps not care what she thought because he meant to see she didn't return from the observatory alive?

Then Connor smiled and a shiver slid down Emily's spine like a snake. "Certainly not," he said. "She'd be bored as a corpse."

Emily shuddered.

"Surely you realize that people who aren't interested in astronomy find gazing through a telescope a deadly dull pastime. We shall have a much more enjoyable time by ourselves." He laughed at her agitation. "I promise I'll behave as properly as a priest."

"But we might want someone to serve us." Emily's voice quivered.

"We shall do perfectly well by ourselves. You need not worry about suffering any discomfort. *I* shall act as your servant and see that you have everything a body could desire."

"Oh," she replied sickly. "That won't be necessary."

"On the contrary," he argued, "it is my duty to see that all your hours are as pleasant as I can possibly make them until we are no longer together."

Her *final* hours? Emily wondered queasily. Still, aside from struggling away from his hold on her arm, there seemed little she could do to escape. She drew an unsteady breath as they moved outside, across the lawn, and toward the same overhanging cliff where they had stood earlier that morning.

As they reached the drop Lord Connor stepped back, as if to allow her to precede him, and placed the flat of one hand against the small of Emily's back. As she took a step forward she set her slipper on a loose stone and felt herself slide toward the treacherous edge of the path. Just as she pictured herself plummeting headfirst off the cliff, Lord Connor's strong hands grasped her waist.

14

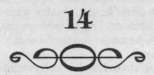

For a split second Emily wasn't certain if Lord Connor meant to pull her to safety or propel her into space. She gaped up at him, paralyzed with fear. Then he smiled and his eyes smoldered into hers.

"Watch your step. It's treacherous going. I should not want anything to happen to you. Here," he said with an enigmatic smile, "I shall hold your hand so you will not stumble again."

Emily's fingers tingled where he grasped them.

"The path runs down there—you can see it plainly. It isn't at all hard to follow, but it isn't wide enough for two abreast. Don't worry. I will trail you within arm's reach to ensure your safety."

He pointed and Emily saw that there was, indeed, a narrow path through the grass. It wound along the hillside and came to a stop at the beach. She swallowed a gurgle of hysterical laughter.

What was the matter with her? She had never been so fanciful while at the academy! There was no danger here. Lord Connor was a charming, handsome man who obviously meant her no harm, even if he *was* a smuggler. Feeling utterly silly, she moved out ahead of him, admiring the tiny white and purple flowers that grew along the rocky cliff face, their tenacious roots clinging determinedly to what little soil they could find, and enjoying the feel of her hand, extended behind her and clasped in his strong grip.

When they stepped onto the sandy beach, Emily noticed a little dinghy nestled in the water with its prow resting against the shore. The back of the boat rose and fell in the whitecaps breaking along the edge of the sand. Cracker

Jack stood at attention beside the vessel. Taking the picnic basket from Lord Connor, he stowed it under one of the seats.

Before Emily knew what he was about, Lord Connor stepped forward, placed a hand around her back and one behind her knees, and swept her into the air. She gasped and flung her arms around his neck, all her fears returning with a vengeance as she wondered if he had meant to drown her all along, rather than push her off the cliff.

He grinned roguishly, his golden hair falling over his brow and his eyes sparkling mischievously. "I know, I know. I promised to behave like a priest, but no self-respecting holy man would allow a lady to soil her lovely yellow slippers."

Although her heart was pounding so hard she could scarcely catch her breath, Emily managed a weak smile as Connor stepped into the prow of the boat and placed her carefully on one of the benches. "Th-thank you," she stammered, her heart thumping at the opposing sensations of fear for her life and the pleasure of being nestled against his warm, solid body.

"Don't mention it," he replied with a gallant bow. "Okay, Cracker Jack," he said to the old sailor as he picked up a long oar. "Let's go."

The trip to the island went swiftly. Emily threw back her head, glorying in the wind against her cheeks and the graceful swaying of the little boat. Connor smiled at her, and she sighed blissfully. "For the first time in my life I can see why men become sailors. How wonderful this feels. Is it the same in a large ship?"

"Quite similar, although one doesn't feel the waves quite so strongly. You don't feel even slightly queasy?" he asked curiously.

"Not a bit."

"You must have inherited that trait from the captain. Lady Caroline couldn't abide the sea; it reportedly made her feel green about the gills even to look at the surf hitting the shore. But then, few people are natural sailors. It would be interesting to see how you fared on a longer journey.

"You know," he continued in a wistful tone, "the skies on the ocean are magnificent. Dark as black velvet, with stars as brilliant as a child's eyes at Christmas. I've often wondered what it would be like to keep a telescope on board. Of course, one would have to take precautions to keep the salt spray off the equipment. Perhaps we might try it someday."

Although Emily did not answer, her heart sang. As they drew close to the island, Connor turned his attention to positioning the bow of the dinghy correctly. A few swift oar strokes brought them close to, but not touching, the rocky shore.

Once again Connor plucked Emily up into his muscular arms as if she weighed no more than a feather. Striding through the waves, he stepped onto the beach. For a moment he held her tightly as he gazed down at her.

"Be careful," he said then as he lowered her from his arms onto a large boulder. "The rocks are slippery from the water and as sharp as a razor if you should fall." Turning back to Cracker Jack, who stood expectantly in the dinghy's prow, he took the picnic basket from the old sailor's gnarled hands. "Thank you. I'll signal when we're ready for you to come back."

Cracker Jack frowned, but sat back down and picked up the oars.

"Isn't he coming with us?" Emily asked.

"No. But you have nothing to fear. Remember, we shall be accompanied by a priest all evening," Connor assured her with a wink.

Emily blushed but did not reply. Once again a nervous flicker rose in her belly and she wondered if Lord Connor were truly a heavenly priest or a satanic devil bent on her destruction—moral if not physical. And which, she wondered further, did she want him to be?

Grumbling, Cracker Jack began rowing back to the ship. His voice floated over the waves. " 'Teddn't proper. Lord love 'em, just 'teddn't decent leavin' 'em alone an' them not 'itched. 'Teddn't proper a-tall."

Emily allowed her gaze to drift up the rocky windrow. It was not so much an island, she saw now, as an enormous volcanic mound that had been thrust up out of the water and subsequently eroded to leave the current mass. High atop the mound of stones rested a man-made tower, built of the same rock that composed the island.

A path had been carved through the rocks, making their climb easier than she had expected. Still, by the time they reached the hill's crest she was breathing heavily, and her lovely yellow gown felt more than a little damp from the physical exertion. The stiff wind blowing around the observatory cooled the fabric, and she drew a pleasured breath.

"The breeze feels wonderful," she declared. Turning, she gaped at the tower rising above them, a hundred feet into the air. "Good heavens! It's huge! From the shore I didn't realize how big it is."

"Yes. It had to be very high in order to protect the telescope from the ocean's salty spray. As you must know, salt is very corrosive and not at all good for machinery, much less mirrors made mostly of copper. They tarnish so easily. Someday, of course, we hope to use glass to replace metal in the mirrors, but at the present time it is impossible to make glass as smooth and flawless as metal. But I suppose you already know all this."

"Yes." Emily replied with a smile, following as he led the way through a small door and up a winding set of stairs.

They seemed to climb forever, round and round and round. At last Connor paused at a second door, and reaching toward the wall, moved a stone, revealing a hidden cache. Inside lay a small silver key. Removing it, Connor slid the stone back into place.

Emily held her breath as he opened the tower door and stepped aside to let her pass before him into the observatory. As her eyes came to rest on the massive telescope, she breathed out slowly. "It's just as I dreamed it would be. If only my girls could see this. One or two of them were as fascinated by the stars as I.

"You know," she added, "one of my fondest dreams has always been to open schools for girls all over Britain; schools that concentrate on the sciences rather than art and needlework. Wouldn't it be wonderful if they could all be outfitted with scopes as marvelous as this one?"

"It would indeed," Connor agreed solemnly.

Jerking her head up, Emily searched his face for mockery. Seeing none, she smiled again and returned her attention to the huge cylinder and the mounting apparatus.

A wooden framework suspending the forty-foot telescope in the air sat on a circular pivot. The pivot rested on steel ball bearings, which enabled the entire structure to be turned in a complete circle with the greatest of ease.

Emily looked up at the ceiling. Also constructed of wood, it was dome-shaped and looked as if it was made of numerous plates bolted together. She frowned. "I understand how the telescope moves, but how do you remove the ceiling cover?"

"I'll show you." Moving toward a metal crank that sat near one wall, Connor rotated the crank until the entire ceiling rolled back like the cover of a desk.

"Incredible," Emily said, eyes wide with awe.

Still smiling, Connor moved away from the lever and ran a possessive hand over the lower part of the telescope's barrel. "It gets better. Just wait until you look into the night sky with this beauty. The rings of Saturn are as clear as anything, and you can see Cassini's division quite clearly."

"The wide, dark space between the rings," Emily replied easily. "I believe it was discovered by Giovanni Cassini in 1675, was it not?"

"Once again I am impressed. Your knowledge is truly extensive," Connor said with approval.

She flushed happily under his approbation. "I've read about the division before but was never able to see it with my scopes. They were not powerful enough. I can hardly wait!"

"If you are excited about that, you'll be really excited to hear about my surprise," he said secretively. "I recently purchased the most current copy of Mechain's object list, and I have it with me."

"Mechain? Isn't he the man who extended Charles

Messier's deep-sky object list? A list of things you can only see with a telescope?"

"You are partially correct, although he also listed things that are visible to the naked eye—the Great Nebulae, for example. Some of the other objects in his book are visible with powerful opera glasses or a ship's lens, and, of course, there are those objects you can see only through a high-powered telescope."

He pulled the treasured pamphlet from his coat pocket and handed it to her, watching like a mother hen as she leafed through the pages. After a time he cleared his throat. "I'd like to publish something similar, someday," he said confidingly.

Emily glanced up from the book, thinking how at odds with his appearance his scientific bent seemed. He looked so at ease in his fashionable clothing, with his stylishly windswept hair. She returned the booklet. "I believe you will," she replied sincerely, wishing she might be at his side to help.

Connor tucked the book back into his pocket. "I'd love to discuss stars all day, but the afternoon is getting away from us. Where do you suggest we start searching for the treasure?"

Emily looked around, trying to quell the feeling that searching for a treasure he had likely already found—if he *had* stolen her map and replaced his with a silly rhyme— was ridiculous. Even if he meant her no physical harm, she thought firmly, all the evidence still pointed to his guilt on that matter.

"Really," she murmured grimly, "it doesn't look like there's anywhere to hide a treasure here."

"I agree. Of course, the captain could have made a hiding place in the rocks like the one that conceals the observatory key, but he'd have needed help, and anyone who had helped hide a treasure would certainly not have kept his own counsel. No, I don't feel that there is anything of value here. Except the telescope." He looked at Emily and smiled. "And you. Shall we have our picnic instead?"

Wondering if his flattery was meant to deflect her attention from suspecting his true motives, she sighed and nodded.

After spreading a woolen blanket on the stone floor, they settled down to a variety of cold cheeses, sweet-smelling bread with fresh, salty butter, and tangy red wine.

"Miss Hawke," Connor said suddenly, discarding a bread crust and looking into her eyes. "Do you not think we might have done with this 'my lord' and 'Miss Hawke' formality? We have made a pact of friendship, after all. I should prefer to call you Emily, and hear you call me Connor."

Emily studied him. Did he really consider her a friend, or did he think her a mere pigeon? She did not trust her voice to answer. Nevertheless, she nodded.

"Excellent." He smiled, then brushed his hands on a cotton napkin and stood. "I know it isn't dark, but shall we use the telescope to look toward the mainland?"

"Yes, I would like that," Emily said as he moved away and began arranging the equipment.

Momentarily he looked up with a troubled frown. "Something seems to be wrong. I can move the barrel up and down, but it won't budge from side to side. See?" He wiggled it and the barrel slid easily toward the heavens and down again. "The rotation device must be jammed."

Moving toward the large metal box that contained the mechanism, he reached down and gripped the handle on its top. At that moment he glanced idly toward shore. His eyes narrowed. "What is that?"

Emily got to her feet and went to stand beside him. "What is what?"

"That. On shore. It looks like a carriage heading toward the castle."

Emily followed his gaze. "It does. I wonder if we have visitors."

"To the best of my knowledge we've never had visitors at Hawke's Nest. Not in all the time the captain owned the place. I hope there hasn't been an accident nearby or some such. Wait here. I'm going to signal Jack to bring me the ship's glass so we might get a better look." Connor moved swiftly out the door.

Emily again sat on the blanket and listened to his boots clatter down the stairs. In about fifteen minutes he returned, a ship's glass in one hand. She watched as he extended it, removed the lens cover, and peered through the narrow end of the tube toward the mainland.

"It *is* a carriage. It's stopping at the castle. People are getting out. A woman . . . and what looks like a maid . . . and other servants."

Suddenly his cheeks faded to dead-white. He drew a sharp breath and nearly dropped the ship's glass. Emily's heart lurched as he lowered the lens, still staring toward land with an expression of pure shock.

"Bloody hell!" he whispered. "What is she doing here?"

15

Standing, Emily moved to take the glass from Connor's stiff fingers, lifted it to her eye, and peered toward shore. A woman in a cranberry-colored traveling gown, with golden curls halfway down her back, stood on the castle steps. "Who is she?"

Connor turned blindly. "It is Bettina. My brother's wife. What the devil is she doing here without Markus? What the devil is she doing here at all? Come on. We've got to go back. Now."

Hastily he closed the observatory roof, shoved the remains of their picnic into the rattan basket, thrust it under one arm, and ran down the steps a second time. Emily watched him go. Then, clutching the ship's glass, she followed, trying to ignore the sick feeling of dread that had taken up lodging in the pit of her stomach.

They seemed to reach the mainland in far less time than it had taken to reach the island. Emily's pleasure in the breezy, sunlit afternoon had vanished, leaving in its wake the sensation of being wrapped in damp wool.

All during the return trip she had watched the emotions flash across Connor's face. First he appeared horrified, then elated, then simply dumbfounded at the prospect of seeing his beloved again after so many years.

Emily felt her heart disintegrate into a million pieces.

When had she begun to feel so warmly toward Connor? When had his bright blue eyes and teasing smile become so important to her happiness? Oh, she had known she was attracted to him, but when—when had she fallen in love with him? There was no doubt in her mind that the elusive emotion that had crept over her when she least expected it was love. Her heart gave another painful thud.

As if he knew what she was thinking, Cracker Jack looked at Emily sadly. He shook his head. Blinking rapidly, Emily turned her face away from the old sailor's knowing, sympathetic gaze.

Perhaps somewhere in the back of her mind she had hoped that, despite their pact of friendship, she and Connor would become much more than friends. She wanted to speak, but could think of nothing to say. She wanted to shake him, to scream, "Look at me! I've fallen in love with you and would take you even if you had nothing! Even though you are a smuggler! And a thief! Don't go back to the woman who betrayed you and broke your heart like you're breaking mine!"

But her lips stayed closed.

What could she possibly say that would change his feelings for the exquisite female—for now they were close enough so Emily could see that the blond woman was, indeed, the most beautiful creature she had ever seen—who had caused him such pain all those years ago?

She could not keep her glance from stealing to Connor's face. He was now utterly expressionless. Was it her imagination that, though he was silent and his expression was deadpan, his eyes glowed with an inner fire, sparkling like the sun skittering over blue ocean waves?

She dragged her gaze away and studied her hands, blinking rapidly to dispel the sharp tang of tears. Her chest ached. She swallowed the lump that had risen in her throat.

Raising her eyes again, she stared at the ethereal figure who had run forward and was skipping down the hillside path toward them, apparently unwilling to waste a moment waiting for her former love atop the cliff.

As she ran across the beach, Lady Duncan suddenly saw Emily seated in the back of the boat and came to a halt so abruptly that she nearly fell. Her vivid blue eyes, so like Connor's, turned flinty and assessing. Then she seemed to catch herself and, straightening her smile, resumed her charge.

"Connor! Connor darling! It has been so long! Far, far too long!"

Emily watched miserably as Connor stepped from the dinghy and firmly set his feet in the sand as his beautiful sister-in-law threw herself at him and wrapped her arms around his neck. For a moment he seemed to hold her close against his chest, then forced her away so he could look down into her face. "What has happened, Bettina? Why have you come? Where is Markus?"

Emily watched with astonishment as Lady Duncan opened her hands, arms still clasped about Connor's neck, and dug her long almond-shaped nails into her palms, causing tears to spring to her huge blue eyes.

"Oh, Con," she wept prettily. "I don't know how to tell you this. There has been a terrible tragedy."

She wrapped her arms more tightly around him. Reaching back, Connor tugged her hands apart and dropped them. "Tell me."

"Your brother," the blond gasped tearfully, "is dead."

For a long moment Connor said nothing. Then he asked in a voice just above a whisper, "How?"

"A duel. He became convinced that I was . . . having an affair," Lady Duncan finished, waving her hands like skittish white doves. "He challenged the man to a duel and was shot through the heart."

Connor took a deep breath. "I see," he said abruptly. "And what brings you here? I should think you would be at Duncan Towers. In mourning."

He gazed pointedly at Lady Duncan's modish, cranberry-velvet traveling gown, and Emily caught her breath hopefully. Did he doubt the sincerity of Lady Duncan's grief?

"Why, I *am* in mourning," Lady Duncan asserted, looking surprised. Then she glanced down at her dress. "Oh, you mean this old frock? I know the color is hardly the thing to wear after one so dear to me has recently died, but I was so torn apart that I knew I must come directly to you. I didn't have time to have a new black wardrobe prepared. I trust there is a seamstress in the closest village?"

"I'm afraid I don't know."

"Well, that's all right." She looked past Connor at Emily. Her ice-blue eyes glinted coldly. "I'm sure your . . . er . . . little friend here knows how to wield a needle. I can see by her gown, which is at least twenty years out of date but looks as good as new, that she must have considerable talent for refurbishing old clothing."

Emily's cheeks burned, but her retort died on her lips as Connor's voice cut through Lady Duncan's pretensions like a knife.

"My 'little friend' just happens to own the estate grounds on which we stand. I would thank you to show her more respect."

Lady Duncan flushed and appeared taken aback. She eyed Emily speculatively, then looked back at Connor.

"I am sorry. I had no idea. Please," she said coolly to Emily, while keeping her gaze on Connor's face, "forgive my hasty tongue. I assure you I would not have made such a mistake if my dear brother-in-law had introduced us, as propriety demands."

"He hardly had time, Lady Duncan," Emily replied with barely concealed hostility. "I am Miss Hawke."

"You know who I am?" the blond said in some surprise.

"Yes. While we were on the island Lord Connor mentioned that you were his brother's wife. It naturally followed, since he has—had—only one brother, that you are Lady Duncan."

"Ah," Lady Duncan remarked. "An intelligent female. How pleasant for my brother-in-law." She laughed mockingly. "Poor Con. You must be so glad to see me, so that you might have more . . . feminine company."

Connor leaped into the breach. "Actually, although you are welcome here, I find Miss Hawke's intellect quite refreshing, Bettina. Shall we walk up to the castle? I'm sure you would like to rest after your long journey. Cracker Jack," he called over his shoulder, "bring the picnic supplies up when you come, please."

Taking his arm possessively, Lady Duncan propelled him forward, leaving Emily behind. Feeling utterly wretched, Emily watched them go.

"I wouldn't worry, miss," Cracker Jack said from behind her back. "I'm sure 'Is Lordship 'as better taste than to be taken in by a tart like that. Woman's no better than she should be, less'n I miss my mark." Moving forward, he helped Emily out of the dinghy.

Fearing she would sob if she tried to speak, Emily nodded and silently moved after the pair. Their voices drifted back on the breeze.

"It is *so* good to see you, Con."

"It has been a long time."

"I would like to stay for several weeks if you and Miss Hawke will have me."

"That will depend upon Miss Hawke. It is, after all, her home."

Emily had to admit they made a handsome couple. Their blond curls were almost of a like shade, although Connor stood many inches above Lady Duncan, whose artfully tousled head came only to his shoulder. Disconsolately, Emily looked at her own feet for the remainder of the climb.

When he and Lady Duncan reached the top, Connor turned. "Miss Hawke, allow me to give you a hand."

"No, thank you, my lord," she said coolly, brushing past his outstretched arm. "I have managed to climb the hill without your aid, and do not think another three feet will do me in." She moved stiffly across the emerald lawns toward the castle. Behind her, Lady Duncan gave a ridiculing laugh. Emily glowered.

Maggie, hands set firmly on her hips, stepped out of the kitchen door as Emily entered the castle. "Miss! There's people all over the place! Not one of them 'as spared me so much as a glance or a by-your-leave! I can't get anybody to tell me 'oo they are."

Emily scowled. "I can well believe it. If they are all as snooty as Her Ladyship, it's understandable. The party belongs to Lady Duncan, Lord Connor's sister-in-law. Apparently His Lordship's brother was killed in a duel. Lady Duncan came to Lord Connor because she was extremely distraught and needed comfort."

Maggie threw a censorious glance at the beautiful woman on Lord Connor's arm. "The comfort part I can believe, but she don't look like she's in mournin'. She looks like a pocket Venus, decked out in all that scarlet finery and 'angin' on 'Is Lordship's arm like a lamprey."

"Maggie!" Emily remonstrated, hiding her agreement behind mock disapproval. "Her Ladyship's clothing is none of your concern. I'm sure she will dress more properly when she has had a new wardrobe made up in Lizard. As for Lord Connor, he is an adult and is fully capable of deciding whether he wants the woman hanging all over him or not."

Maggie stood her ground. "Lady Duncan left London too soon to buy a black traveling gown?" she growled. "Any shop in Town could have sold her one, premade. I worked as a seamstress once, so I know they're always prepared for such emergencies."

Emily shook her head in wonder. "Really, Maggie, you have had your share of professions, haven't you? But we shall say no more on the matter of Lady Duncan. Be silent, now; here they come."

Connor held the door open and Lady Duncan sashayed into the room. "The kitchen, Con?" she said peevishly. "I hope you don't make it a habit of wandering through the servants' area."

"It was the closest door and I knew you wanted to go to your room as quickly as possible. I also wanted to speak to our cook. Maggie, would you ready a bedroom suite for Lady Duncan? And do you think you could prepare something special for this evening's meal? To celebrate Her Ladyship's visit?"

The maid eyed him with disfavor. "A celebration, is it? And 'ere I was thinkin' somebody 'ad died."

"Maggie!" Emily said sharply.

"Beg your pardon, my lord and lady," the maid muttered, bobbing a scant curtsy as her green eyes took in Lady Duncan's frilly red gown. Her lip curled critically.

Lady Duncan raised her huge blue eyes to Connor's. "I cannot believe you have such rude servants. If she were mine, I'd have her dismissed. Or at the very least, beaten."

"Beaten?" Connor repeated uncomfortably. "I hardly think that will be necessary. Besides, she is Miss Hawke's personal maid and is merely acting as cook until we find a replacement."

Lady Duncan brightened. "Perhaps *she* can sew a few things for me." Turning, she looked down her nose at the maid. "I will call for you later."

At last Emily's temper overflowed like a rampant volcano. "I'm afraid Maggie is kept quite busy," she snapped. "She won't possibly have time. You did bring your own maid with you, did you not?"

"Well, of course," Lady Duncan sputtered. "But she can hardly be expected to dress my hair and keep my clothes pressed as well as do odd jobs."

"Then you must resign yourself to wrinkled gowns," Emily said with a cold smile. "Come. I will take you upstairs and you can direct *your* maid to prepare a chamber for your stay."

"But Lord Connor promised that your maid would—"

"Lord Connor was mistaken," Emily retorted as she strode from the room without a backward glance, leaving Lady Duncan to follow or to be left behind.

16

Lady Duncan was installed in a chamber in the west wing, just beyond Emily's apartment. She remained in her room all afternoon.

When it was nearly dinnertime, Emily stood gazing at her reflection in the cheval glass. She was draped in an elegant gown of ivory satin with a full skirt and overdress of silver gauze that Maggie had laid out for this evening. Its bodice was embroidered with seed pearls in the shape of lilies, and it had a short train that came to a point in back. Tight lace sleeves also ended in points against the backs of Emily's hands.

The gown's waist was quite high, and there was a little diamond-studded bow nestled beneath the breast. Despite a frilly lace fichu tucked in its border, the bodice was much lower than any Emily had ever worn before. She regarded her image doubtfully.

Maggie, on the other hand, eyed her mistress with pleasure. She had insisted on helping Emily dress for this "celebratory" dinner, and had prepared the meal ahead of time to facilitate matters.

"Oh, miss," the maid whispered breathily, "you look just like a bride."

"A bride? At my age? I hardly think so." Emily blushed and the color spread like a rosy veil across her breasts, scandalously bare above the gauzy fichu. "You don't think the decolletage a bit low?" she asked nervously, tugging at the neckline.

"Not a bit of it. Besides," the maid said as she pulled the bodice back down, "Lady Duncan 'as nothing upstairs to speak of, and you showin' yourself off like this is sure to put 'er in a pelter. Didn't you notice 'ow flat-chested she is? Looks like she 'as a board stuffed down her bodice. Lord Connor won't be able to 'elp but notice the difference between you."

A gurgle of laughter escaped before Emily snapped it off and picked up an ivory-handled swan's-feather fan. She waved it rapidly in front of her face to cool her high color. "Do you think I need any jewelry? I don't have much, but I do have a string of small pearls Mrs. Harriman gave me when I had been on her staff for three years."

"No. You look fresh and lovely just as you are. And unless I miss my guess 'Er Ladyship will be drippin' in gems. 'Er kind always overdresses. Given your exquisite gown and superb bosom, Lord Connor will be unable to keep 'is eyes on 'is plate tonight. That should put a pricker in 'Er Ladyship's drawers."

"Well," Emily replied with a muffled giggle, "if you're absolutely sure my bodice isn't too low, I'd best go down. Jack rang the second dinner gong some time ago, so I'm already a bit late." She moved toward the chamber door, which had been repaired earlier that morning.

"Yes, you'd better. I'll come with you. I left a chocolate mousse in a pot of ice water to chill and it needs checkin' on."

Connor and Lady Duncan were already downstairs, Emily noted as she entered a small withdrawing room. Someone must have cleaned the chamber upon Her Ladyship's arrival. Although the red and gold Chinese brocade furniture still seemed a trifle dusty, the worst cobwebs had been dusted from the fireplace mantel, and the few figurines scattered about on low tables gleamed.

Her eyes went instantly to Connor. He looked marvelously masculine in a stark white waistcoat, jacket of sea-blue superfine wool that brought out the color of his eyes, and woolen breeches that disappeared into boots shining like black satin. Then her gaze slid to Lady Duncan, who returned her glance with disfavor.

Lady Duncan had chosen a frilly gown of bright pink. Her pale curls were threaded with ribands of the same shade, and, as Maggie had predicted, she wore an elaborate diamond necklace around her neck. More gems covered her earlobes, wrists, and fingers, and sparkled amid her blond curls.

Emily felt Connor's gaze drop to her decolletage. After a lengthy inspection he cleared his throat and raised his eyes to her face.

"Miss Hawke, you look stunning."

"Thank you," Emily replied, suddenly too shy to meet his gaze. "I am sorry I'm late. Shall we go in to dinner?"

Lady Duncan surged to her feet, flounced over to Lord Connor, and seized his arm possessively. Connor smiled wryly and held his other arm out to Emily, who, despite the urge to wrench the other woman's arm from its socket, managed to return his grin. Inside the dining room Lady Duncan claimed the chair on Connor's right, leaving the left for Emily.

Although the conversation was not glittering, the food was delicious. Maggie had outdone herself. Later, as they sat over bowls of chocolate mousse, Lady Duncan looked across the table at Emily.

"So, Miss Hawke," she said in a tone that left no doubt that she was outrageously curious but trying desperately to conceal the fact, "tell me why I have not heard of you before now. One would think a woman of property and Quality would have been seen among the *ton*. You are Quality, are you not? I am certain Lord Connor would not dream of associating with a woman beneath his station."

Emily smiled tightly. "I do not think it likely you would have heard of me, my lady. Until a week ago I was an instructor at Mrs. Harriman's Academy for the Betterment of Young Ladies."

Lady Duncan's eyes widened. "A schoolteacher? How very odd."

But before Emily could reply, Connor spoke. "Miss Hawke's father was my mentor and business partner. He recently died. Miss Hawke has come to the castle to learn more about him and to collect her inheritance."

" 'Collect her inheritance'? I should have thought a better place to do that would have been at a banking establishment."

"Yes, well," Connor replied easily, "as I also said, she wanted to learn more about her father."

Lady Duncan's eyebrows flew to her hairline. "You mean she knew nothing of him? Doubly odd."

"There were peculiar circumstances," Connor stated firmly. "*Personal* circumstances."

Lady Duncan's face showed her displeasure at being reprimanded. "I see." She returned her attention to Emily. "And now that you have inherited your father's estate, do you intend to return to the academy to teach, Miss Hawke, or take up a position as a woman of substance? Perhaps we shall be graced with your presence in Town this year for the Season's entertainments."

Emily felt her cheeks warm. She looked down at her dessert and tried to control the trembling of her hands. Then she held her head high and answered proudly, "I'm afraid I will be unable to take up my teaching position again. Although I would like nothing more than to return to the school, there was some ... trouble. As for staying in London for the Season, I am not the type of woman who really enjoys such things."

"Not the type of woman?" Lady Duncan cried. "But my dear, *all* women enjoy parties and balls and such—at least unless they are afraid they will not be accepted." Her blue eyes widened speculatively. "Or unless they have something to hide. Please, tell me more of this 'trouble,' if you will."

"Bettina," Connor began, "I hardly think that is any of our bus—"

Emily shook her head. "It is all right, my lord. I do not mind telling my story. There was a gentleman whose daughter was enrolled at the school. He made improper advances and then threatened to spread damaging rumors about me if I did not comply. Naturally I refused, and realizing that such rumors would be damaging to the school, gave up my position for the good of the academy."

Lady Duncan's eyes shone. "Who was this offensive gentleman? He should be ostracized from polite society." She sounded more as if she thought Emily's attacker should be given a medal.

Emily shrugged. "I suppose it can't hurt to tell you, now that I have left the academy and he cannot harm my friends. His name is Lord Marsden."

The delight vanished from Lady Duncan's face, and her pretty, bow-shaped mouth dropped open. "Lord Marsden? Impossible! He is every inch a gentleman! I know him very well. He is a good friend of mine, in fact. He stood as my husband's second during the duel." She paused to cross herself. "God rest Markus's poor soul."

"Perhaps Lord Marsden behaves as a gentleman as long as there is no fear of reprisal," Emily retorted. "*I* found him repulsive, and hardly thought his actions proper."

Lady Duncan's mocking smile gave evidence to her disbelief. "Well, my dear, *I* have never known Lord Marsden to act in any way other than as a gentleman should. Although he is a very attractive man and, I suppose, because of that attractiveness, some women might make fools of themselves in ways that he might misconstrue as encouragement. I am certain he merely mistook some action of yours—"

"Encouragement!" Emily gasped.

A slight movement from Connor's direction made her clamp her mouth shut and look at him. He had placed his napkin beside his dish. His hands were clenched into fists. When he raised his eyes they were like chips of blue glass.

When he spoke his voice was barely audible and edged with steel. "Why did you not tell me of this before, Emily?"

"You did not ask, my lord. Besides, it happened in the past, and really matters not."

Connor slowly opened his hands and stretched his bloodless fingers. His eyes never left her face. "You are wrong. It matters a great deal that you have been so insulted."

Emily's heart quivered at the furious glow on his face. "Th-thank you, my lord. But I'd prefer to forget about it. Besides, I am hardly likely to see the man again, am I?"

Lady Duncan's lips twisted up like a crocodile's smile. "Good God, I should hope not, if he is as evil as you say.

I should think you'd be terrified into palpitations at the very thought."

Then, smiling, she turned toward Connor. "Enough of this subject. I want to hear all about *your* life during these last few years, Con darling. You cannot know how much I have missed you."

Emily gaped as she saw Lady Duncan jab her own eye with a fingernail. Connor, his attention still focused on Emily, had not noticed. When the blond woman lowered her hand, her eyes were filled with sparkling tears. She looked exquisitely beautiful and infinitely fragile.

Emily felt a surge of loathing like none she had ever felt before. Was Connor blind? Could he not see through the woman's tricks?

"Truly," Lady Duncan continued with a broken sob, "I do not know what I shall do with myself now that Markus is gone. Duncan Towers seems so empty. I know you did not approve of my leaving too precipitously to have a suitable wardrobe prepared, Con, but I simply could not stay a moment longer. I missed Markus so much, and everything at the Towers only reminded me of him."

"You mustn't worry about what to do, Bettina," Connor replied absently, obviously still infuriated about Lord Marsden. "You are welcome to stay here for as long as you wish."

Emily suppressed an urge to stab his hand with her fork.

"Oh, thank you," Lady Duncan gushed. "I am hoping that when I return to Duncan Towers you may be persuaded to return with me. Naturally, now that you are Lord Duncan, however, I shall remove to the Dower House."

Connor froze. His eyes took on a peculiar expression.

"My lord," Emily said quickly, "what is it?"

He drew a deep breath and exhaled slowly. "In all the commotion, it hadn't even occurred to me that Markus had no son, leaving me his heir."

"No, nor daughter either to warm my old age," Lady Duncan mourned. "I can only hope to catch—" She broke off and amended hastily, "Er, find another man, when and *if* I ever get over losing my darling Markus, so that I might still have children."

Connor stared at her blindly, obviously hearing nothing but his own thoughts swirling about his head. "Of course you will, Bettina. A woman as beautiful as you could not possibly remain a widow. Any man would be proud to have you by his side."

Emily cringed at Lady Duncan's triumphant smile.

Unable to stand much more of the effusive Lady Duncan, Emily was more than happy to retire to her chamber early. Once again a steaming cup of chocolate awaited her pleasure on the bedside table.

After removing her elaborate gown, Emily sat in her chemise on the dainty Chippendale chair near the dressing table and sipped the hot liquid. It tasted oddly bitter, as if Maggie had not put enough sugar into the brew. However, not wanting to hurt the maid's feelings, and since there was nowhere to dump it other than out the window, where it might drip on the castle walls and show from below, Emily forced it down and placed the cup back on the bedside table.

Maggie returned shortly thereafter, having moved her small pallet into the dressing room that connected off the main chamber, and made her way to her own bed. Within moments her gusty snores filled the apartment.

Unable to sleep with all the noise, Emily lay atop her plush feather bed, her mind whirling.

Connor was now Lord Duncan, and it was obvious that Lady Duncan intended to have him for her own. Of course, there was the problem of affinity, that being the illegality of a man's marrying his brother's widow, to contend with, but Emily didn't doubt that Lady Duncan would find a loophole somewhere in the law, even if it meant seducing a magistrate to get her way.

When Connor finally belonged to Lady Duncan, Emily knew *she* might as well be dead, for it would kill her to see the man she loved in that witch's claws. She tried to convince herself that Connor was an adult and, as such, was fully responsible for his actions. But how could any red-blooded male resist a woman as provocative as Lady Duncan?

For the hundredth time since Lady Duncan's arrival Emily felt a wave of inadequacy rush over her. Her Ladyship was so ... elegant. And *she* was so ... *in*elegant.

Giving an agonized sigh, she rolled to one side and pounded her pillow in an attempt to make it more comfortable. How could she even think of sleeping when she was very likely going to lose the one man who could make her happy? She sighed again and rolled to her back. The mattress felt uncomfortable, as though the bed were filled with rocks instead of feathers. Muttering with irritation, she thrust the coverlet aside and sat up. The mattress was so thick and high that her feet dangled over the edge of the bed, not touching the ground. This made her feel like a little girl, and again she couldn't help comparing herself to Lady Duncan's sophistication and thinking herself less than adequate.

Jumping off the bed, she moved restlessly to the fireplace, tossed another log onto the dying embers, and watched the flames leap back to life until the room was well-lit.

If only Connor were here now. If only he would tell her that *she* was the one he wanted, not Lady Duncan.

As if conjured up by her imaginings, she heard footsteps outside in the hall. She held her breath and moved close to her door. Cocking her head to one side, she listened carefully. Her heart pounded with excited expectation.

But the footsteps moved away.

Biting back a cry of disappointment, Emily put tentative fingers on the door handle and turned it softly. She froze as the door creaked slightly, but then she continued to push it open soundlessly and stuck her head around the jamb. Her blood seemed to freeze in her veins.

A figure moved noiselessly down the hall toward the east. It held a candle high and was surrounded by an eerie glow.

Was it Connor perhaps, going after the treasure now that the household was safely abed?

Opening the door further she stepped out into the hall, her feet sinking into the deep carpets. She could feel the stone floor even through the plush fabric, and wished she had put on her slippers. But not wanting to lose the mysterious figure, she ignored the chill and followed.

It was not until she had trailed the figure to the end of the east wing that she realized her mistake. As the figure paused near Connor's door, it turned and glanced behind. Gasping, Emily leaped into the shadows, praying she had not been seen.

Lady Duncan!

The woman knocked gently and the door opened. The firelight in Connor's room threw a brilliant cast on his old love. She was resplendently alluring in a red velvet dressing gown. For a moment Connor merely gazed down at Lady Duncan, then the woman moved into the bedchamber, and the door closed.

Turning, Emily fled back the way she had come, her breath coming in great heaving sobs as tears cascaded down her cheeks. When she reached her room she hurled open the door, slammed it shut without disturbing Maggie's energetic snores, and threw herself across her bed. Covering her head with her pillow, she allowed pain to roll over her like a thundercloud.

Despite her belief that she would be unable to sleep for the rest of the night, less than five seconds later—even before the tears had dried on her cheeks—she was unconscious.

17

Connor leaned lazily against the doorjamb. In his right hand he held a glass of brandy—the last of an entire bottle. However, despite imbibing freely he didn't feel even slightly in his cups; rather, he felt more sharp-witted than ever.

He smiled down at Bettina. His masculinity was gratified to see desire flame in her eyes. Not taking his eyes from hers, he swallowed some more brandy, enjoying the feel of it as it burned a path down his throat. Although it had not been planned, he had been expecting this little visit.

How like Bettina to think she could win him over so easily by offering him what she had likely offered every gentleman in London. He had no doubt that the man his brother had fought in the duel had indeed, despite Bettina's arguments to the contrary, been her lover. He assumed the man had been married, and thus unable to wed Bettina after Markus's death, and that was why she had come here.

Thinking back to when she had claimed to adore *him*, he recalled her passionate demands that he make love to her even though they were not yet betrothed. He was glad, later, that he had not succumbed, although at the time it had been a rare fight with his morals. He'd always wondered if his refusal was the real reason Bettina had chosen to marry Markus. Had Markus given in so easily that Bettina knew she would be able to rule him for life?

Despite his dislike for his brother, Connor felt a sincere regret that Markus had lost his life over such a worthless piece of flesh as Bettina. Beautiful, she was. Worth tumbling over a bed or even a pile of hay, she was.

Worth dying for, she was not.

He felt a stab of remorse at the thought of Markus attempting to defend such a licentious woman's honor. Poor bloody fool.

Now, had she been Emily, Connor thought as he looked down at Bettina's face, he would not have hesitated to throw down the gauntlet to protect her honor. Why, he'd been prepared to seek out Lord Marsden the moment he'd heard of the rascal's attack on his little schoolmarm. He'd been more than willing to run the villain through with a rapier, though he'd known Emily for barely a sennight.

He took another large swallow of brandy.

But it was highly unlikely, he reasoned, that other than the occasional need to protect Emily from a house mouse or long-legged spider, the man lucky enough to wed her would ever need to engage in battle. The thought of infidelity would never even occur to the lovely schoolteacher. Now *there,* he mused, *there* was a woman who would be faithful till the death. Sweet Emily.

He tossed back the last of his brandy.

Still, Connor thought, he could not deny that at one time, he, like his brother, had also thought Bettina worth possessing at any cost, including bloodletting. He'd have gladly killed his own flesh and blood if he'd thought it would make Bettina love him.

Indeed, when he first caught sight of her through the ship's glass, arriving at the castle, he'd been overwhelmed with uncertainty about how it would feel to be with her again. It had been wondrously liberating to discover that, aside from a mild glimmer of disgust at the way she'd hung all over him so recently after her husband's death, he felt nothing at all. The love he'd buried in the past didn't even whimper from the grave.

He had outgrown her.

Gazing down at the woman who had broken his heart so many years before, he let his eyes wander over her hair, gleaming like fairy-spun moonbeams as it curled wildly about her elegant face. It was quite beautiful. Her lips were full and red, made shiny as her pointed pink tongue flicked out to moisten them. They were quite inviting. Why, then, did he feel no lust at all?

Bettina drew a sharp breath, raising her scant breasts like an offering. Inevitably Connor found himself comparing her meager chest to Emily's ripe bosom.

The memory of the schoolmarm's velvety, luxuriant cleavage pressed intimately against the gauzy fichu she'd worn at dinner caused Connor's lower half to clench urgently. He drew a sharp breath of his own and turned slightly so that Bettina would not see the evidence of his desire and mistake it for interest in her.

Too late.

Bettina leered at him hungrily, and Connor took a step backward as she advanced into the room, closing the door behind her. As she raised both hands and untied the bow of her dressing gown, she laughed huskily. The robe fell lightly to a luxurious puddle at her feet.

The sight of her naked body made Connor's stiffness melt like a candle left out in the sun. He studied her dispassionately. When she spoke he almost laughed out loud.

"You want me, don't you Connor? You've always wanted me. As I have always wanted you. Take me. *Take me, my darling. Now.*"

Narrowing his eyes, Connor considered her offer. He did not delude himself into believing that he had suddenly become so much more appealing in the last few days than he had been when he'd watched her speak her vows to his brother so many years before. It could only be his new title that had caused his sudden allure.

Suddenly he felt very tired and irritable. "What do you *really* want, Bettina?" he demanded shortly. "Tell me and then get out."

For a split second she looked stunned. Then her huge blue eyes grew even larger. "But my love, I already told you. I want *you.*"

He smiled wryly. "Now that Markus is dead, you mean? I wasn't good enough for you all those years ago, but now I'm suddenly irresistible? I wonder why."

Instead of explaining, Bettina reached out and grasped one of his hands, lifting it to one tiny breast and squeezing her hand around his. Connor suppressed a sudden queasiness. Good God, had he really wanted to marry this woman? He must have been insane.

"My darling," Bettina murmured thickly, "is it so difficult for you to comprehend my desire for you? You are a man; I am a woman; and I have never forgotten our past embraces. How often, when Markus held me in his arms, did I imagine it was you loving me in his place? Oh, Con, it was always you that I loved. You must know that I only married Markus because my family demanded it of me."

The moment she removed her hand from his, he dropped his arm back to his side. "I know nothing of the kind. I don't know what you expect, Bettina, but you may as well leave," he said quietly. "Nothing is going to happen here tonight."

She paled. "But Con! I love you. I want you. It was always you I wanted. Please, my beloved! Do not send me away!"

Connor fought for patience. "For God's sake, what do you want, Bettina? For me to get you with child? For that is what may happen, you know. How would you 'catch' another husband then? Or are you barren, and is that why you were able to cuckold my brother time and again?"

Bettina gasped and her cheeks flamed. "You wrong me, sir! I came here tonight because I thought you, like me, might have regretted our unfortunate parting years ago. I came here tonight to give myself to you in love and the hope that we might spend our futures together!"

Connor sighed. "Bettina, while I am willing to forgive, I cannot forget what has already passed between us. I loved you with the very breath in my body when you chose my brother over me. But now . . . I no longer feel the same."

"But you must! You loved me once, surely you can love me again if you but try," she whimpered pleadingly. "What will I do if you do not want me? I did not want to tell you this, but Markus had nearly bled the Duncan estates dry before his death. His creditors have been hounding me unmercifully."

Connor sighed and rubbed a hand over his eyes. "I see. You need money. Well, my dear, so do I."

"You? But you are successful! My sources told me you had a thriving shipping business!"

"Your sources? You had me spied upon?" He laughed shortly. "I fear your sources failed to give you the latest." He quickly told her about the captain's wish that the business be sold.

By the time he finished, an expression of resignation had washed over Bettina's pinched face. "So you cannot help me," she said flatly.

Connor felt a wave of sympathy. "Not yet. But I hope I will be able to do so, soon. When—if—the shipping business is sold, I will be quite plump in the pocket. Then I promise to pay off your creditors and settle an allowance on you. All you need do is tell that to your creditors, and, rather than risk the wrath of the new Lord Duncan, they should leave you be."

Bettina looked ready to weep. "Thank you, my lord. Well, I had best return to my room. I will leave in the morning," she said, retrieving her dressing gown from the floor and slipping into it.

"Fine. Good night, Bettina." He opened the door and she disappeared down the hall.

Connor watched her go, thinking how different the night would have been if Emily had been his midnight visitor. With a heavy sigh he wandered to a cupboard and pulled out another bottle of brandy.

Emily rose early the next morning, feeling slow and puffy, probably, she decided, from the combination of going to bed teary and waking too soon. Her sleep had been so deep she didn't even remember dreaming, and it seemed as if she had barely lain down when morning had come. This, she noticed quickly as she glanced out her window, was impossible, as the sunny landscape was now dark, wet, and forbidding, with frequent bolts of lightning rending the sky.

Maggie had already left the chamber, and the tempting scents rising from belowstairs indicated that she was busily cooking breakfast.

Rather than wearing one of the newly divested gowns, Emily threw on her old black bombazine, which perfectly emphasized her dark mood, and walked out into the hall.

It didn't appear as though anyone else was up and about. She drew a relieved breath. Her heart still ached from what she had witnessed last evening, and she hoped it would be some time yet before she had to face Lord Connor and his long-lost love after their night of bliss.

As she entered the dining room, a flash of lightning momentarily brightened the glass walled chamber. Sheets of rain obscured the view of the landscape.

She sat down at the table as Maggie came out of the kitchen, a steaming platter of eggs in one hand, and a dish of buttermilk rolls balanced atop a tray of bacon in the other.

In contrast to the storm the maid smiled sunnily. "Good morning, miss. Sit down and I'll serve you."

"You seem remarkably chipper this morning for one who has just had her cooking requirements tripled, Maggie."

"Oh, it's not that much trouble cooking for a few more," Maggie replied gaily.

Emily eyed her suspiciously. "You'd never have guessed that last night."

A fresh smile broke over the maid's freckled face. "Yes, but last night I 'adn't learned that Lord Connor 'ad 'ired Andy—you know, the cart driver's boy—to 'elp Cracker Jack with the 'ousehold."

"Andy? You mean he and Mr. Crabbe were unhurt by the accident? How wonderful!" Emily frowned as she remembered Connor's veiled suspicions about the two mens' involvement in the carriage accident. If he really had cause to think the men were evil, why then would he hire them now? Then she banished the thought as Maggie continued speaking.

"I don't know about Mr. Crabbe, but Andy was apparently thrown from the cart before it fell. Although 'e was knocked out cold 'e wasn't wounded. 'E woke when the men from Launceston came to take care of the wreckage and the dead animals, and rode back into town with them. Then 'e came 'ere to see if Lord Connor 'ad any work available, and 'Is Lordship 'ired 'im. I'm so 'appy I could dance for joy!"

Upon hearing Connor's name Emily put her elbows on the lace tablecloth, and settled her chin into the palms of her hands. She sighed gustily. "His Lordship is a most accommodating man."

Maggie frowned. "Is sommat the matter, miss? I thought you liked Andy."

"Oh," Emily replied glumly, "Andy seemed very nice. I'm just not feeling well this morning. But I don't mean to put a damper on your good spirits."

Maggie's face creased with displeasure and suspicion. Clamping her hands on her hips, she glared at the door leading to the hallway. "It's that Lady Duncan, isn't it, miss? She's done somethin'."

Emily looked up dully. "What makes you say that?"

"Oh, anybody can see she's the type that just isn't 'appy unless she's causin' trouble." Maggie shook her head. "What's she done? I'll bet it 'as something to do with Lord Connor."

Emily blinked back tears. "Lord Duncan, you mean."

"Of course. I keep forgettin'. Please, miss, don't look so glum. Surely you know you looked far more beautiful than 'Er Ladyship did last night. And you can bet Lord Connor thought so, too."

While Emily realized it was not proper etiquette to spill out her heart to a maid, she needed an understanding ear too badly this morning to mold her actions to convention. She gave Maggie a meaningful look. "Mayhap he did, but that didn't keep him from accepting what was freely offered last night."

Maggie pulled up a chair. "Tell me what 'appened."

Tears rolled down Emily's cheeks. She sniffed. "I am not at liberty to say."

An expression of comprehension crossed Maggie's face. "I think I can imagine," she said sagely. "Oh, dear. I'm so disappointed in 'Is Lordship. I would never 'ave believed 'e could 'ave sunk so low if you 'adn't told me yourself."

Emily wiped her eyes with her fingers. "I don't know what's the matter with me. It isn't as if either Lady *or* Lord Duncan will matter in my future. Why should I care what they do together? If His Lordship loves Lady Duncan, I must wish them well and go on with my own life. They were in love once, after all. They probably belong together."

Maggie pursed her lips. "Oh, I don't know about that. If you ask me, Lord Duncan seems to care *that* deeply for you even though you've only known each other a short time. And it's obvious as a cat's whiskers that you care for 'im. Don't you?"

"I don't know what I feel," Emily answered tremulously. "Half of the time I hate him with all my heart."

"And the other 'alf?"

Emily breathed out heavily. "I love him so much I think I'll die if he chooses Lady Duncan."

Maggie smiled. "I thought as much. I'm going to say something now that might make you very angry, miss."

"Please, if you think it will help, say what you like. I couldn't feel any more wretched than I already do."

"Very well," Maggie said. "I've watched the two of you for the past few days, and I think that you'll agree, if you really think about it and if you're honest with yourself, that you can 'ardly blame Lord Duncan for keeping 'is distance. After all, *you* were the one who suggested a pact to remain only friends," she finished with a cagey smile. " 'Tweren't 'Is Lordship."

A deafening peal of thunder punctuated the maid's words.

"Maggie!" Emily cried, remembering the carriage ride and the maid's energetic snores. "You were supposed to be asleep! I didn't know you were listening! How could you be so dishonest?"

The maid shrugged. "I didn't want to interrupt you and 'Is Lordship's little 'eart-to-'eart. It was the first sign that you weren't out for each other's blood. So I kept my eyes closed and let things work themselves out."

She pinned Emily with a relentless stare. "But *you* were the one who laid down the rules, miss."

"But when I told His Lordship I only wanted to be friends, I didn't mean that I wanted to be just friends forever! That is, I don't mean it now. Oh, Lord," she wailed, bursting into fresh tears. "I don't know what I mean anymore!"

" 'Is Lordship is a man, and they tend to take everything literally, not to mention that they are very fragile emotionally," Maggie said knowledgeably. "Still, it's my guess Lord Duncan is as much in love with you as you are with 'im. 'E probably just doesn't want to offend by breaking 'is word about being only friends. Nothin' is more precious to a man than 'is honor."

"What can I do?"

"I know what I'd do, but then I'm not gentry. If 'twere me, I'd go to 'im and tell 'im exactly what's on my mind. I mean," Maggie said bluntly, "what 'ave you got to lose? At least, even if it didn't result in weddin' bells, you'd know you tried."

"I couldn't possibly," Emily said emphatically. "Suppose he laughed in my face?"

"Suppose 'e did?" Maggie said sharply, obviously losing patience. "At least then you'd know 'ow 'e felt. Honestly, you Quality are odd folk—all this shilly-shallyin' about so you don't step on each others' toes. It's a wonder you ever marry at all. But then, most marriages between gentry are arranged, aren't they?"

Emily nodded.

"So what's it to be? Are you goin' to go after the man, or are you goin' to let Lady Duncan get 'er cat's claws into 'im?"

"I can't. I wish I could, but I just can't."

Maggie let out an annoyed grunt and turned away. "Then I guess you'd best forget about 'im. You can't catch a fox without settin' a trap." Glancing back at Emily's devastated face, she added sympathetically, "I wouldn't worry if I were you. I'm sure everythin' will turn out for the best in the end. It always does. As for Lord Duncan, if 'e really prefers 'Er Ladyship to a woman as sweet as you, then I say 'e deserves exactly what 'e gets."

"No man could deserve Lady Duncan. Even Lord Marsden. Well," Emily amended with a weak smile, "perhaps Lord Marsden."

Maggie grinned and changed the subject. "You'll never guess who was in my kitchen this mornin'. Milo! 'E was as gentlemanly as you please. Sat right there where you are and ate a nice big plate of bacon and eggs. When 'e finished 'e gave me a little bow, and even washed 'is own plate. 'E isn't nearly so frightenin' once a body gets to know 'im. And 'e's really quite 'elpful. 'E is the one who takes you your chocolate each night. I didn't even ask; 'e just came in one day, picked up the cup, and took it to your room. Imagine!"

Emily smiled halfheartedly.

Glancing around as if to ascertain they weren't overheard, Maggie added confidingly, "just between the two of us, I'm trying to turn 'im up sweet so that 'e gives *me* a diamond like the one 'e gave you. If it takes 'avin' a chimp in my kitchen, so be it!" She looked gratified at Emily's more genuine gurgle of laughter. "There now, you're feeling better, aren't you, dearie?"

"A little. Thank you, Maggie."

"I tell you what," the maid said. "You eat an 'earty breakfast and then take a walk in the fresh air. It will 'elp clear your mind. No more 'eavy thoughts on such a lovely mornin'. And after your walk you can start 'untin' for the treasure!"

Emily nodded. "I will. I'd better start looking, since it seems His Lordship will be rather occupied until Her Ladyship leaves. If she leaves," she added darkly.

Maggie filled a dish with food and placed it on the table in front of Emily. "It could be some time before she can, if this rain keeps up. Andy tells me the road back to Lizard is completely washed out."

Then she went back into the kitchen, leaving Emily alone with her thoughts. A sound at the doorway made her look up. Lady Duncan returned her surprised stare with a crafty smile.

"My lady!" Emily said sharply. "I didn't hear you come in."

"Apparently not. What is this about a treasure?"

Emily bit her tongue to keep from cursing. "Oh, that. It's nothing, really, just village tattle. There's supposed to be a buried treasure somewhere around here. It's just a rumor."

Lady Duncan's eyes bored into her. "Just a rumor."

"Yes."

"I see." Lady Duncan turned toward the sideboard and served herself a heaping portion. "I'm starved. I had quite a night."

Emily tried to ignore the sharp pain in her heart. "Did you?" she said with studied indifference.

"Oh, yes. I visited Lord Duncan. It is always so nice to have time alone with old friends."

Emily flushed. "I hardly think that is any of my business, my lady. What you and His Lordship do is none of my affair." She cringed at her unfortunate choice of words.

Lady Duncan gave her an assessing glance over her loaded fork. "Do I detect a slight possessiveness in your tone?"

"Absolutely not. I couldn't be less interested in what either of you do in your spare time."

Lady Duncan bit into a slice of crisp bacon, then shoved the whole thing between her lips and continued with a full mouth. "Mm. Delicious." Picking up a biscuit, she took an enormous bite even though she had not yet swallowed the meat. "By the way," she said in a muffled voice, "does that nasty white bird belong to you?"

"Polly? No. She was the captain's."

"Horrid creature. When I passed her cage in the main hall this morning she nearly gave me heart failure. Screamed something in my ear—something like *'Riches in earth are fine, but God's greatest treasures lie in heaven.'* Simply dreadful. If I were you I'd have the loathsome beast killed and roasted."

For the first time Emily felt a surge of affection for Polly. She smiled sweetly. "Oh, I couldn't do that. She is quite a good watch-bird, you know. Keeps the castle free of vermin. Now, if you will excuse me, I find I have quite lost my appetite."

She half-rose, then sank back into her seat. "My lord!"

Connor leaned lazily against the doorjamb. "Am I interrupting a private conversation?"

"Of course not, Con," Lady Duncan replied. "Do come in and have some breakfast. Miss Hawke's maid is quite a good cook. Try some of the bacon. It is tasty, if a trifle dry."

With grace and understated aplomb, Connor moved to serve himself, then sat at the head of the table, glancing indifferently from one woman to the other.

"So there is a treasure in this castle, is there?" Lady Duncan demanded without preamble. "I must confess I was wondering what you two could possibly have found to enthrall yourselves out here in the country. Of course, I myself have always preferred London, but I imagine a country mouse ... er ... lady like Miss Hawke is more comfortable in pastoral surroundings."

Having heard nothing but Lady Duncan's first statement, Connor flashed Emily an astonished stare. "And to think you were upset with *me* for telling *Maggie!*"

Emily shook her head admonishingly. Dropping her eyes, she studied the cold food on her plate. "Only of the legend of the Norman treasure, my lord. Lady Duncan overheard Maggie asking if I intended to search for it this afternoon. Naturally I told her that such a quest would be absurd, since the story is naught but a village yarn."

"Quite right," Connor replied, picking up on the circumstances. "What do you intend to do this afternoon, Miss Hawke?"

Swallowing the lump in her throat, Emily raised damning eyes and looked from him to Lady Duncan and back again. "I do not know, my lord. But might I suggest you take Her Ladyship on tour of the castle? I'm sure you would both like the opportunity to ... become further reacquainted. I'd suggest a picnic but I doubt you'd enjoy it much in this storm."

"Oh," Lady Duncan said quickly, "a tour sounds lovely."

Lowering his brows, Connor studied Emily. "I would enjoy that if you could be persuaded to come with us."

Then, noticing the way Emily was dressed, he stared. Why was she wearing that dreadful black bombazine gown again when he knew full well that she hated it as much as he did? He would have understood her wearing it if they'd been grubbing about in search of the treasure, but he was baffled about why she thought it suitable garb for the breakfast table. She must be trying to make a statement, but what? And why?

Then he frowned. It had been *her* idea to remain only friends, hadn't it? Maybe she was revolted by his attraction to her—she would have to be blind not to have seen it, for God's sake—and this was her way of stopping things before they began. Could she feel his interest in her and be trying to turn his regard toward Bettina?

Emily lowered her eyes. "I am sure I shall be quite busy, my lord." Although she had barely touched her breakfast, she pushed away from the table. "And now if you will excuse me, I have things to which I must attend."

When she had gone, Lady Duncan smiled prettily. "Well, Con, as you must have deduced from the weather, I'll be here for a few more days."

"That is fine," Connor said. "I fear I, however, will be quite busy and you will have to entertain yourself during your stay. I'll show you the library, if you like. It is quite extensive." Then he, too, rose from his breakfast. "I hope you do not mind eating alone, Bettina. Like Miss Hawke, I find I have completely lost my appetite. Since it is her wish that I do so, I will call for you at your chamber this afternoon to take you sight-seeing. Be ready at two."

Eager to begin treasure-hunting so she might get Connor off her mind, Emily wasted no time. She spent the first half of the day going from bedchamber to bedchamber, but found nothing but an ample supply of dust. Then, giving Lady Duncan's maid the excuse that, as hostess, she wished to examine the chamber to ascertain its comfort, she searched that room as well. It, also, rendered no answers.

The only chamber she was unable to gather the nerve to search was Connor's. Although she stood outside his door for a long time, she finally moved away without so much as touching the door handle.

Walking back through the hall, she tapped and pounded on every rusty suit of armor she saw, just to make certain the captain hadn't dropped his treasure into one of them. As she got down on hands and knees and hammered on the last leg of the last suit, only to have it return her efforts with a rumbling metallic echo, she sighed. Brushing off her skirts, she clambered to her feet.

She spent the next hour in the kitchens, but didn't stay there long since she found Maggie's amused snickers each time she lifted a pot lid or peeped into a cupboard vastly annoying. Then, since it had grown late and was nearly time for dinner, she asked Maggie to send up a tray and retired to her room for the night since she was unable to bear the thought of watching Connor and Lady Duncan mooning over each other. She was not completely alone after finishing her dinner, however, as Milo made a brief appearance in order to bring Emily her nightly cup of chocolate.

The storm had not abated by the next morning. Emily rose early and made her way to the library, where she began leafing through innumerable dusty tomes whose grime filled the air with a dank gray cloud that made her sneeze. A diligent search only turned up several books which would have to be replaced or discarded, as they now served as snug homes for families of mice.

When one of these animals, a tiny female with several naked pink babies to protect, reared up on its hind legs and bared its yellowed teeth, Emily grimaced and beat a hasty retreat. The next time she saw Connor, she decided irritatedly, she'd suggest that he and Lady Duncan have a go at searching the remaining volumes.

Then, as dark had once again fallen without her noticing how late it had become, she decided to repeat the previous night's action of taking a tray in her room. Later she retired without having seen anyone but Milo, who this time

brought not only her nightly chocolate, but her entire dinner tray, as well.

The next sensible place to look, she decided as she left
her room the next day, dressed once again in her black
gown, was the fifth tower, the one in which her father had
spent hours gazing out to sea during thunderstorms like the
one presently battering the coast. She could almost imagine him sitting at a stone table in the dark tower, a candle
by his side as he counted out his ill-gotten doubloons.

As she moved down the hall, looking in first this room,
then peering through that doorway, she quickly realized
that there seemed to be no way to get to the tower at all.

Then she smiled. Why hadn't she realized it before? It
was so obvious! There must be a secret passage! The treasure would surely be found in the tower room. It might
even be hidden in the passage itself. Wouldn't it put
Connor's nose out of joint if she found the treasure while
he was busy philandering with Lady Duncan?

The thought of him brought a pang to her heart and her
smile vanished. Despite her pain at his adoration for his
old love, as well as the possibility that he might have stolen her half of the treasure map, she could not bring herself to hate him.

Retracing her steps a second time, she ran her fingertips
over every likely looking bit of carved wood or stone that
she could see. None of them triggered the mechanism she
expected to spring open at any moment. Finally she threw
herself down on one of the old chairs lining the hallway.

If only she had her section of the map. Who knew but
that it might have made sense of the mysterious verse in
Connor's half? And why shouldn't she have it? she
thought then. Why was she trying to act honorably, when
Connor was not? Surely she deserved as good a chance of
finding the treasure as he.

Standing, she strode back to Connor's chamber. Outside
his door, she paused, wondering if the valet, Nipper, was
within. Biting her lip, she knocked briskly. When no one
answered, she reached down and turned the handle. It was
not locked.

18

Just being in Connor's bedchamber made Emily tremble like the last leaf on an autumn tree. Her heart pounded and her hands shook as though she had the palsy. She very nearly backed out of the room. But, she thought then, in for a penny, in for a pound.

A low fire still burned in the grate. The room was overwhelmingly masculine. Rich but not opulent, it appeared to suit Connor to perfection. Several sea chests lay scattered about the room, along with bookshelves, bureaus, and nightstands. All were made of dark, uncarved mahogany, decorated with brass handles and intricate dragon patterns inlaid with opal. The last bit of firelight made the opal chips gleam crimson, cobalt, emerald, and amethyst.

Were they things Connor had brought back from his travels, Emily wondered, or things he had stolen from another merchant's ships during one of his smuggling ventures?

The walls were covered with indigo velvet that echoed the deep blue in the opal mosaics. On the floor a plush blue and gold carpet with splashes of crimson invited one to take off his shoes and cavort barefoot across its richness. With a pang of love so sharp it was more painful than pleasurable, Emily imagined Connor doing just that.

Over the mantelpiece the steady beat of an unadorned brass carriage clock lent an aura of peace and tranquility to the chamber. Near the hearth a low mahogany table sat between a pair of leather armchairs.

If she closed her eyes, Emily could almost see Connor sitting in one of the armchairs before the fire, his long legs stretched out langorously, a snifter of brandy in one refined hand. As he sat there he would turn toward her, his golden hair glittering in the firelight, his blue eyes gleaming with ... with ... what?

She didn't dare to imagine desire in his eyes, but all the same, she knew it would be delightful.

Then she shook her head violently and turned away from the enchanting delusion. Connor was not the handsome hero of her dreams, and even if he were, he would never look at her with anything but the eyes of a friend. Her hasty pact had seen to that.

Besides, he was a smuggler. He was a thief. He was a womanizer. He was the kind of man who consorted with his own brother's widow—and the former Lord Duncan not even cold yet!

Straightening her shoulders, Emily moved toward a low chest of drawers and tried not to notice the rich scent of Connor's cologne lingering in the air. Had he worn the sensuous fragrance today to impress Lady Duncan? Had he worn it for numerous other women? Women he thought of in terms other than "just friends"?

Realizing she was clenching her jaw so hard her teeth ached, Emily steeled her resolve and pulled open a drawer. Bits of elegant jewelry, a hairbrush of teakwood and boar bristle, a bottle of that musky cologne, and a few other trifles lay scattered over the white cotton cloth covering the drawer's inner surface.

Her half of the treasure map was not among them.

For a moment Emily allowed herself the luxury of gazing at Connor's personal possessions. Of thinking about how recently that brush had caressed his luxurious golden hair. Of how that bottle of scent had been tipped and pressed against his hand. Of how his sensuously tapered fingers had smoothed the light, lemony fluid over his beautifully sculpted neck and freshly shaven cheeks.

Picking up the crystal bottle, she opened it and held the stopper, carved into a ship's anchor, to her nose. The heady fragrance made curls of heat twist through her belly. She hastily closed the bottle and replaced it in the drawer.

Her fingers tingled as she brushed aside the rest of his personal whatnots, trying to ignore a few shimmering gilt hairs trapped in the brush, strands that begged to be removed and tucked into a locket or between the pages of a copy of Shakespeare's sonnets.

Again she shook her head irritably. Really! She had to stop behaving like a lovestruck moonling! Her half of the map was probably somewhere in this room, and she meant to have it.

Quickly she rifled through the remaining drawers, but found that they held only carefully folded items of clothing. Leaving the chest of drawers, she turned to Connor's bureau. In no time at all she had sifted through it as well—again without success.

As she pushed the last compartment shut, a sound from the hall outside made the blood drain from her face.

"Good morning, Cracker Jack. What are you doing up here?"

Emily gasped. It was Connor! What might he do if he found her snooping about his quarters? Her knees threatened to give way. Oh, Lord! This was simply too, *too* dreadful!

"I was just changin' the candles in the wall sconces, my lord," Cracker Jack intoned. "Since they're lit each night, they melt before dawn."

"I see. How is Andy working out for you? Is he taking care of all the odd jobs you need help with?"

"Oh, 'ee's just fine, Lor' love 'im. Trouble is there don't seem to be much for me to do anymore. I'll tell 'ee, by noon today the lad had finished every task I gave 'im this mornin'—things I didn't expect 'im to finish till tomorrow."

"Good. You just relax and enjoy what free time you have."

"Thank 'ee, sir!"

"And Cracker Jack?"

"Aye, sir?"

"I don't want you mentioning it to Andy, but I'd appreciate it if you'd keep an eye on him and let me know if you see any odd behavior. Will you do that?"

"Certainly, but what do 'ee expect me to see?"

"I don't know, but he was present when Miss Hawke

and I had our carriage accident, and we may learn what he knows about the event, if anything, if we watch him closely. That, my friend, is the main reason I hired him."

"Aye, sir."

Scuffling footsteps echoed off down the hall—Cracker Jack wandering away. Emily's brow wrinkled as she wondered why Connor would want his own partner in crime watched. Perhaps Cracker Jack, having been the captain's close friend, had been kept ignorant of Connor's shady dealings, and asking him to watch Andy was Connor's way of keeping the old sailor from being suspicious of Connor himself.

Her eyes froze on the door handle and, unable to breathe, she heard it click as the latch released. Heart in her mouth, she watched it rotate.

Then, knowing she had not a moment to lose, she burst into action. Moments before the door swung fully open she flicked aside one of the blue velvet curtains and dashed behind it, praying to all the gods she could think of that Connor would not notice the swaying drapery.

The instant he stepped into his chamber Connor realized something was amiss. Closing the door soundlessly, he let his gaze drift over the familiar terrain. As accustomed as he was to Nipper, he knew it was not the valet whose presence he now sensed.

He narrowed his eyes. Nothing appeared out of the ordinary, but the prickle on the back of his neck made him certain that someone had been there and was, quite possibly, still present. The clock ticked softly on the mantel. Its murmur seemed somehow ominous.

As thunder rumbled in the distance and rain slashed at the bedchamber windows, Connor stepped to his bedside table. Reaching beneath it, he pressed a hidden button, exposing a concealed compartment. His fingers curled around the loaded revolver stashed within.

Holding the gun's nose toward the sky, he edged toward his bureau, opened it, and saw that his things had been thoroughly disturbed before being replaced with care. Further investigation showed that his desk had also been searched. For what? And by whom?

Suddenly his gaze was caught by the slight swaying of the curtains concealing the castle's bare stone walls. Shutting the drawer, he turned. He moved forward, lowering the revolver until it pointed directly at the place he presumed the intruder's chest would be.

With one hand, he grasped the thick indigo velvet, soft as a wealthy man's shroud. Jerking the cloth back, he thrust the pistol forward and pressed it against the trespasser's delectably ample breast.

Delectably ample breast?

He stared, astounded, as Emily Hawke slumped against him. Her already pale face turned the color of bleached linen and she swayed, then crumpled into a heap at his feet.

After dropping the gun back into its hidden compartment, Connor shut the drawer and gathered the unconscious woman in his arms. He rose and carried her to his bed, then hurried to his bureau and poured some cold water from a delft pitcher into its matching basin. He opened a drawer and pulled out a handkerchief, moistened and wrung it out, and hurried back to Emily's side. She was just beginning to stir.

"Wh-what happened?"

As she tried to sit up he gently pushed her back down. "Not so fast. Lie still. You fainted. What are you doing here, Emily?"

He watched as the woman's deathly pale cheeks turned a healthy pink. She did not answer, but lay biting her lower lip and staring up at him as if he were Beelzebub himself. He felt a surge of concern at her obvious horror.

Lifting his moistened cloth, he laid it against her cheek. "It doesn't matter. We can discuss it later. There. Does that feel better?"

"Yes, Thank you." Emily lowered her eyes. "Oh, my lord. I am so sorry. I don't know what you must be thinking, but I fear the facts can be no better. I must tell you the truth. I was searching for my map."

She flicked him a glance but his expression was indecipherable. She continued shamefully, "Even though you'd denied it, I was certain you'd stolen it and then substituted that ridiculous rhyme for your half. Thus, I was sure you already knew where the treasure was, and I wanted an equal chance of finding it."

He still did not speak, and she rushed on. "And then you seemed so happy to see Lady Duncan. And you wanted to take her on a tour of the castle. And I saw her go to your room in the middle of the night. And you've spent every day since with her, instead of helping search for the treasure, which I thought must have been because you already knew where it was. And I felt ... I felt ... Oh, heavens. I am truly sorry, my lord," she wailed.

A sudden elation surged through Connor. He smiled. "You said you'd call me Connor. Not 'my lord.' " He shifted to sit more comfortably on the bed next to her. "I told you I didn't steal your half of the map, Emily."

Her blush deepened. "I feel ridiculous. I should have believed you."

He raised a brow. "Why? You know nothing about me but trivialities. If our positions were reversed I confess I'd have searched your room long before now—although you didn't make a very thorough search. You missed finding my revolver."

"Well, I'm hardly an old hand at this, you know."

"I can see that. But you know, I do take issue with two things you said."

"What?"

"I most certainly did *not* want to take Lady Duncan on a tour. I did so because you suggested it. Since she was sitting right there when you asked, I could hardly refuse. But let us get one thing straight once and for all, Emily. As far as I am concerned, Lady Duncan may go to hell and back without me. She may go anywhere she likes as long as she does not involve me in her activities.

"*You,* on the other hand," he finished, "had best inform me if you intend to enter my chamber again without warning. You never know what you might find, and I warn you now that I will not be held responsible for my actions if you show up unannounced."

"I promise I will," she answered fervently, "if you will only forgive me."

"You are forgiven. And secondly, as far as I know Lady Duncan has spent her days, after I gave her a tour, reading in her room. Like you, I have been searching for the treasure. It is a wonder we haven't run into each other, but this *is* a huge place."

"It certainly is. And thank you for being so understanding. My lord?" Emily asked then, breathlessly.

"Connor."

"Connor, are you very angry with me?"

"Should I not be? By rights I should turn you over my knee and punish you for coming into my room like a thief in the night." He grinned. "Or morning."

As the words left his mouth he was overcome with a desire to do just that. To have Emily bent over his lap, pressed against his loins, to feel her ripe bosom against his thighs, to see her delightfully round bottom aiming at the sky—

He broke off the thought while his desires were still under control. "But naturally I shall not. You had quite a scare. You could have been killed. I might have shot you."

The thought of Emily bleeding her life away on his floor nearly brought him to his knees. His entire body convulsed, and without thinking of the consequences, he picked her up again, pressing her against his chest. "Good God, Emily. If I had shot you I would have wanted to die myself."

"But you didn't. I'm all right." Emily's voice was a mere whisper. "And I'm so sorry about all this."

He pushed her from him slightly so that she had to tip her head back to meet his gaze, then he drew a ragged breath as he stared down at the lovely eyes gazing so trustingly into his. *Emily,* he thought wildly, *darling Emily. If only you knew . . .*

Then he froze. Knew what?

That he burned to touch her, to run his lips over her beautiful impish face, across her delicate high-boned cheeks?

That his hands itched to unbutton her gown, beginning

at the high collar, opening the fabric just enough to allow his tongue to slide over her enticing cleavage, those glowing orbs whose perfect rounded tops he'd seen peeping at him from her bodice the night before at dinner?

That his manhood ached and stretched fully against his thigh until he wanted to press her back into the bed and make her his so that she might never leave him?

Dear heaven, he thought. He wanted her to know all this and more. But he had no right. She was his friend, and that was all she wanted to be. He would not alienate her by trying to force her to be more than that. He would not estrange his best friend. Yes, he admitted silently, it was true—a woman, one of those creatures he thought he would mistrust for the rest of his life, had become the dearest friend he had ever had.

Somehow, he decided abruptly, he would keep Emily by his side and never let her go. She need never know he loved her.

Loved her?

By God and all that was holy! He loved her! he realized with a jolt. More than he'd ever loved anyone or anything in his life! He knew he had so polluted his heart with his pain over Bettina that he had failed to see the most beautiful thing in the world. Now that his hate for his brother's wife had changed to a kind of sympathy, his heart was free to explore other emotions.

He drew a sharp breath and fought the urge to claim Emily's lips with his own.

Because of the love he felt for her, he would take no chance of frightening her away from Hawke's Nest. Curbing his passions, he regretfully laid her back against the pillows, then brushed her long black curls, which had come loose from her coiffure and curled in a becoming tangle around her face, away from her silver-green eyes.

He dropped the damp handkerchief onto the bed. Backing away, he said shakily, "I shall leave you now. Feel free to search my entire room again, if you wish. Let us have nothing between us, Emily. You have no idea how dearly I value you . . . and your friendship," he finished lamely. He stared at her lovely mouth. "No idea at all.

"Lie there until you have recovered from the shock of my frightening you." He retreated toward the door. As his hand touched the doorknob, he turned back and said falteringly, "Emily, Emily, I—" then whirled around and rushed out of the chamber without finishing the sentence.

Emily watched him go, her composure in tatters. Rising, she picked up the moist handkerchief and pressed it against her scorching cheeks—burning not with embarrassment at having been discovered in her clandestine search, she admitted honestly, but with desire and longing. At last she laid the damp cloth on his bureau and fled to her own room.

Once in her chamber she threw herself into a chair and sat staring at the wall as minutes ticked into hours. By afternoon, when she had sat there so long she began to feel as though she were sprouting roots, she raised her head and heaved herself to her feet.

Determined to put all her uselessly romantic dreams aside, since Connor obviously wanted only her friendship, and she had no desire to shame herself by begging for more, she forced her thoughts back to the treasure hunt and set about examining her own room a second time. She had already gone over it once before searching all the other chambers, but maybe she had missed something. And even if she had not, she thought wistfully, it would help turn her mind away from Connor.

Lifting the coverlet on the bed, she bent down and peered underneath the mattress. Nothing. No trap door. No doorway to a secret passage. Rising, she moved to push aside the thick curtain draperies hiding the bare stone walls. Naught there, either.

Her gaze slipped thoughtfully to the floor. With a great deal of grunting and gasping, she managed to slide the heavy rug aside—and found only cold solid stone beneath.

Finally, feeling very tired and wanting nothing so much as a hot bath and a long nap, she moved toward the bell-pull that hung alongside Lady Caroline's picture. Why did she have the unmistakable impression that she was missing something, something right there in this very room?

With her fingers inches away from the bell cord, she

gazed up at her mother's portrait, studying Lady Caroline's exquisite face. *Tell me, mother,* she pleaded silently. *Help me find the treasure so I might leave this place and heal my broken heart. I cannot bear being so close to one who does not love me.*

Lady Caroline gazed back silently, and for a moment Emily imagined that there had been a flicker of encouragement in the painted eyes.

Suddenly she gasped. Could it be? Had the answer been in front of her nose all this time?

19

Prepared for another grave disappointment, Emily put out a trembling hand. Carefully lifting one side of her mother's portrait, she peeked around the edge. There, behind the painting, stood a narrow door.

As another crack of thunder echoed over the castle battlements an excited squeak escaped Emily's lips. Wrapping her arms around herself, she danced about the room.

When she had regained her composure, she stepped back and studied the painting, trying to decide the best way to move the massive picture to expose the hidden door. The painting probably weighed well over two hundred pounds. There must be a secret device that made it easy to push aside.

As her fingers slid over the heavy gilt frame, Emily heard an audible click, and the portrait swung out into the room, suspended on a brass bar. Gazing at the exposed door, but seeing no handle, Emily decided that it, like the painting, must also have a hidden catch.

Running her fingertips over its rough surface, she poked and prodded every little bump and hollow but found nothing. Just as she was about to give up, her fingers met a little ridge on one side of the door and, triggering it somehow, caused the door to glide open automatically. She stared at the door's edge for a moment, amazed to see that it was nearly a foot thick.

Then she looked past the door at the shadowy passage beyond.

She peered through the murk, wishing she could see further into the tunnel. Of course she couldn't go into the dark passage by herself like one of the heroines in the Minerva Press novels of which Mrs. Harriman had been so fond. That would be the height of stupidity. Those heroines had inevitably gone where no man with two guns and a large dog would have ventured.

Still, while realizing that the heroines' actions were indisputably imprudent, at the same time Emily felt an unexpected kinship with those characters. Like them, she wanted to throw caution to the wind and rush into the passage without delay.

Pulling her lower lip between her teeth, she nibbled uncertainly. If she had any sense she would close the hidden door, secure the painting, and go in search of Connor so that he might accompany her.

But what could happen to her if she sneaked one little peek? The treasure could be just inside the doorway! How exciting it would be if she were the one to find it, all by herself.

Surely one glimpse would hurt nothing.

She hurried to her bedside table, grabbed a partially burned candle, held it against a glowing coal in the grate until the wick flared, and then scampered back to the passage. Teeth chattering with excitement, she held the tiny light high and stepped into the pitch blackness beyond. She had gone only a few steps, however, when she heard an odd whirring noise.

Spinning about, she turned back just in time to see the secret doorway slide shut with an ominous thud.

The blood that had been making her heart pound with excitement now congealed in her stomach like cold bread pudding. A moldy-smelling draft made her candle flicker dangerously.

Setting the light on the floor, she began examining the closed portal. Since there was no handle on this side, either, she knew there must be another secret catch.

Running her fingers over the doorframe in the hopes that the mechanism would be in the same place as on the other side, she searched for several moments. When her search yielded nothing she gave a sob of dismay, balled her hands into fists, and pounded on the door with all her might.

"Help!" she screamed at the top of her lungs. "Maggie! Anybody? Let me out of here! Help!"

As she had expected, there was no response. How could there have been? Neither Connor nor Lady Duncan was likely to venture uninvited into her room, as she had into theirs, and Maggie was probably belowstairs preparing the evening meal.

Certainly Cracker Jack, Nipper, and Andy would have no cause to seek her out, and Milo only visited in the evenings, when he brought her chocolate. Which meant that, unless she were content to sit and wait for Maggie to return to the chamber for the night, or until Connor noticed she was missing and started a search, she was stuck there.

But would anyone realize she was gone before her candle burned itself out?

Again she pummeled and searched, searched and pummeled relentlessly, until her candle had burned down half an inch and her hands throbbed. The scent of rancid tallow was strong in the close, musty air, and a wisp of acrid smoke rose from the tip of the flame, making her eyes sting and smart.

She threw the thin wax taper a calculating glance.

Suppose she sat there until her candle burned out, waiting for Maggie to come up to bed, and then the little maid couldn't hear her beating on the door? What then? The scenario was not unthinkable; as she had seen, the door behind the painting was extremely thick. Also, she observed, judging from how rapidly her candle was melting as well as the large amount of dark smoke filling the passage, the taper was obviously made of inferior wax that would be completely liquefied within the hour.

In that case, Emily thought fearfully, she could even *die* here, starving slowly while she waited for someone to rescue her. This passage, after all, had probably not been used since her father's death. What were the odds that anyone else knew its location?

On the other hand, if she blew out her candle while waiting for Maggie to rescue her, she had no way to relight it. That would serve nothing, apart from saving a candle.

The thought of being lost in the darkness made goose-flesh stampede over her arms as if an army of tiny black spiders had dropped from the passage ceiling and skittered over her flesh.

Then she almost laughed aloud with relief. It was so simple; she had frightened herself with thoughts of doom for naught. All she needed to do was follow the passage up to the fifth tower—since that must be where it led—and shout for help from the window at which her father used to watch thunderstorms.

Taking a deep breath, she picked up her candle, cupped a hand in front of it to keep it from extinguishing, and moved carefully down the narrow corridor. In another hundred paces the path split into two separate passages, one going right and the other forking off to the left.

Pausing, she held her candle at the mouth of each, but saw nothing more than the heavy stone walls, like those that made up the rest of the castle, snaking off into the darkness. Finally she shrugged and turned right.

Surely, she thought some time later, she had been moving long enough to have come to the tower by now. Perhaps she should have gone left. But, she noted, glancing down at the candle, which had melted to a mere stub, there was not enough of it remaining to allow her to retrace her steps.

She'd have to keep going and hope the passage ended soon. A rush of panic fluttered over her as she thought of reaching a dead end and being lost in the darkness forever. Suddenly the floor took a sharp downward turn.

Emily eyed the descending passage uncertainly but kept moving. She tried not to notice as her candle began to sputter and the tiny yellow flame neared her bare flesh. Then, just as abruptly as it had sloped, the floor changed from granite bricks to a shiny dark substance, almost like glass.

Stone. It was damp stone.

Running a hand over one wall, she realized that their granite bricks had also changed, replaced by moist limestone. An eerie, mind-numbing silence filled the air and weighed heavily against Emily's ears until she opened her jaw wide to relieve the ache.

When she first heard the voices she thought they must have been in her imagination. As the corridor made a sharp turn, however, instinct made her hesitate and peek around the corner before moving forward.

Ten or twelve men stood talking among themselves in the bright light of several blazing torches lining the walls of a broad stone chamber. Sick with relief, Emily clasped one hand to her breast and sagged against the wall. For the moment she was so happy to see other people that she felt faint and breathless.

Then, just as she opened her mouth to call for help, she noticed how oddly the men were dressed. A few of them wore red-and-white-striped shirts, and two had gold hoops through their earlobes. Their faces were scruffy, as if they had not shaved in weeks.

Stepping back to shade her candle flame behind the tunnel wall, Emily snapped her mouth shut. Smugglers. They must be smugglers.

Connor's comrades, perhaps?

Peering around the corner, she watched one of the men curiously. Something about him seemed recognizable. If only he would turn toward her so she could see his face.

As she watched, a scuffle erupted and a second familiar-looking man leaped upon the first with a long, gleaming blade. Emily craned her neck but could see only the attacker's back. Moments later the first man slumped to one side, motionless.

Gasping, Emily covered her mouth to keep from crying out as she recognized him. It was Mr. Crabbe, the cart driver! Scanning the group, she looked for Andy, the cart-driver's apprentice. He did not appear to be present.

Then the murderer turned toward her, and Emily realized why he had also looked familiar. It was Connor's valet, Nipper!

Backing away swiftly, she tiptoed for fifty or sixty paces, then began running as soon as she thought she was out of earshot. Her candle flared sporadically as she ran on, breathless with panic, until she reached the fork in the passage.

There disaster struck.

Catching her toe on a bump in the stone floor, Emily fell, rolling against the slick floor and banging her head into the side of the corridor. Leaping from her hands like a frightened toad, the candle bounced off the far wall, where it flickered and snuffed out.

Emily lay still for several moments until the pain in her head subsided. Then she stood. Turning this way and that, she peered through the darkness in utter confusion. Which passage led back to her room? Which one led back to the smugglers?

Nearly overcome with panic and fear, she stood motionless in the blackness for a long moment. Then she put her hands out to her sides, pressed her fingertips against the stone walls, and moved as swiftly as she could in the direction she hoped led to her chamber.

Then she saw it—a low glimmer of light. A torch.

Fear clutched at her throat like the hand of death as Emily deduced that she had, indeed, chosen the path back toward the smugglers and would meet them head-on at any moment. Her head buzzed and she bent low, breathing deeply to keep from fainting. If she passed out now, she had no doubt that the smugglers would make certain she never regained consciousness again.

The faint light from the approaching torch made it possible for her to see a few feet in either direction. It also let her see that, oddly, her pursuer was alone. As the footsteps neared she stepped into a natural niche in one side of the wall. Pressing herself as flat as she could, she held her breath.

The man passed within a foot of her without noticing her trembling form.

As his footsteps faded into the distance Emily opened one eye and gazed after him incredulously. Then, realizing she still had no light and still didn't know for certain which passage led back to her room, she chewed her lip and considered her options. At last she squared her shoulders.

There was really only one thing to do. She had to have the smuggler's torch.

Swallowing her terror she moved silently after her quarry, watching the floor for some weapon with which to disable him. She nearly cried with relief when she spied a likely looking bit of timber.

Picking up the board, she hefted it assessingly.

Suddenly the man paused and cocked his ear to one side as if he had heard Emily's movements. She froze, suddenly glad she was wearing her old black gown. In it, she must be practically invisible in the murky light.

As soon as the man started moving again Emily ran forward as fast as her legs would carry her and brought the timber down on his head with a loud *CCCRRACKK!* The man dropped the coveted torch and it rolled to a stop, still burning, several feet away. As he fell, he half-turned. His eyes went wide with astonishment.

"E-Em—" he mumbled as he hit the stone floor.

"Connor!"

Gaping at the crumpled figure, Emily knelt beside him. "Connor! Oh, darling, I'm so sorry! I didn't know it was you. Oh, please, please wake up. Have I killed you? Are you dead?" She sobbed hysterically. "If you're dead, Connor, I'll just kill you!"

Pressing her fingers to the side of his neck she felt for a pulse, then drew a relieved breath. She took his head in her lap and cradled it gently, running her fingers over the planes and hollows of his face and smoothing back his golden hair.

After several minutes he stirred. "What happened? Did the roof cave in?"

Emily wiped away an errant tear. "No. I hit you—by mistake. I'm so sorry."

"Emily? For God's sake, what are you doing down here?"

It was then that Emily remembered that Connor was one of the smugglers. God alone knew what he would do to her if he knew she'd seen Nipper commit a murder!

Thinking quickly, she stammered, "While searching my room for the treasure, I found a door behind my mother's painting. I only wanted a peek before I came to find you, but once I got inside the door closed behind me.

"I was walking down this path when I dropped my candle. It went out, and I tried to get back to my room in the dark. When you came down the passage so silently you frightened me. I didn't know who you were. I overreacted. I only knew I had to have your torch if I was to get back to my room."

Connor lifted his head, then groaned and clasped it with both hands. "I see. Well I am glad I found you even though I'll have a devil of a headache."

"How . . . how did you know where to look?"

"I went to your room when you didn't come downstairs for supper. That was several hours ago. When I knocked and you didn't answer I thought you must be sleeping. Once supper had passed and you still hadn't come downstairs, I got the strangest impression that you were in danger. I brushed the feeling off as silly fancy for as long as I could, and when I couldn't stand it anymore I went back to your room and forced the door."

Emily couldn't help herself. With a gurgle of laughter she said, "Never tell me you broke my new door!"

He grinned self-consciously. "Only the lock. When I entered your room I noticed your mother's painting hanging slightly ajar and saw the hidden door. I found the mechanism to open it, but no sooner had I stepped into the corridor than it slid shut again. However, unlike you, I found the opening mechanism on the inside so we won't have any trouble getting back out."

"Oh," Emily exclaimed, "the painting! Of course! I was worried that Maggie wouldn't realize where I had gone and that she wouldn't hear me through the thick door, but I didn't even think that the painting, since it was attached to an iron bar that swung independently of the hidden door, might still be hanging loose. I could have waited right there rather than try to find my way out."

Connor laughed, then winced with pain. "Yes. Well, you do have a tendency to act first and think later. Not very schoolmarmish qualities, you must confess."

"No they aren't," she replied musingly. "Do you know,

I don't think I've acted at all like myself ever since I arrived here."

Reaching out, Connor traced her cheek with a finger. "Well, I find your impulsiveness quite intriguing."

"You do? Even though I bludgeoned you?" She eyed the bump on his head doubtfully.

"Well, that part I could do without. But I must tell you that your arrival in my life has made it far more exciting. I mean, your hiding behind the curtains in my room and getting lost in secret passages while searching for treasure, and our tumbling down muddy hillsides and almost getting bashed by falling statuary. Quite a change from one monotonous sea voyage after another. I could get used to such an eventful life."

As if encouraged when she did not pull away from his touch, he dropped his hand and caressed the sensitive skin of her throat. The pads of his fingers felt callused and rough, proving that he was not just an idle gentleman but also a strong, physical male.

Seeing the glow in his eyes, Emily suddenly felt shy. She pulled away and the warmth in his eyes faded abruptly. "Well," he said huskily, "we ought to get back. We can explore this passage another day, but just now it is getting late."

Emily's pleasure evaporated as she remembered that he had, no doubt, already explored the passage during his smuggling activities. "Of course," she replied bleakly.

In no time they stood at the little door that led into Emily's bedchamber. Connor reached out. "You see? Up here at this corner there's a little bump. You press it and"—the door swung open—"*voilà*. But please don't go into the passage alone again. The door locks automatically when it swings closed, as you discovered earlier, and you might not be able to find the button to release it by yourself."

What he meant, Emily assumed, was that he didn't want her running into his partners.

As they stepped into the bedchamber, Connor slid the painting back into place. Eager to be out of the passage, Emily pressed close behind him, expecting him to move away from the door. When he turned and met her breasts with his firm chest, she drew in her breath sharply. For an instant he gazed down at her intently, his eyes seeming to turn an even deeper blue.

Despite Emily's chagrin at his being a smuggler, it seemed the most natural thing in the world when he lowered his lips to hers.

20

Connor's lips were like nothing Emily had ever experienced, hard and soft at the same time. Without warning her body burst into erotic flames and she pressed herself hard against his muscular chest.

His shoulders were like rock beneath the palms of her hands. She snaked her arms about his neck to pull his mouth closer. The faint scent of lemons rose from his slightly roughened cheeks, and she heard him murmur her name.

A half-sob rose in her throat as she curled her arms more tightly about his neck and shoulders, pressing herself against him wantonly, wishing she could make him a part of her so that they would never be separated. In that moment Emily realized she didn't care if he was a smuggler, a murderer, or that he had probably, despite his protestations, stolen her half of the map so that he could cheat her out of her share of the treasure. She loved him as he was, and nothing could ever change that.

A low moan escaped her lips, answered by a rough growl from his. Then, to her sheer delight, his lips left her mouth and wandered over her cheek, down her neck, and paused at the small hollow at the base of her collarbone, his tongue glissading eagerly over her skin.

As one of his hands slid from her back around to the front of her waist, rising to lift one breast in his palm, she shuddered with delicious abandon. His fingers tightened, gently squeezing her entire breast, and then teased her nipple to a hard, throbbing point of fire. Burning hunger swept through her and she arched into his hand, mindless of anything but his touch.

The caress was over as quickly as it had begun. Emily looked up to find Connor breathing as if he had just run a race, and gazing down at her in horror.

"Emily, I . . . I am sorry," he said huskily. "I do not know what came over me. I—"

At that moment the bedchamber door burst open and Maggie ran into the room.

Emily thrust away from Connor's arms, cheeks aflame. Then, seeing the expression on the maid's normally complacent face, Emily rushed to take her by the hands. "Good heavens, what is it, Maggie?"

"Oh, Miss Emily! It's so wonderful! You're goin' to be so 'appy."

"What is wonderful? What has happened?"

"There's a letter for you downstairs, in the library. It's from Mrs. 'Arriman. She sent me one, too, and I'm sure yours contains the same news. Please, you must come now and read it!"

The three of them hurried to the library, where Emily found the sealed letter and tore it open. As her eyes scanned the single rather messily scrawled sheet, they filled with tears of relief. "My God. He's dead. Lord Marsden is dead."

Maggie danced around the room joyfully. "Yes, 'e's dead, the ruttin' bastard! 'Is 'eart gave out while 'e was chasin' one of Lady Milcox's maids round a table in 'Er Ladyship's London town 'ouse! Oh, Miss Emily, now you can go back to the academy and 'e'll never bother you again!"

"He's dead," Emily repeated. And he wasn't the only one, she added silently, remembering Mr. Crabbe, who'd met his fate at Nipper's hands. She shook her head bemusedly. "It's true. I can return to the school. If you will both excuse me now, I'd like to retire to my room. I think I need some time to be alone."

Connor's voice stopped her as she moved toward the door.

"Emily?" he said questioningly, a tremor evident in his deep voice. "Emily, I know you must be happy to be free to return to the academy, but you won't be departing directly, will you?"

Emily gazed at his handsome face, suppressing the agony she felt at the thought of leaving him. "No, not immediately. I cannot until the storm abates. But I think it best for all concerned that I go as soon as possible."

"But what of the treasure?" he demanded. "You can't run out on me. I need your help."

Emily's chest constricted. Of course he did not want her to leave; they were supposed to be treasure hunting. How foolish of her to suspect for one moment that he had wished her present for any other reason. "You know this place far better than I," she said brokenly. "I'm sure you'll be able to find it by yourself. I'll be happy to tell you where I've already searched, to make your task easier."

"Perhaps I could find it alone, but I thought we agreed that two treasure hunters were far more likely to find the booty than one. We still need to examine the secret passage more carefully, and we should also try to find the entrance to the fifth tower."

Emily caught back a sob. Why did he insist upon keeping up this charade? Why not admit he had stolen her half of the map and already knew where the treasure was? Why did he insist they keep on searching? Had he failed, despite his thievery, to locate the loot, and that was why he wanted her to remain and help him look? And why would he want her back in the passage, since it was filled with his fellow-smugglers? Oh God! She was so confused!

"I don't care about the treasure," she cried. "You can keep it all. I will have my mother's jewels, once we contact the captain's other solicitor, and the gems from her gowns. They are more than enough for me."

"That is totally unacceptable," Connor said grimly. "Half of the treasure is yours, and you are going to have it."

"I don't know what else to tell you," Emily answered wearily. Pausing briefly, she then suggested, "How about this: if you find the treasure while I am gone you keep all but one fourth. It is only fair that we reduce my share since I will not be present to help search for it."

Connor's expression turned stony. "I shall not agree to those terms unless you stay one more week to help me look."

A huge knot formed in Emily's throat but she managed to croak, "As you wish. I will stay for one week. But after that you must let me go without further trouble. And I'd prefer that you search the passage," she said then, certain that Connor already knew what it held, and not wanting to go back among the murdering smugglers. "I left part of the library unexamined," she explained hastily. "I will be occupied with it for some time."

Sweeping past Connor without giving him time to reply, she bolted through the door and down the hall, just before tears streamed from her eyes and rolled down her cheeks. As she rounded one corner she nearly collided with Connor's valet, Nipper, who was kneeling on the floor, tapping on a suit of rusty armor. He jerked back and caught her as she nearly fell over him.

"Careful, ma'am," he said. "You could hurt yourself running about like this."

Tearing herself away with a gasp of terror, Emily kept running and did not stop until she slammed her bedchamber door behind her.

For a moment she stared wildly about the room as if she had never seen it before, then she threw herself across the bed. Swiping the tears from her wet cheeks, she rubbed her hands against her bombazine skirts.

When she had cried herself out, she sat up and noticed that another steaming cup of hot chocolate waited on her side table. What an angel Maggie was. She must have known that Emily, in her shock, would retreat to the bedchamber after hearing of Marsden's death and had prepared the soothing brew before she made her announcement. There was no sign of Milo, though Emily knew he must have brought the drink.

Picking up the cup, Emily sipped slowly, then made a moue of distaste upon discovering that it was even more bitter than last night's brew. But its heat was comforting, so she drank it down. Then, moving toward her large, heavy bureau, with much grunting and perspiring she slid it across the floor until it covered the lower half of her mother's painting. No smugglers were going to sneak up on her!

Drawing a hand across her forehead, she then lay back down on the bed. Thank God she could return to the academy. It was wrong to be happy at another's unfortunate demise, but she could not restrain the flood of relief that washed over her like a cleansing tide as she contemplated Marsden's death.

It was so lucky that she had somewhere to go to give her fragmented heart time to heal. She knew she had to leave the castle before she confessed her overwhelming love for Connor, feelings she could not deny and couldn't keep to herself much longer. She had to leave before shaming herself utterly.

But how could she keep her devotion hidden for a week? Seven long days? One hundred sixty-eight endless hours?

Mournfully she remembered the glint in Connor's eyes and the fervor in his kiss. To be sure, he had responded to her passion with passion of his own. But she had to admit that that probably meant nothing; he was a man, wasn't he?

His response did not necessarily mean he felt any more for her than he had professed: friendship. His kissing her had most likely been an impulse, something he had done without thinking. She had pressed her bosom into his chest and he had reacted as any virile man—which Connor certainly was—would.

While still reliving the precious moment when their lips had touched, the moment she would cherish for the remainder of her spinsterish life, she fell asleep.

Maggie gazed after Emily, then turned gleaming eyes on Connor. "You needn't pretend I didn't see you kissin' Miss Emily, my lord, 'cause I did. And now I want to know what you intend to do about it."

Connor returned the maid's pointed stare, trying to ignore the ache in his chest where his heart felt as if it had turned to lead. "What can I do? I do not think she would thank me were I to try to stop her from leaving Hawke's Nest. She finds me nothing but a bother and a bore and I have no doubt she will be much happier back at the academy."

He sighed, thinking of their kiss. While Emily had been in his arms he had thought the embrace a portent of a wonderful future together. Now it seemed more like a death knell. He swallowed and blinked rapidly.

"Cor, you're both mad." Maggie shook her head so that her frizzled red curls bounced. "The pair of you 'ave no more sense between you than a cat's belly full of dead mice."

Connor bestowed his most freezing stare. "I beg your pardon?"

The maid laughed. "Now don't go gettin' all 'igh and mighty with me, my lord. I am not afraid of you. I am not even in your employ; I still work for Mrs. 'Arriman. You'd better be glad that I'm one to speak my mind, since I seem to be the only straightforward person 'ere."

"You are right," Connor agreed sadly, turning away. "I had no call to snap at you, and I am sorry. It's just that I find Miss Hawke the most infuriating female on the face of the earth. Infuriating and wonderful. It will tear me apart to lose her."

Maggie smiled. "Of course it will. As it will tear 'er apart to leave. It is often that way when two people love each other."

Connor spun around. Had he behaved so conspicuously that everyone knew his feelings?

Maggie clamped her hands down on her hips. "Don't try to tell me you don't love 'er. I've seen the way your eyes light up at the sight of 'er, and 'ers when she sees you. I know Miss Emily better than almost anyone, as I've known 'er since she first came to the academy. And I know she's as much in love with you as you are in love with 'er."

Connor's heart began to pound. "How do you know?"

"Oh, sir. She was *that* angry and 'urt when she thought you were bowled over by Lady Duncan. 'Ad 'erself all in an uproar over it. Told me 'erself 'ow she felt, she did."

"She told you she loved me?"

"Aye. And if you are stupid enough—beggin' your pardon, my lord—to stand there while she packs up and goes back to the academy, then you're a bigger fool than I thought you."

"What am I to do? You heard her just now. She seems to want to leave. I fail to see what I can do to stop her."

Maggie threw her hands into the air. "God 'elp us, but the Quality are an 'opeless lot when it comes to matters of the 'eart." Connor growled, and she rushed on. "Claim her as your own, my lord. She wants you desperately, only she cannot tell you that, bein' as she's a maid and you're a man and you're both Quality. Now, if 'twere me, I'd 'ave 'ad you roped and tied long afore now. But you gentry are different, always 'iding behind what's proper and what's not."

Connor looked doubtful. "But *she* is the one who insisted we remain only friends. It was not I."

"Aye, and she 'as regretted it since the moment the request slipped from between her lips."

Connor felt a weight lift from his heart. Clapping his hands on the maid's shoulders, he grinned broadly. "Maggie, I could kiss you!"

Maggie smirked. "I don't think my Andy would approve of that. Me and 'im 'ave got what you'd call an 'understandin' that as soon as 'e gets a decent-paying job, we'll be married. But," she added thoughtfully, " 'twould be nice if you could find us both a place in your London residence. You know I'm not one for living in the country. And Andy will live wherever I say, if I can only get 'im to the altar."

"You've got yourself a deal!"

Releasing her, Connor retired to his own bedchamber. First thing in the morning, he thought as he fell asleep, he would claim the captain's daughter for his bride.

21

As it happened Connor did not get a chance to ask Emily for her hand in marriage the next morning, or, indeed, all that week, for when she was not talking nonstop about where she had already looked for the treasure, she was nowhere to be found. And when Connor attempted to broach the subject of his love for her, she ran the other way—always having some excellent excuse.

The rain finally abated on the last evening before Emily's departure back to the academy. She left the dining table early (as she had done for the last six nights), and went to her room. There, she locked the door, which Cracker Jack had mended yet again, behind her with the large brass key that matched the one in Milo's possession. She had not been able to retrieve the chimp's key, but since she did not intend to be at Hawke's Nest much longer, she was not overly concerned.

Her nightly cup of hot chocolate waited on her bedside table, and she picked it up. After three or four large sips she shuddered, shaking her head from side to side as goosebumps rose on her arms. Gods! Each cup for the last six days had seemed bitter, but this had to be the worse yet! It burned, and left her tongue slightly numb. She would have to speak to Maggie about using more sugar.

She set the cup down with a thump. Not even for Maggie's sake could she force the terrible stuff down. Moving to the dressing table, she poured a cup of water from the pitcher beside the washbasin, brushed her teeth, and swished the minty tooth powder around her mouth until the bitter taste was gone.

Then she prepared for bed, thinking that, since she and

184

Maggie were to leave early the next morning, a good night's sleep was definitely in order. Not to mention that it would disallow any possibility of running into Connor elsewhere in the castle in the middle of the night, a prospect her treacherous body found infinitely appealing but her mind knew was not even to be considered.

Relaxing against the plush feather mattress, Emily gazed up at the swaths of fabric lining the ceiling. Her body felt weightless, like a cloud or a butterfly drifting on a summer breeze. She slid deeper into the pillows, enjoying the sensation and trying to keep from thinking about her sad fate.

Quite abruptly, she realized she felt far more sleepy than she had upon entering the room. Then, she had been almost jittery.

When she first heard the faint clanging sound, like metal on metal, she lay still, wondering if she were dreaming. She tried to move, but, although certain she was still conscious, she found that she was unable to do more than wiggle one toe.

The noise persisted. With great difficulty Emily finally succeeded in turning her head. Her eyes widened as the brass handle on her chamber door clicked and the heavy oak portal swung open a foot.

Milo's hairy head appeared around the edge of the door and he peered at her curiously. Then, as though satisfied she was asleep, he crept into the room on tiptoe, tucking his brass bedchamber key into his coat pocket.

The chimpanzee continued across Emily's chamber in the direction of Lady Caroline's portrait, pausing as he reached it and glancing back toward the bed. Then, moving the heavy bureau aside with an ease that made Emily's eyes pop open wide, he released the painting's hidden catch and swung the portrait away from the wall.

From Emily's perspective she could see that the inner door to the secret passageway was already open, as if someone had been waiting just inside for the moment the portrait would be removed.

She tried to wriggle into a sitting position. With supreme effort she managed to rise to one elbow just as three dirty, bedraggled men swarmed through the hidden door, came to an abrupt halt, and stared at her with obvious consternation.

It was the smugglers! They must be searching for the treasure!

Unable to awaken the scream sleeping in her throat, Emily returned the smugglers' gaze, staring silently despite her mind's terrified clamoring. What was wrong with her?

As one of the three men crossed the room, picked up her chocolate mug, and stared down into it, everything became clear. The bitter taste had not been due to Maggie's oversight, Emily realized. She had been drugged! Without a doubt someone had trained Milo to put a sleeping potion in her chocolate and then, when she had fallen asleep, enter the chamber in order to release the portrait while she slept.

Emily felt queasy. How many nights had she lain thus while the smugglers had traipsed through her room? How could she so foolishly have thought they couldn't come past the bureau blocking the portrait?

Scowling fiercely, one of the men stepped toward the bed. "The boss ain't gonna like this one bit." Turning, he glared at Milo. "You stupid ape, didn't you remember to put the laudanum in her chocolate?"

Rocking back and forth, Milo bared his teeth and growled.

Another man spoke up. "Shut up, Gibbs. Don't get 'im riled. 'E'll wake up the 'ole house. I knew we should have drugged all of 'em, 'stead of just 'er." He smiled comfortingly and took a banana from his pocket. "There, there, Milo. You done good."

Milo reached into his own pocket, extracted a small, empty glass vial, and exchanged it for the fruit, which he peeled and began to eat.

The third man, who had a gold ring through his ear, moved toward Emily with a leer. "Well, seein' how she's up, we might as well have a bit o' fun with her."

Milo immediately tensed, springing forward until he stood between the smuggler and the bed, brandishing the naked banana like a sword. His fierce attitude left no doubt that he would attack the first man to touch her. Emily breathed a sigh of relief and praised God she had given the little chimpanzee a kiss when Connor had suggested it.

The would-be rapist snarled but retreated. "Well, we don't really have time for dalliance, anyway," he muttered. "Let's get on with it. Ike, you take her through the tunnel and stick her in the tower. We'll kill her later. Right now we have more important things to worry about."

As if seeing that the danger to Emily's virtue had abated, Milo stepped aside and began to eat his fruit.

Due to the effects of the laudanum, Emily had collapsed back against the pillows. Grunting, Ike slung her over his shoulder like a sack of millet and moved toward the passage. As they passed through the hidden door Emily's borrowed night rail caught on the secret catch and tore, leaving behind a bit of fabric.

Certain her one chance at survival lay with the chimp, Emily threw an agonized, pleading glance toward Milo, who returned her gaze with one of surprised dismay and dropped his half-eaten banana on the floor.

The trip through the passage seemed much shorter this time. When they reached the underground chamber where Emily had first seen the smugglers, the man carrying her made a sharp right, moved into a second chamber, and then carried her out through a natural stone arch into the night.

Despite her groggy state, Emily gasped with surprise.

Why, they were not in the captain's fifth tower at all, as she'd thought the third smuggler had meant when he'd instructed the second man to take her "to the tower." Instead, they must have passed under the sea until they'd come to Star Island.

High above, the observatory stood like a sentinel guarding Emily's prison. It was only visible for a moment, however, before the smuggler carried her toward a small cave on one side of the island, dropped her roughly on the sandy ground, used a bit of rope he'd picked up in the main chamber to tie her up, and gagged her with his filthy neckerchief. Then, without a word, he returned the way he had come.

Connor had also decided to make an early night of it. His heart was heavy as he trudged up the stairs and moved toward his bedchamber.

Why had Emily avoided him in the short time they'd had remaining? Did she despise him so much? Or was she simply trying to save his feelings because, contrary to Maggie's insistence, she did not return his love?

Just as he reached his chamber door, an object struck him in the ribs and he fell backwards with a crash. Milo, now seated on Connor's chest, leaned down to peer into his face. "Milo, what the devil—"

His voice failed as the chimpanzee emitted a torrent of hysterical shrieks. Then the ape bounded off Connor's chest, grasped his hand, and pulled him determinedly down the hall toward the west wing. Something, Connor deduced, was dreadfully wrong.

"All right, all right. Just a minute," he said, pulling free and entering his chamber long enough to retrieve his loaded revolver from the hidden drawer and drop it in his coat pocket. Then he sped down the corridor after the chimpanzee.

A shudder of fear ripped through Connor's chest as the chimp paused before Emily's open door and leaped from side to side, agitatedly pounding his chest. Connor stepped cautiously into the dark chamber. "Emily?" he called warily.

When Milo tugged on his hand and pointed, Connor realized the chimp was indicating a shred of fabric hanging on the passage door. His stomach roiled as he saw it was a bit of lace from Emily's night rail. He nodded his understanding. "All right. Just give me time to light a candle."

The tunnel seemed to go on forever. As Connor raced through the passage, with Milo scooting along ahead of him, he passed the fork and came to the first large chamber. There, Connor caught a glimpse of a low rowboat bobbing in what appeared to be a water-filled cavern. A second, smaller chamber adjoined the first on the right.

Milo scurried on ahead through both rooms, with Connor following as quickly as he could. Then, suddenly, they stepped out under the nighttime sky.

Connor squinted and tried to get his bearings. "What the—where are we?" He glanced up. "Good God! The observatory!"

Milo scurried toward the hillside, screeching emphatically. At first Connor thought the ape was trying to show him where someone had been buried, and his heart pounded with abject terror. Then he heard a faint moan.

Breathless with relief, he noticed a heretofore unseen crevice, a tiny cave. There in the shadows, huddled in the sand, lay Emily.

As he ran toward her, a muffled sound made him hesitate and turn. Three men, who must have been in one of the caverns he and Milo had run through and had followed as they passed by, surged forward. They were dressed in sailors' garb but looked much dirtier than ordinary seamen.

Lifting his revolver from his pocket Connor cried, "Halt, or I'll shoot!"

Either they did not hear, or they thought they could reach him before he pulled the trigger. Connor managed to discharge a bullet into one man's chest moments before the other two seized him.

Twisting in their grasp, he snarled, "Smugglers. I should have known. Filthy dogs."

"Shut your trap, boyo," snapped a fourth man, who had come up behind the others. "You should have left well enough alone."

At hearing the familiar voice, Connor's eyes widened. "Nipper! Never say you are one of these devils. Cracker Jack mentioned he thought you were up to something, but I never believed it."

The valet laughed roughly. "Aye, mate, the old man had the right of it. Understand that I don't want to kill you, but I must. You know too much now." He glanced at his com-

panion. "Give me your knife, Ike, and then hold him while
I cut his throat."

Pulling himself erect, Connor prepared to meet death
fearlessly. As the man named Ike slid a lethal-looking
blade from his belt and handed it to Nipper, Connor turned
to gaze at Emily. Her gray-green eyes were enormous in
her pale face, and tears streamed down her cheeks.

Resigned to his fate, Connor pushed all fear of rejection
away and said quickly, "I love you, Emily. I wish we had
more time together, but I must tell you this simply: I love
you and I have since the moment I met you. Take care, my
darling. I will see you on the other side."

"Stop yer yammerin'," growled Nipper.

Just as the valet took a step toward Connor, Milo, who
had been standing off to one side, erupted in a tornado of
activity, sweeping one long-fingered hand toward the
ground and up again, flinging a large quantity of sand into
the valet's eyes.

"Aargh!" Nipper cried, dropping his blade and clawing
at his face.

Instantly Connor jammed an elbow into each of his cap-
tors' ribs. As the two smugglers gasped and doubled over,
releasing his arms, he slammed his fist into the valet's
face. Turning about to face the two men who'd been holding him, he saw Milo smash a large chunk of lava rock
down on the second man's pate.

Lifting one booted foot, Connor thrust hard into the remaining smuggler's stomach. Gasping for breath, the man
slid to his knees. Clasping his fists together Connor raised
them over his head and brought them down on his combat-
ant's neck. The smuggler dropped like a felled ox.

Turning, Milo ran back into the main rock chambers
and returned seconds later with bits of rope. After handing
these to Connor, who gazed at the chimp in amazement at
the animal's apparent understanding of the situation, the
ape stood to one side, grinning and chortling to himself.
As Connor finished tying the captives, the ape held out
one hairy hand.

Connor shook it gravely. "Good work, my friend." Then
he moved to kneel beside Emily, rapidly removing her

bindings and the dirty kerchief from her mouth. "Are you all right?"

"As well as can be expected," she choked, "but my mouth is as dry as the Sahara. Thank God Milo found you." She held out her arms to the ape. "Milo! You saved my life."

The chimpanzee fairly flew across the sand, then threw himself into Emily's arms and planted a moist kiss on her cheek. She hugged him tightly. Finally she stopped cuddling the gleeful ape and turned a serious gaze on Connor. "My lord, in regard to your proffered sentiments of a moment ago, there is something I must say."

Connor flushed and shrugged. "It is unnecessary. I am sorry if I embarrassed you, but I was unable to go to my grave without telling you my feelings. You don't need to say anything."

"But—"

"No," he said quickly, "be silent. Maggie told me you returned my affections, but I know she must have been wrong. I tried to convince myself she was right, but since you have avoided me at every turn for the last week I know I can no longer delude myself. But don't worry; although I will always love you more than anything in this world, I will never trouble you with my feelings."

Pivoting on one foot, he began moving back into the inner chambers. "I will give you a moment or two to compose yourself and will wait inside until you are ready for me to escort you back to the castle. Please don't take overlong; there could be more smugglers about."

"Con, wait," Emily called softly. "Please."

Scarcely daring to look at her, Connor turned his head. Her eyes were luminous and her mouth curved gently. Afraid to speak, he waited silently.

Emily drew a shaky breath. "I don't want you to say anything until I have finished." He nodded, and she smiled sweetly. "Maggie was right. I do love you—Oh, how I love you! I did not dare speak of it before now, because I believed you could never return my affection, and . . ." She hesitated, then rushed on, "And because I mistakenly thought you were one of the smugglers."

Hope sprang into Connor's chest and he spun about to face her. Then the second half of her announcement hit him. His eyebrows drew together. "A smuggler? Why would you think that, for God's sake?"

Quickly, Emily explained. "While I realize, now, that I read a great deal into what were, in reality, innocent events, at the time there seemed to be numerous reasons to believe you were a smuggler. These happenstances, combined with my mistaken belief that you had been behind both the carriage accident and the incident with the falling gargoyle, made it easy to think the worst of you, especially when you asked Mr. Simms about what would become of the treasure if one of us died."

Connor opened his mouth to object, but she raised a hand.

"First, there was the incident when we arrived, when you quizzed Cracker Jack about the cook's reason for leaving. While I did not think anything of it at first, later I wondered if you hadn't been quizzing him in an effort to discover how much he knew. Yet, I never believed he was a smuggler. I thought that, being the captain's closest friend here at Hawke's Nest, he would have been kept in the dark so he could not inform the captain, whom he knew would not have approved.

"Second, there was the fact that the captain was a pirate, and you and he were business partners. I thought perhaps you had been seduced into thinking that illegal activities were somehow romantic, or harmless. After all, you were very young when you met him, and it would not have been impossible for you to have some kind of hero fixation on him and want to follow in his tracks whether he desired it or not. His having discovered your smuggling activities would have explained why he wanted the business sold: to save you from yourself.

"Third, there was my stolen map. While you insisted you hadn't taken it, and while we still do not know what became of it, you must admit that given my suspicions of you already, you were the most likely candidate for blame.

"Fourth, when I told you I had seen the ship in the harbor, signaling to the castle, you told me that it might be very dangerous for me to tell what I had seen. I took that as a thinly veiled threat." She laughed. "If you only knew how terrified I was that day we went on the picnic. I thought you had reconsidered when you previously rescued me from the falling gargoyle and had decided to murder me, after all.

"Fifth, while lost in the hidden passage, I stumbled upon the smugglers." She paled and her smile vanished. "I saw Nipper murder Mr. Crabbe. Since they were both smugglers, it followed that you were, as well. And when you hired Andy, after voicing suspicions about both him and Mr. Crabbe after the accident, I assumed you knew he was a villain too. If you knew he was evil, and hired him anyway, I believed it could only be because you were also evil. I assume he is also a smuggler, but is not here at the present time.

"And sixth, when I got lost and you came looking for me in the passage, I assumed you knew what was at the end of it. I thought that, being my friend, you were hastening after me to stop the smugglers from killing me if I happened upon them.

"So you see, given all my 'proof,' I really had good reason to suspect you."

Connor shook his head. "Hearing your list, I could almost believe it myself. But there are some things that bother me. Why would I have placed myself in danger in the carriage and gargoyle accidents? And why, when you insisted you leave the castle after Marsden's death, would I have tried to keep you here? Or lure you back in the passage, if I knew it would be dangerous? Wouldn't I have wanted to keep you out of it, at all costs? Why wouldn't I have agreed that it would be most prudent for you to leave Hawke's Nest as soon as possible?"

Emily's smile returned. "As for the two accidents, I never did understand how you could have been behind them. They were the main flaw in my reasoning. As for why you would have wanted me to remain at the castle and keep searching for the treasure, I thought perhaps that, despite your possessing both halves of the map, you had still been unable to find the loot and needed my help."

Connor smiled bemusedly. "I am not a smuggler, love. You know that now, don't you?"

Emily grinned back. "Oh, yes. Even my overactive imagination couldn't explain why your own men would have pretended they didn't know you, and then try to kill you, back at the observatory." Then her smile faded. "But I want you to know, Connor, that it wouldn't matter to me if you *were* a smuggler. I love you with all my heart. Nothing could change that."

Flinging an arm around her waist, Connor pressed her so close to his body that neither could breathe. "My love?" he said at last, relaxing his grip slightly.

"Yes, darling?"

"Will you make me the happiest man in the world?"

She pulled away to gaze at him, searchingly.

He kissed the tip of her nose. "Marry me, schoolmarm."

Emily's answer shone in her eyes, and Connor lowered his face to hers to claim her lips in a long, passionate kiss. When he raised his head, both of them were shivering with desire. "Come, my love," he murmured at last. "Let us go back to the castle. It may not be safe to linger here."

Despite the possible danger, it was a far longer journey back to Hawke's Nest than it had been for either of them earlier, due to the overwhelming necessity of stopping to swear eternal devotion to each other and share long, achingly sweet kisses after each promise of love. However, at last they arrived at the hidden door and stepped through into Emily's room.

Suddenly Emily frowned. "Oh, dear. There is something we haven't considered."

Too happy to think, Connor merely gazed at her. "What is that?"

"The treasure. We still need to find the treasure, or you will lose the most important thing in your world. Your shipping business. Unless you will consent to let me sell my mother's jewels. If there isn't enough money from that, perhaps you could purchase part of the business, at least."

"Ah, my sweet schoolmarm," Connor replied, dropping a tender kiss on her lips, "I have the most important thing in the world right here in my arms. And I told you before: Your mother's jewels will not be sold. If I lose the company, then so be it."

Again they kissed, stopping only when Milo entered the room behind them, closed the portrait door, grinned, and made rude smacking noises with his thick lips.

"All right, old man," Connor said with a chuckle, "we'll stop. For now." He looked at Emily. "It is almost dawn. Do you want to get some more sleep—in my room of course, since I doubt you'd be able to relax in yours and all the others are too dusty to bother with—or would you like to go downstairs for a bracing cup of tea? I want to find Cracker Jack and have him tend to the captive smugglers."

Emily shuddered. "I know I won't get a wink of sleep until they are gone. Just give me a moment to put on one of my mother's gowns and I'll accompany you downstairs. But don't leave me—just turn your back."

Connor gave her a rakish look, but did as she requested.

Once she had changed, Emily and Connor left her bedchamber and began searching for Cracker Jack, while Milo trailed along behind. They had just reached the main staircase when an unfamiliar sound made them hesitate.

"What was that?" Emily whispered.

Connor shook his head, placed a finger to his lips, and leaned over the balustrade. His mouth dropped open. Curious, Emily also peered down into the main hall.

Far below, Lady Duncan was on her hands and knees pounding on the wall below Polly's brass cage. The bird clacked her beak balefully, peering hopefully at Lady Duncan's skinny backside.

Emily blinked. "She must be looking for the treasure."

Connor nodded. As he and Emily reached the bottom, Lady Duncan surged to her feet, her face flaming.

"My lord! Miss Hawke! I was just . . . that is . . ."

"I think we all know what you were doing, Bettina," Connor replied smoothly. "Find anything?"

"Not a damned thing." Lady Duncan shook her dainty blond curls disgustedly. "I've hardly seen either of you for the past week, and I got tired of reading, so I decided to try *my* luck at treasure-hunting. It kept me from climbing the walls while I waited for the damned rain to cease so I could be on my way. You aren't angry with me?"

"Why should we be?" Emily said. "We've already gone over most of the castle. If there is a treasure here, it will probably remain hidden for another five hundred–plus years."

Lady Duncan suddenly glanced behind Emily and Connor and let out a horrified squeal. "Gracious heaven! What is that? Get it away from me!"

Emily turned to see that Milo had just descended the last few steps. Upon noticing Bettina, whom he had not seen 'til now presumably because she had spent most of her visit in her room, he puckered his lips and dashed forward.

Lady Duncan shrieked and, whirling about, ran several feet. "Get it away from me, Con! Don't let it touch me!" She leaped up to stand on the table below the hanging bird cage. "Get away from me you dirty little mon—"

"No!" shouted Connor.

"—key!" Lady Duncan finished just before losing her balance.

She swung her arms wildly, her fingers grasping for purchase. Since the only available handhold was Polly's cage, she clung to it as though it were a lifeline—until its small chain came free of the ceiling and both woman and bird crashed to the ground in a flurry of petticoats and feathers.

Polly burst out of the broken cage door and took to the wing, echoing Milo's enraged cries with her own deafening squawks.

Connor threw up his hands. "That's done it," he remarked exasperatedly to no one in particular—which was just as well, since both women had dived for cover and there was no one to hear him. Then, as Polly swooped determinedly near his ear with a loud snap, he, too, took to his heels.

22

Pandemonium reigned supreme. Standing atop a chair, beside a cupboard filled with fine china and porcelain miniatures, Milo roared with fury and tried to smash every unsecured object he could reach, while Polly dive-bombed the three humans, threatening to tear out their hearts with her massive beak.

Clapping her hands over her ears, Emily crouched beneath a low table, while Connor hid behind the velvet draperies lining the walls.

The only one not fortunate enough to find a safe haven was Lady Duncan, who ran mindlessly back and forth across the hall, her full silk skirts trailing behind her like streamers.

As she passed Milo, who had been concentrating on hurling a group of Dresden shepherdesses into the cavernous hall fireplace, the chimp put out one hairy hand and grasped the rear neckline of her delicate silk gown. A tremendous splitting sound cleaved the air and Lady Duncan's entire body jerked backwards so that she nearly fell. When she had regained her balance she stood, blinking down in dismay, as she realized she was scandalously clad in a mere chemise.

Milo screeched with delight and wrapped the shredded, filmy gown about his shoulders like a cape. As Lady Duncan gaped down at her disrobed body, Polly skimmed through the air like an avenging angel. The bird's brilliant yellow crest stood up like a blade and her pupils dilated and contracted rapidly.

As Polly's talons entwined in Lady Duncan's carefully styled coiffure and her gigantic black beak snapped at the terrified woman's ears, Lady Duncan screamed and raised both hands to fend off the bird.

Milo found this vastly amusing. Leaping about and screeching wildly, he pulled the gown from his shoulders and waved it like a flag. Then, in a frenzy of titillation, he searched for something else to throw.

Finding nothing left to brandish, as he had already seized everything small enough to pick up and hurled it into the fireplace, he barreled across the room, shimmied up the thick chain holding the cup-shaped bronze chandelier he used as a bed, and threw himself into it. With the light careening from side to side, he disappeared from view and then reappeared a fraction of a second later with his hands filled.

The next moment the air was thick with debris as Milo bounced small objects off various parts of Lady Duncan's anatomy with the accuracy of a small boy skipping stones.

By this time Lady Duncan was on all fours and scrabbling for the main exit, with Polly still clinging tenaciously to her head. As she reached the entryway she leaped to her feet and swung the heavy double doors open so hard they crashed against the walls. When she ran down the front steps and began sprinting across the wide lawn, Polly released her and took to the air.

Swooping back through the doors, the bird came to a rest on the top of her shattered cage. There she muttered irritably, *"And God threw the harlot into a fiery pit, hotter than the sun."*

Seeing that the fun had come to an end, Milo swung down from the ceiling, ambled across the room, and seated himself in a plush Louis XIV chair. There he gazed about as if surprised by the shards of porcelain and other refuse littering the floor.

Emily stayed beneath her table for the time being, watching as Connor slipped cautiously from behind the velvet draperies. When he had successfully moved out into the center of the room and had not been attacked, she inched her way out to stand beside him. "Do you think Lady Duncan will be all right? I hope Polly didn't hurt her badly," she said nervously, keeping her eyes on the peeved bird.

Connor glanced out the open doors. "I doubt she sustained permanent—" He broke off abruptly and his mouth dropped open. He sank to his knees.

"By all that's holy," he murmured, looking over at the ape, who had propped his chin on the arm of the chair and was watching indifferently. "You little devil. You had it all this time."

Milo suddenly seemed profoundly interested in his nails.

"Had what?" Jumping up, Emily hurried over to see what the fuss was about. Then she, too, sank to her knees.

"The fabled Norman treasure. He had it hidden in his bed all along," Connor said softly. "If he hadn't been overcome with the desire to throw something at Bettina, we'd probably never have known it existed. Unless he took it up there himself, it's probably been in that chandelier for hundreds and hundreds of years."

Emily gazed at the floor. There, like flowers in a spring meadow, lay a heap of unset gems, elaborate necklaces, rich gold bracelets, and ropes and ropes of pearls the size of wrens' eggs.

Glancing at Connor, Emily noticed that he had picked up a delicate gold crown. Although no stones adorned the circlet, it was made of the most exquisite filigree she had ever seen, in the shapes of flowers and birds. "Oh, how beautiful," she whispered reverently.

"Yes, it is." Settling back on his heels, Connor smiled oddly. "There must be tens of thousands of pounds worth of treasure just here on the floor." He glanced up at the chandelier, which was nearly four feet in circumference. "I cannot even begin to guess how much is still inside."

Emily ran her fingers over a rope of rose-colored pearls the size of large grapes and sighed blissfully. "Do you think we'll ever find the captain's treasure as well?"

Connor shook his head. "I doubt it. Unless I miss my guess there never was one. I believe all his wealth, like mine, was tied up in the shipping business. He must have merely been playing matchmaker. That's the only reason I can think of why he would give us that utterly absurd "map"—because there *was* no treasure."

"His insistence that the shipping company be sold was damned odd, too," Connor added. "If I hadn't known he'd been examined for mental stability by a competent physician only a short time before his death, I'd have to wonder how sound his mind really was.

"That's all water under the bridge now, though. We've almost searched this place from top to bottom, and if he had had a treasure, we'd have found it. I am certain the chandelier is the only place we did not think to look, and there aren't any more lights like that one in the castle. And I think, given our wandering in and out of the passage, that we can be quite confident that there is no treasure there.

"During the last week, when you were avoiding me"—he smiled as Emily blushed—"I even searched all the fireplaces. Nearly got stuck in a couple, and ruined some fine clothes I had made up by Weston last time I was in Town. No, it looks like the captain just wanted to see us thrown together long enough so that we'd fall in love. And he got his wish." He smiled tenderly. "I love you more than life, schoolmarm."

"Oh, Con," Emily whispered.

Still clutching the crown, Connor slid across the floor toward her. Reaching out, he ran one large palm over her ebony tresses. "Sweet Emily. You had me so frightened when you said you were going back to the academy. Promise you'll never leave me."

Happy tears filled Emily's eyes. "You have my solemn oath, my lord."

Lifting the Norman crown, Connor placed it on her head. He smiled and caressed her cheek with the rough pad of one finger. "Queen of my heart."

"Well, well, well," a familiar voice said from the front doors. "Isn't that sweet?"

Emily caught her breath, trying to remember where she had heard the voice before. As her memory cleared, the blood drained from her face. Assailed with sudden dread, she whirled about. "Mr. Simms!"

"The same," the solicitor said with a nod as he entered the hall. In front of him, stiff with rage and indignation, walked Cracker Jack. A revolver was pressed against the old sailor's spine. A second gun waved in Emily and Connor's direction.

Simms smiled amiably at Connor. "How wonderful. You have found the Norman treasure. I am profoundly grateful to you; I was becoming worried when my men had failed to find the captain's treasure after so long. I had begun thinking I might have to give up the search and go away empty-handed."

Bringing Emily with him, Connor surged to his feet. "Simms! So you are the brains behind the smugglers' brawn."

"Oh, yes," Simms agreed. "As I have been for years. In fact, it was my suggestion that the captain try pirating to begin with. It was I who found fitting men to sail his ships. It was I who sold his goods to some of my other disgustingly wealthy clients, men who would pay any price for good French wines and silks. And it was I who recommended Mr. Nipper to the captain to act as your valet upon your return home from the university. I found him in Newgate."

"I see," Connor said steadily, eyeing the revolvers. "He was a damned fine manservant. Did he have experience, or was he merely a common criminal?"

"Oh, he was a real valet. He had stolen a king's ransom in gold from a former employer. He was more than happy to serve me after I saved him from the hangman's noose and promised him untold riches. Of course, the captain never knew Nipper was anything but a harmless servant."

Simms's face contorted with sudden fury. "I did so much for that old bastard. But what gratitude did I receive? Do you think he left me a single ship so I might continue business? Do you think he paid me back for all the money I made him? Not on your life!

"Instead he left me a note suggesting that I would be better off giving up smuggling altogether when he was gone. Insisted I would never be able to handle things without him." He spat. "Selfish son of a bitch. It wouldn't have killed him to have left me one little ship. But no, he wanted everything to go to you and his precious daughter. Including his fleet.

"Every single stinking ship," he hissed. *"That* is the thanks I got for all my hard work."

Connor's eyes narrowed with dawning comprehension. "Are you saying Captain Hawke never wanted the shipping business sold? That somehow you falsified his will?"

"No. There was an amendment I was supposed to read to you in the event you did not find the treasure. But since I intend to kill you both before you ever leave Hawke's Nest, you needn't concern yourselves with it. Really, my lord, how could you have thought the captain would ever have sold something that was so precious to both you and him?"

"If he did not intend to sell, why this charade?" Connor demanded.

Simms rolled his eyes. "He wanted you and his daughter to be together long enough to form an attachment. Apparently he believed that if he gave you a quest, something that forced you to work together, you would fall in love. And he was right, which proves that you are as great a fool as he was."

Emily saw that Connor was circling slowly to the left. Although she didn't know what he planned, she burst into speech to keep the solicitor's attention occupied.

"Did you also take my half of the treasure map, Mr. Simms?"

The solicitor spat. "Aye. Nipper stole it off your bureau on your first night here, when he and Cracker Jack entered your room to see why you'd been screaming. And a fine lot of good it did me. It was just a single sheet of paper inscribed with a child's nursery rhyme about wishing on a star. Obviously nonsense."

Emily frowned. "I do not understand why you didn't simply keep the maps, back in London. Or why you did not merely read them before giving them to us."

"Couldn't keep them. You are forgetting the captain's 'mystery solicitor,' whom he hired at the same time we went into the smuggling business. Cagey old devil. He never did trust me." His mouth worked furiously. "And he never told me who the solicitor was. Wisely, I might add. Otherwise I'd simply have gone to the man's office, murdered him, and burned his office to destroy his copies of the captain's documents. You will recall, of course, that I tried to get his direction from Lord Connor, but was unsuccessful.

"Also, I could not read your treasure maps before giving them to you, because their envelopes were sealed with wax impressed by the captain's signet ring—which disappeared along with his body when he was lost in the storm. As he always used that particular seal and none other, I knew Lord Connor would have been immediately suspicious, had I given him a map sealed with plain wax.

"So you see, the only way I could gain access to the maps, which I mistakenly believed would help me find the captain's treasure, was to give them to you and let you come to Hawke's Nest.

"Oh, I did not intend you to actually arrive here. You were meant to be killed in the carriage accident my man, Crabbe, organized. Then he was to bring the maps to me.

"But once you'd escaped alive, I deemed it best to let you live. I could have killed you any time, but it seemed wiser to let you search for the treasure. There was always the chance, as has conveniently proven the case, that you would find it for me."

"What about Andy?" Emily asked. "You mentioned Mr. Crabbe, but you did not tell us if Andy was also a member of your gang."

"No. He is Crabbe's nephew, whom Crabbe intended to bring into our brotherhood once he arrived here. We're always on the lookout for young blood. Men in our occupation have a habit of dying early and leaving us shorthanded.

"Enough talk. Let's get moving." He waved his revolver in Emily's direction.

"There is no need for violence, Mr. Simms," Emily said quickly. "There is plenty of treasure here for all of us. Why don't we simply sort everything into equal piles?"

Simms cackled disparagingly. "Why should I share any

of it with you when I can have it all?" Giving Cracker Jack a rough shove so that the old seaman fell forward, he laughed again. Emily winced as Cracker Jack's knees slammed against granite. "Get over there with them, old man, or I'll blow your brains all over this room."

Connor had nearly managed to get around to Simms's other side when the solicitor whirled about. "Thought to trick me, did you, my lord? Get your aristocratic ass back over there with the others."

Returning to Emily's side, Connor pushed her behind him. "What are you going to do now, Simms?"

"Once I get you all back into the hidden passage, I am going to shoot both you and Cracker Jack with the two bullets in these pistols," Simms informed him nonchalantly. "Then, before strangling Miss Hawke I shall . . . enjoy her company in memory of the love I felt for her mother."

Emily bit off a cry and he threw her an amused glance. "Yes, my dear. I quite worshipped Lady Caroline. That is why I was so shocked by your physical appearance when I first saw you in my London office. But Caro preferred her husband, if you can believe it."

"You'll never get away with this!" Emily whispered.

"I think I shall," the solicitor said matter-of-factly. "At any rate, for a fortune like this I'm willing to take the chance. When you're dead I'll hide your bodies in the passage, take the treasure, and sail away."

Connor's hands clenched into fists. "Surely it is not necessary to kill Miss Hawke. How can one woman harm you?"

"Aside from her knowing about my history of smuggling and watching me commit two murders, you mean?" Simms asked with a slight grin.

Emily cleared her throat, and tried to sound braver than she felt. "Am I correct in assuming it was Milo who drugged my chocolate?"

"Yes," Simms replied. "That came about quite accidentally, as a matter of fact. You see, since we thought you'd die in the carriage accident, we did not expect you to make it to the castle. So when you did arrive, and were given the captain's old room, through which we'd been entering in order to search for the treasure ever since Cracker Jack informed Nipper that he suspected him of the peculiar happenings at the castle, we had to think of something."

"But why train Milo?" Connor questioned. "Wouldn't it have been easier for Nipper to have drugged Emily's tea and let himself into the room?"

"We thought of that, too. After a lengthy discussion, we decided that it would be much safer to use the chimp. Imagine, for example, if it had been Nipper whom Emily had seen on her first night here. The cat would have been set among the pigeons, so to speak, because he could have had none but evil designs to be sneaking around in a woman's bedchamber. No, there was far too much at stake to risk him getting caught.

"So we used Milo. He is quite remarkably intelligent. It was a simple thing to train him to pour a small vial of laudanum (of which we kept a large supply on hand) into your chocolate, open the secret passage, and exchange the empty vial for his daily banana, which my men had waiting for him on the other side of the secret door. Being an animal, once he was trained to do the act it never occurred to him to empty the vial anyplace but in your chocolate."

"So when we were in London and you told me you didn't know where Milo was, you were lying," Connor deduced. "He was with you."

"No. Nipper happened upon the chimp wandering the beach the same day you arrived, apparently just getting home after some escapade, and took him to the shack in which I have been staying for the last few days. He began training Milo right after your arrival, and the chimp was ready almost immediately. Milo has been doing a wonderful job, as my men have reported daily.

"When no one came to the cottage this evening with news, I decided to come to the castle to see what had happened. I half expected my men to have absconded with the loot."

"How do you plan to get away?" Emily inquired. "You cannot possibly carry all the treasure away on horseback or in a carriage."

"On the ship you noticed in the harbor several nights ago, I presume," Connor commented. "It must have been Nipper who signaled from the fifth tower to the ship. I assume that is when he reported on the state of his search."

"Again, you are correct," Simms agreed amiably.

"Your crew must consist of more than the four men we saw," Emily stated flatly. "Won't the other smugglers get suspicious when their fellow seamen do not return? And what about when you make several trips to and from the ship, loaded down with booty? Surely they will realize you have the treasure."

"They won't need to be suspicious," Simms said with a cheerful smile. "I intend to tell them all about our good fortune. When you are dead I will signal them to come up through the passage and carry the jewels back to the ship so that I don't have to.

"Then, when we are close to London, I will find some excuse for why we must hide the treasure along the coast, after which I'll lace their grog with arsenic. When they are dead, I will exchange their sailors' garb for street clothes and hurl them overboard. That way, if any of their bodies happen to drift inland no one will connect them with me. My ship will drift until someone sees it, and, soon as I am rescued, I will report a terrible storm and say that everyone but myself was lost."

"No one will believe you," Emily said.

"Perhaps not, but they will have no proof to show otherwise."

"Won't your men figure out that you're up to something?" Connor asked.

"Not until it's too late," Simms said confidently.

"What about the gargoyle that fell," Connor inquired then. "Were you behind that accident as well?"

Simms shook his head. "No, though I would have been, had I thought of it. It must have been merely due to the excess of rain we've been experiencing, and the age of the stone." Straightening, the solicitor waved his revolvers. "Come along. Time grows short. If the three of you will move toward the stairs we will go up to Miss Hawke's room and get this business over with. We must make haste if I am to sail with the tide."

"Yes, it would be a pity if you were delayed, after all your careful planning," Connor agreed.

Emily was amazed at how cool Connor seemed. She was shaking in her shoes. Was this how their lives would end? With their bodies moldering away in a hidden passage that might never be discovered again? Would their love die before it had ever had a chance to mature?

She swallowed to clear away the tightness in her throat. Throwing Connor an agonized glance before moving across the room toward the stairs, she reached out for his hand. Cracker Jack followed close behind as they started climbing.

Gazing after them, Milo hopped down from his chair and ambled out of view.

Halfway up the grand staircase, a sound made them all turn back. Emily caught her breath to see Maggie wander into the hall, swinging a basket of eggs on one arm and holding Milo by the other.

"Maggie!" she screamed. "Run, Maggie! Get help!"

Before the maid could reply, Simms called out coldly, "I wouldn't, my dear. Good work, Milo." He threw Connor a cocky grin. "See? Even that filthy animal knows who will come out the winner in this little match. I didn't even have to train him to round up everyone else who must die."

Emily could have sworn the chimpanzee glared at the solicitor before leaving Maggie's side and returning to the Louis XIV armchair beside the hearth.

Not batting an eye, Maggie shook her head. "Come get me, you rotten bastard."

"Do as I say or I'll shoot you where you stand," Simms snarled.

Maggie stood her ground. "Disable one gun and be left with only one bullet?" she retorted. "I doubt even you are as stupid as that."

Lips tightened to a white line, Simms moved toward the maid. Emily pressed a hand to her mouth. As Simms reached the middle of the room Connor drew in his breath sharply.

Following his gaze toward the opposite side of the room, Emily saw that Maggie's beloved Andy had crept into the hall and was making his way toward the chain holding up the bronze chandelier. When he released the large metal hooks that held the chain in place, the fixture began to sway back and forth. Simms had just reached the center of the room when the faint creaking made him look up.

Immediately, Andy released the chain. When the dust settled, only the solicitor's legs protruded from beneath the enormous fixture. They were not moving.

Once he was certain the danger was past, Connor pulled Emily into his arms and held her so tightly she could hardly breathe.

The last thing that registered in Emily's ears before she was swept away on the wings of desire was Cracker Jack's raspy voice.

"Lord love 'em," the old seaman chortled, "ain't love grand?"

EPILOGUE

Emily and Connor sat on a soft blanket at the base of the observatory on a spot where the rocks had been cleared away to leave a wide swatch of golden sand. The sun, just beginning to dip below the horizon, cast multicolored rays of light over the small island, glinting off the lenses of Emily's new spectacles and the gold locket she wore around her neck, part of her mother's jewels that the new solicitor had sent down from London. Her new jonquil-yellow gown glowed red-orange in the sunset.

"Happy, darling?" Connor asked.

"Oh, yes." Emily sighed, snuggling deeper into the curve of her husband's arm. Then, glancing over at the large group of girls playing tag on the beach, she smiled. "The students are having a wonderful time, aren't they?"

The students were girls from the four scientific schools she and Connor had set up around Britain—academies that centered their curricula on the sciences: math, physics, chemistry, and astronomy. Although the schools' attendance was small, Emily was confident it would grow as the years passed, especially since Etta Lou was spreading the word among her fellow headmistresses. Thus far they had all seemed surprisingly positive about the prospect of adding the sciences to their schedules.

It had been Connor's idea to bring the girls to the island for astronomical observations through their huge telescope. The event was to take place twice a year, with half of the girls from all four academies each time. This was their first visit to Star Island.

"It certainly seems so," he agreed. "Milo appears to be enjoying himself as well."

Emily laughed at the chimp, who was distributing kisses among the girls. "Indeed. You know, he's become a pleasure to have around now that you've convinced him he needn't pour disgusting things into our nighttime chocolate in order to get a banana. And the girls adore him.

"He also seems to appreciate our letting him make the captain's old bedchamber his own, ever since his chandelier was smashed. He'll never know we did so just to keep him from barging in on us every night since we couldn't discover where he hid the key.

"Besides, I am quite pleased with our new apartments, in the fifth tower. I'm amazed we didn't realize sooner that the fork in the secret passage led there. And who'd have suspected that the captain would have decorated the chamber so lavishly? It is no wonder he never fussed about his inability to visit the observatory here on Star Island, what with the excellent telescope he had rigged up in the tower."

Raising her face to the sun, she sighed again. "I am so glad you suggested these outings. It is so pleasant here."

Connor grinned. "If I had not, I probably would never have seen you. I know you'd have forever been running off to teach astronomy lessons at the different schools. It's much better for me to have you give specialized lessons at Hawke's Nest.

"I also had to consider the fact that, although you installed very good telescopes in each school, none was as powerful as our own. And of course I knew you missed teaching."

"You are most perceptive, my wonderful lord," Emily whispered, kissing his cheek. "I am especially glad that, since we only hold these events twice a year, I am able to go on seafaring journeys with you, as well as work on our list of deep-sky objects."

"I enjoy both endeavors," Connor agreed. "But I especially enjoy the sea voyages when we take a telescope along. I was right about your having inherited the captain's ability to sail without becoming seasick.

"Oh, I almost forgot," he said then. "I fear I shall have

to insist you skip your astronomy class next April. You'll need to reschedule it for March or May."

"Why?"

Reaching into his pocket Connor pulled out a sheet of cream-colored vellum. "Because we have had a summons from our regent," he said with satisfaction. "It seems he is having his first star party in that month. April is the best month for the event, of course, since the skies get dark earlier than in summer months and it isn't as cold as in winter."

Emily's heart pounded eagerly as she unfolded the paper and scanned the scrawled message. "Con! How did you manage it?"

Connor shrugged. "Although I had planned to request an invitation, I had nothing to do with this. Apparently the regent heard about your schools and decided you would be an asset to his first party. You know, his recognition will make your academies very successful."

Emily sighed joyously. "I never knew I could be so happy. I truly have everything I ever wanted in the world."

After looking about to make certain they were not being observed, Connor bent to press a warm kiss to her lips. "As do I. But there is one thing that bothers me about having the schoolgirls here at Hawke's Nest."

"What is that?" Emily asked, concerned.

He traced her lips with the tip of one finger. "I have to keep a dignified distance from you until they leave."

"Mm," she murmured deliciously. "They will be gone in two days, my love. And they cannot follow us into our bedchamber."

His eyes glittered. "Thank God."

Emily noted his visibly rising passion and felt an answering swirl of heat in her lower parts. Raising a hand, she traced the scar on his forehead before dropping her fingers to trace his whisker-roughened jaw. Then, glancing over at the girls, who were drifting in their direction, she sighed and got to her feet.

Connor also gave a disappointed sigh, but stood up. "We had best get the telescope ready for the night's festivities," he said resignedly. "But I expect you to be properly grateful this evening for all my efforts."

"I will do my best." Suddenly Emily started. "Wait a minute. Wasn't there something wrong with the telescope? Remember the trouble you had raising and lowering it?"

Connor frowned. "Now that you mention it, I do. I hope I can fix it before the sun goes down. It would be horrible if these first lessons were a failure because the telescope was broken."

Clasping hands, they climbed to the observatory.

When they entered the main room Connor squeezed Emily's fingers, then dropped them and moved to the box. For a moment after he lifted its lid, he stood very still. Then a slow smile spread across his face.

Hurrying forward, Emily peered into the large box. Her heart gave a lurch. Reaching down with one trembling hand, she took a handful of gleaming gold doubloons out of the mechanism box and sifted them through her fingers.

"The captain's treasure," she whispered. Then she gasped. "Good Lord, how could we have missed this? How could we have been so blind? There were clues all over the place."

"My God, you're absolutely right!" Connor shook his head and laughed. "When I think of all Polly's remarks about heaven and the stars and suns and moons, I could kick myself for not seeing it sooner. And of course the verses on our treasure maps could only have pointed to the observatory."

Emily dropped a handful of coins back into the box with a clink. "Wait a minute," she said suddenly. "There's a paper here as well."

Connor leaned forward. Reaching out, he brushed the gold aside and fished out a piece of parchment. "So there is," he said, unfolding it slowly. His eyes skimmed the writing quickly, and a deep chuckle rumbled from his chest.

"What does it say?" Emily demanded. "Let me see." Taking the paper, she began reading.

My Dear Children,

So you have done it. You have found the treasure. I suppose it would seem a bit pompous to say I knew all along that you would, but I did.

What I did not know was whether you would also discover that you loved each other. While it would have been easier merely to have divided my wealth between you, it would not have brought you together for a long enough period of time that you might fall in love.

I pray you will forgive an old man's sentimental heart, but, as you two were the dearest people in my world (yes Emily, you also were dear to my heart even though I stayed away from you for your own good), I had to attempt the impossible: to bring the two of you together. If you are not yet in love with each other I hope you will give some thought to a dying man's last wish. May God bless and keep you,

CAPTAIN ERASTUS HAWKE

Connor smiled fondly. "That old rascal. Did you read the part about 'a dying old man's last wish'? He wasn't leaving anything to chance, was he? I hope, wherever he is, he knows his plan succeeded."

"Yes. And he got his wish more than you yet realize, my love." Emily smiled crookedly. "It looks like we'll have a nice nest egg to leave our children." She glanced over at Connor and blushed.

Connor caught his breath. "Are you trying to tell me something, darling?" he asked hopefully.

The half-smile spread fully across Emily's face. She nodded, then gasped as Connor caught her up in his arms. "I take it you are happy about the development?"

"Happy does not begin to touch the depths of my feelings," he replied. His eyes glistened and he released her only long enough to brush at them. "I want a dozen children, at least. And I want them to grow up loving one another as much as we love them."

"How could they help it," Emily whispered, "when our home is filled with so much happiness?"

"Oh, Emily," Connor murmured. "Darling, wonderful, irritating little schoolmarm. I never dreamed I could love anyone as much as I love you. I thought I was doomed to go through life distrusting women after what happened with Bettina."

"You have forgiven her now, haven't you?"

"Yes." Then Connor grinned. "Although, as you know, I wrote to Mr. Jensen, the captain's 'mystery' solicitor and our new legal counsel, instructing him to give Bettina an allowance until she wed, I do not think she will be collecting for long. She has fallen madly in love and writes that we should expect wedding bells any day. I left the letter in the library, if you'd like to read it. I suppose I should resent her marrying so soon after Markus's death, but I cannot really blame her. He was not an easy person to love."

"Unlike you, my lord," Emily said sincerely.

Reaching up, she wrapped her arms around Connor's neck and pulled his lips down to hers for a long, deep kiss. Both were breathless when they heard the schoolgirls' footsteps clambering up the tower stairs for the astronomy lesson. Stepping apart, they looked into each other's eyes, certain that nothing and no one could ever separate the love that bound their hearts together as one.

Avon Romances—
the best in exceptional authors and unforgettable novels!